THE STAR ALLIANCE

Ken Lozito

THE STAR ALLIANCE

ISBN: 978-1-945223-02-0

The author greatly appreciates you taking the time to read his work.

Published by Acoustical Books, LLC
KenLozito.com

Cover art by Jeff Brown
http://www.jeffbrowngraphics.com/

Discover other books by Ken Lozito

ASCENSION SERIES:

The Star Shroud
The Star Divide
The Star Alliance

SAFANARION ORDER SERIES:

Road to Shandara (Book 1)
Echoes of a Gloried Past (Book 2)
Amidst the Rising Shadows (Book 3)
Heir of Shandara (Book 4)
The Warden's Oath (Short Fiction)

CHAPTER ONE

IT WAS SIX o'clock in the morning, and Edward Johnson was being escorted to the infamous West Wing of the White House. A few hours before, he'd gotten the call that President Halloway wanted to meet with him that morning. He had met Susan Halloway when she'd been a senator and a rising star in politics, but this was his first summons to the White House.

As he and his escort walked the long corridors, Ed noted that despite the early hour the White House was already abuzz with activity, and he suspected the quiet moments in this historic seat of power were few and far between. His thoughts returned to the meeting ahead as the aide who was escorting him came to a halt and spoke to one of the Secret Service agents posted outside the Oval office. The agent nodded, but Ed knew the Agency had already vetted him long before he had been allowed to enter the White House.

The door opened, and the aide stepped just inside the doorway for a brief moment, then turned back toward him. "The President will see you now."

Ed nodded his thanks and stepped inside, taking stock of the place he'd only seen in pictures until then. But the pictures weren't nearly as impressive as standing in the actual office of the president. Ed felt like he was marching through history with each step he took across the plush carpet of the vast room. His eyes slid toward the Resolute desk where ninety years before John F. Kennedy Jr. had played at his father's feet. Ed closed his mouth and brought his attention back to the present.

"Madam President," Ed said.

"Mr. Johnson, it's been a long time," President Halloway said. "Thank you for coming on such short notice. I believe you know Dr. Philip Gray."

Ed shook hands with Dr. Gray. He knew *of* him. Dux Corp had indirectly funded Gray's research in particle physics, but Gray was more advisor than scientist these days. "Please call me Ed," he said.

Susan nodded. "I'd apologize for waking you in the middle of the night to bring you here, but I knew you were already up."

"Hardly anyone sleeps all that much at Mission Control since we've had initial contact with Michael Hunsicker," Ed said.

The president took her seat behind the desk, while Ed and Dr. Gray sat on the plush chairs facing her.

"I've been expecting your call," Ed said to the president.

"Really?" Dr. Gray said. "You expected a call from the president?"

Ed glanced sideways at Dr. Gray but kept a majority of his attention on the president. "Yes, and if I hadn't been called, I would have initiated contact."

Philip Gray's mouth hung open in a half bewildered smile.

"Indeed," President Halloway said, "and it would have been a call I'd have been remiss to ignore, especially when it came from the head of

Dux Corporation and a member of its inner circle."

They shared a moment of acknowledgement, each confirming the other's powerful positions and influence, but any head of Dux Corp hadn't reached such levels of influence by being bullheaded.

"Thank you for seeing me, Madam President," Ed said.

President Halloway smiled, and tiny crow's feet formed along the edges of her brown eyes. She was a handsome woman—not overwhelmingly beautiful but certainly pleasant to look at—and only a fool would underestimate her. Beneath the pleasant exterior was a shrewd and powerful leader.

"Over the next few days, world leaders will be receiving similar briefings of what I'm about to share with you and your staff after this meeting," Ed began.

"Is this regarding the Shroud Network?" Dr. Gray asked.

"In part. NASA and the other space agencies around the world have been working through the Athena's final data burst," Ed said.

"The one from that hacker, Zack Quick?" Dr. Gray said in a tone that bordered on accusatory.

"I won't argue Zack's presence on the Athena Mission. His contribution to the mission has proven invaluable time and time again. The only reason we're aware of the Shroud Network is because of his work," Ed said.

"What is Commander Hunsicker's status?" President Halloway asked.

"He's assured us that he has plenty of provisions, but I assume you'd really like to know about the alien he's taken residence with on Pluto," Ed said.

"That's a big part of it," President Halloway said. "The events of the past few months have made the spaceship Endurance a high-priority item so a rescue mission could get underway. The leak about the alien structure on Pluto and the alien message before that have made many of those on Capitol Hill want to haul Dux Corp leaders and all its subsidiaries before a congressional hearing."

"Understood, Madam President," Ed said.

The president's lips curved upward. "You're very good, Ed. Your reputation is well deserved."

"Bruce Matherson's goal was always for the betterment of mankind. His granddaughter is on the Athena Mission," Ed said.

"So you believe they're still alive?" President Halloway asked.

"Yes, I do," Ed answered. "The events leading to the disappearance of the Athena were confirmed by Chazen."

"The alien," Dr. Gray said.

"They call themselves Boxans. We have no reason not to believe him," Ed said.

President Halloway leveled her gaze at Ed. "Except for the fact that they've been observing us in secret for over a hundred years. And the presence of the Star Shroud doesn't inspire a lot of trust. There is a lot that doesn't add up for me or my military advisors. I would like to open formal communications with the Boxan."

"He won't speak to us in any formal capacity," Ed said.

"Why not?" Dr. Gray asked.

"He said he's not authorized to negotiate for his species. He's some type of research scientist, and the reason he's communicating at all is because of Michael Hunsicker's presence," Ed said.

"I would like to speak with him," President Halloway said in a tone that left little room for negotiation.

Ed nodded. "It's possible, now that we've finished building the device."

"We saw that in your report," Dr. Gray said, and quickly scanned his tablet computer. "A communications device that allows for real-time communication with the alien outpost on Pluto."

"To put it in layman's terms," Ed said, "we can receive calls but cannot initiate a call of our own. The device is basically a receiver. Quite ingenious actually. It has a lot of people in Houston excited. We've shared the design specs with the other space agencies."

President Halloway rose from her seat and walked over to the massive window, gazing out at the meticulous landscape that made up the White House grounds. After a moment's contemplation, she turned back toward them. "What would you suggest we do?"

"I would suggest we offer Chazen our aid without any strings attached. My impression from Michael Hunsicker is that the Boxan is keenly observant. We shouldn't try any ploys or anything," Ed said and paused. "The official offer of aid should come from the global community and not just this nation."

President Halloway raised an eyebrow. "It's the global community that concerns me. We want to put our best foot forward, but we're far from becoming a unified species."

"There is also the issue of the warning," Dr. Gray said.

"Yes, the warning about the Xiiginn. They are another alien species. We don't know much about them other than that the Boxans were shielding us from their presence," Ed said.

"We need more information, and since this—being—is the only one who can enlighten us, we need to start with him. This is a slippery slope we're on, and there are a number of avenues that could pull us into an interstellar war," President Halloway said.

Ed nodded. "I'm prepared to share all we know with you and your staff. The problems we face will affect us all."

"For all our sakes, I hope it's enough," President Halloway said.

A Secret Service agent stuck his head into the Oval Office and announced that the meeting room was ready for them. They filed out of the office, and while Ed knew that the next few hours would shape the world to come, he couldn't help but feel the weight of all that had transpired in this office since the White House had been built. Mistakes had been made and victories won. In the end, he hoped wisdom and guidance would rule this day.

*****

Millions of miles away on a dwarf planet, Michael Hunsicker sat in the control room of the Boxan listening station. Chazen had just engaged the Boxan communicator, which was connected to a receiver back on Earth.

"Houston, do you read me?" Hunsicker asked.

"Loud and clear, Michael. This is Gary Hunter."

A holoscreen switched on and showed Gary's face. Hunsicker smiled. It had been a few weeks since he'd seen another human being, which was nothing compared to the length of time since Chazen had seen another Boxan. Hunsicker glanced over at the Boxan, who gave him a nod.

"It's good to see you, Gary."

"Same here. I was told to extend our thanks to your host," Gary said.

"You are welcome," Chazen said. His deep voice spoke slowly and clearly.

"Now that we can communicate, Chazen has agreed to share a translator program so you'll be able to understand him. Inform the other space agencies to be prepared for a data stream that will contain the necessary elements to implement," Hunsicker said.

Gary Hunter grinned. "Confirm, universal translator program. I'm sure there will be a lot of linguists out there who would like to study it. The European, Chinese, and Russian space agencies will have their comms devices up soon, but for now we've agreed to share a recording of these sessions. The spirit of cooperation."

Hunsicker suppressed a snort. For as long as he'd been with NASA, he'd known scientists were more amiable to the spirit of cooperation than nations. If anything, his experience here on Pluto had taught him that the confirmation of other intelligent life would put some of the petty differences his fellow humans clung to into perspective.

"That's good news," Hunsicker said. "I have another six months of supplies left from what we brought down from the Athena, and Chazen believes he can adapt his supplies for human consumption."

"That's good to hear. We've been working on a resupply mission, and crews have been working around the clock on the Endurance," Gary said.

Hunsicker frowned. "I thought the Endurance was two years away from completion."

"Priorities have shifted. We want to get another manned mission out to you as soon as possible," Gary said.

Chazen stood up and left the control room. Hunsicker watched him go, and Gary waited him out.

"Is everything all right?" Gary asked.

Hunsicker brought his attention back to the holoscreen and nodded. "Yes. He's been away from his home for a long time. I wish we could help him get back to his home world."

"We could, but it would mean he'd have to travel to Earth," Gary said.

"I'm not sure if he'll do that, but we can extend the invitation."

"By the way, we've gotten in touch with your family and let them know you're alive. We'll bring them here to speak with you soon," Gary said.

Hunsicker felt his throat thicken. He'd volunteered for the Athena mission after his wife Caroline had died, but he found that he really would like to see his grandkids again. His eyes grew misty, and Hunsicker swallowed down his emotions. "That would be great," he said.

"We'll get you home, Michael. You've got my word on that. We have a lot of people working on this."

"The Athena is still out there. We can't forget about Kaylan and the others," Hunsicker said.

"We're not, and the fact that Chazen believes the wormhole took them to another habitable system of planets is very reassuring," Gary said. "We'd like to schedule a call so the president could speak with

Chazen."

"I'll let him know," Hunsicker said.

Hunsicker spoke with Gary Hunter for the next hour, answering his questions. He knew there was frustration about the Boxan communication device only being able to be activated from Pluto. He suspected Zack could have figured something out about that. The former hacker was absolutely brilliant and could run circles around the best of them. Chazen had insisted that only the receiver designs could be sent back to Earth, and he was violating certain protocols by doing that much. Hunsicker had no doubt there were efforts to reverse engineer the designs, and he suspected Chazen thought the same.

After the call ended, he left the control room and headed toward the power station. Most of the wreckage from Redford's attempt at restoring power to the Boxan monitoring station had been cleared. The artificial intelligence had been designed to function autonomously and had engaged First Contact Protocols when the Athena crew entered the station and started turning things on. Chazen later explained that the botched startup protocols used in the power station had led to the seismic activity they'd experienced. When the Boxans had built the monitoring station, they had calculated Pluto's orbit and its effects on the planetary surface. The AI running the station had been attempting to compensate for fifty Earth years' worth of planetary shifts, which had led to their frightening experience. While the seismic activity hadn't seemed to worry Chazen all that much, what did have the Boxan concerned was the fact that a wormhole had opened in the first place.

Hunsicker entered the power station and found Chazen working at one of the interfaces.

"The president of my country would like to speak with you," Hunsicker said.

Chazen glanced down at him. "As I've said before, I will speak with your world leaders, but I'm not authorized to speak on behalf of my species."

"I don't think it's anything that formal. Many of my people are eager to learn about you. They know you are stranded here and are working on a way to get us safely back to Earth. Perhaps from there we can help you make contact with your home world," Hunsicker said.

Chazen closed the console he'd been working on and turned away. "The last communication from my home world was clear. No further contact should be attempted. All Star Shroud networks are to go on permanent standby until reactivation is authorized from Sethion High Command."

"Those orders left you stranded here. Don't you want to try and get home?" Hunsicker asked.

Chazen turned back toward Hunsicker. "The only reason for that last communication was because of the Xiiginn attack."

"Right, and the shutting down of the Star Shroud networks prevented the Xiiginn from gaining access to worlds with intelligent species to exploit," Hunsicker said.

Chazen remained quiet.

"I think it's important that you at least consider coming to Earth," Hunsicker continued, "to help quantify the threat of the Xiiginn. I'm here with you, and I'm not sure I fully understand the threat they represent."

"The AI correctly surmised that the Mardoxian potential exists in humans," Chazen said.

"Because Kaylan was able to use the chamber."

"Yes," Chazen said. "This will bring the Xiiginn here."

Hunsicker swallowed. He wasn't sure how much he should push Chazen. The Boxan had gone silent for long periods of time before while they repaired the station. "Look, Kaylan is exceptional. She's the only person I've ever known who could do what she can do. We're not a planet full of people who have this Mardoxian potential."

"That won't matter to the Xiiginn," Chazen said.

"All the more reason for us to work together and perhaps return to Earth. They just want to speak with you," Hunsicker said.

Chazen sucked in a deep breath and remained silent.

"What would you do if you were in our position?" Hunsicker asked.

Chazen glanced over at the reactor chamber, his eyes growing distant for a few moments. "I will speak with your president," Chazen said, and walked away.

Sensing that the Boxan wanted to be alone, Hunsicker didn't follow. The Boxans adhered to well-defined protocols to deal with a number of situations, but Hunsicker guessed that being stranded in an alien star system wasn't among them. He needed Chazen if he was going to survive, and Chazen needed Humans if *he* was going to survive. And survival meant not spending an eternity on this lifeless planet.

CHAPTER TWO

KAYLAN STOOD ON the bridge of the Boxan stealth ship. She'd much rather have been working from the Athena's bridge, but the Boxan scanners were way better than anything they had. They'd spent much of the last few days looking through the wreckage of the Xiiginn cruiser. Initially she'd hoped they would detect Zack's suit computer, but they hadn't found a trace. The cruiser wreckage had spewed out into space, with large chunks being drawn into the gas giant Selebus orbited. The ship hadn't been vaporized in the explosion but had blown apart into pieces. Some of those pieces were as big as the Athena. The escape pods that jettisoned from the cruiser had gathered at a safe distance and were later picked up by Nershal ships from their home world. Those ships had entered into orbit around Selebus, and salvage vessels had arrived to collect the remaining wreckage. Kladomaor wanted to leave, but Kaylan wouldn't leave without Zack. She couldn't leave him behind.

"I don't think there is anything more we can learn by scanning the wreckage," Gaarokk said. "They must have taken Zack somewhere else."

Kladomaor was hunched over, looking over the shoulder of another

Boxan. He turned in Gaarokk's direction and stood up straight. Boxans were eight-to-ten feet tall on average, but their battle armor made them taller still.

"If he's still alive," Kladomaor said.

Kaylan met the Boxan's challenging gaze. "He is still alive."

The Boxan's flaxen-colored eyes softened as he drew in a patient breath. "You haven't been able to detect his location since the cruiser was destroyed."

"I need to have some idea where he is in order to be able to find him. You have us so far from anything it's no wonder I can't find him," Kaylan said. She hated the desperation in her voice, but her frustration had been mounting. She hardly ate and only slept a few hours at a time.

"You might need to accept that he's gone," Kladomaor said.

Kaylan clutched her arms in front of her chest. "I won't leave here without him," she said, and left the bridge.

Kladomaor shook his head, and after a few moments, Gaarokk cleared his throat. Kladomaor looked up and waited for the scientist to speak.

"Nicely done," Gaarokk said.

"Someone needed to say it," Kladomaor said. "If Zack isn't dead, you and I both know he's being used by the Xiiginns, which is a fate much worse."

"We don't even know if the Xiiginns can affect them the way they do us," Gaarokk said.

"There are other ways to make someone do what you want. *We* may not practice it, but the Xiiginns have no issues with torture and genetic experimentation," Kladomaor said.

"All the more reason to try and find him," Gaarokk said.

"We have been. I've been in contact with Udonzari, but with the growing Nershal unrest, the Xiiginns have been on high alert. He doesn't even know where the survivors have been taken. He has his agents scouting all the known facilities on Selebus, and so far—nothing," Kladomaor said.

"If they moved the survivors, wouldn't it make more sense for us to start searching the Nershal home world?" Gaarokk asked.

Kladomaor blew out a breath. "Where would you suggest we start? We're one ship restricted to stealth, which means we can only use passive scans to avoid detection."

"The Humans won't leave here until they find out what happened to Zack," Gaarokk warned.

"Don't you mean Kaylan won't? Hicks has the bearing of a soldier and is someone I think won't shy away from making the tough decisions," Kladomaor said.

Gaarokk pressed his lips together, his eyes drifting downward in thought. "They are an interesting species. There is a strong bond between them. It's almost instinctual that they shove aside differences when one of them is in danger. While some of the others don't quite have Kaylan's conviction and aren't so vocal about it, they are working feverishly hard to try and figure out a way to find him."

"Agreed, their camaraderie is admirable, but they don't realize what's at stake. The Humans are out of their depth. We need to get them out of here and return to the High Council. Only then can we get the support we need to help the Humans safeguard against the Xiiginns,"

Kladomaor said.

"You would sacrifice one of them, leaving him to his own fate at the hands of the Xiiginns?" Gaarokk asked.

"If it means saving more of them in the long run, then yes, I would," Kladomaor said.

"They won't see it that way—" Gaarokk began.

The door to the bridge opened and Ma'jasalax walked in. The Mardoxian priestess had slowly been recovering from her time spent as a prisoner of the Xiiginns. Her loose-fitting robes covered the wounds from where she'd been connected to the machine on board the Xiiginn cruiser. There hadn't been time to figure out exactly what the machine had been doing, but Gaarokk believed the tubes were feeding biological compounds into Ma'jasalax. The question remained as to whether there were any long-term effects and whether any of them would be affected by whatever Ma'jasalax had been exposed to.

Kladomaor gave her a slight nod in greeting.

Ma'jasalax leveled a knowing gaze at Kladomaor. "Gaarokk is right."

"About what?" Kladomaor asked.

"If we force the Humans to leave the Nershal star system, they won't see it as the benevolent act you believe it to be."

"Then they are shortsighted and have much to learn," Kladomaor said, and looked away to examine one of the consoles nearest him.

Ma'jasalax didn't answer right away, and for some reason that grated on his nerves more than he would like to admit. Kladomaor returned his gaze to Ma'jasalax.

"Perhaps," Ma'jasalax said. "Or it could be quite the opposite. *We're* being too *farsighted*. So much of our time is spent accounting for the longevity of our actions that we fail to see the things that are right in front of us."

"Fine. What do you think I'm missing?" Kladomaor asked.

"You've lost soldiers in this war, friends who are gone now and whom you carry within you. The pain of their loss has served you well when facing the Xiiginns; however, that same strength is becoming a hindrance when giving aid to the Humans," Ma'jasalax said.

"I've been trying to help them," Kladomaor said.

"You think because they haven't had your experience with the Xiiginns, you know what's best. It was our arrogance that blinded us to the threat of the Xiiginns in the first place, and now it's our fear of them that will lead us to alienating an intelligent species that needs our help," Ma'jasalax said.

The silence on the bridge became apparent to Kladomaor as he realized the Boxan crew had stopped what they were doing and turned to listen.

Kladomaor's brain raced to oblivion in the blink of an eye. He wanted to lash out at the Mardoxian priestess because her words cut deeper than he thought they could, and he wanted to blame her for sending the initial message to the Humans that had brought them here in the first place.

"I make my decisions based on experience, and my experience tells me the Humans are being irrational and will not listen to reason," Kladomaor said.

"They listen just fine," Ma'jasalax said. "They just don't agree with your reasoning."

Kladomaor's shoulders stiffened, and he resisted the urge to step away. "Then they disagree to their own detriment." Kladomaor glanced around at the Boxans on the bridge, who quickly turned their attention back to the consoles in front of them.

Ma'jasalax stepped closer to him and spoke softly. "If you persist in this line of action, you will drive the Humans away. We need to work with them."

"They need us in order to get back to their star system," Kladomaor said.

Ma'jasalax gave him a patient look. "I know you wouldn't hold that over them."

"If the Xiiginns reach Earth, it could be Sethion all over again," Kladomaor said.

"Our home world is still there," Ma'jasalax said.

"With half the population having gone mad."

"You are living proof that the effects of the Xiiginn influence can be counteracted," Ma'jasalax said. "And you discount the Humans because they aren't as technologically advanced as we are, but perhaps there are other things we can learn from them."

"If the Xiiginns learn of the Mardoxian potential in Humans, they will be hunted down. We've managed to prevent any of our own with the Mardoxian traits from falling into the Xiiginns' hands, but if they were to figure out how the trait works and perfect it into their own genetically altered species, the galaxy would be even more under their shadow than they are right now. I would do anything to prevent that from happening," Kladomaor said.

"I would never question your conviction when it comes to the Xiiginns, but if we're to form an alliance with the Humans, we need to help them even if we don't approve of the wisdom of their actions. As long as those actions don't violate any of our own core values, I don't see why we shouldn't help them, and neither should you," Ma'jasalax said.

Kladomaor was silent while he gathered his thoughts. His instincts told him the Humans were being foolish. The sacrifice of one of their own to help ensure the survival of their species wasn't too steep a price to pay. He understood the loyalty the crew of the Athena had for one another. He respected it, but he also knew their loyalty was something the Xiiginns would use against them. The Xiiginns wouldn't hesitate to use any advantage that would swing the odds of winning an engagement in their favor. He couldn't make himself agree to stay in the Nershal star system any longer.

Kladomaor rubbed the bottom of his chin and glanced back at Ma'jasalax.

"Let me put it this way," Ma'jasalax said. "If we don't help them now, using all the means at our disposal, then why would any of the Humans—or any other species for that matter—have cause to listen to our counsel when the stakes are higher? The current state of the Confederation should have taught us that. We are not all-knowing and—"

"And the other species will not simply listen to us because we think we know what's best for them. Believe me, you've made your point quite clear," Kladomaor said.

"I'm not sure I have," Ma'jasalax said.

"Why is that?"

"Because you still don't believe it. What would you do if, after all this, the Nershals remain allied with the Xiiginns?" Ma'jasalax asked.

"Then I would keep exposing the wrongdoings of the Xiiginns," Kladomaor said.

"I'm sure you would, but consider for a moment that no matter what you did the Nershals remained in their alliance with the Xiiginns. Or better yet, what if the Humans entered into an alliance with the Xiiginns?" Ma'jasalax asked.

Kladomaor's brows pushed forward, and his gaze hardened. "Then we would leave them to their fate."

"Ah, you see, there it is finally," Ma'jasalax said, "an acknowledgement that we cannot control the galaxy, and that sometimes, despite all our best intentions, it may not be enough to impart our wisdom to other species."

"Well then, let's hope both the Nershals and the Humans are smarter than that, or we may find ourselves in a war with them as well," Kladomaor said.

"Indeed, let's hope so, for all our sakes. Now let's try and think of a way we can help the crew of the Athena find their missing crew member," Ma'jasalax said.

CHAPTER THREE

MAR ARDEN STOOD in a darkened room where only the minimal amber glow of holographic consoles provided any light. This amount of light was preferred by the Xiiginns, and there were no other species present in any official capacity. Most species in the Confederation functioned within a visual spectrum much higher than the Xiiginns. His species was at home in the darkness and could see stunning detail even with a minute amount of light. And darkness in this area of their base was a key necessity second only to the secrecy of its location. The nights upon this moon were long, which was something all Xiiginns relished. The star in their home system was old and nearing the end of its cycle in cosmic terms, much dimmer than the star here in the Nershal star system.

A chime from the door sounded just before it opened and in walked Kandra Rene, one of his most promising students. Her long platinum-colored hair was tucked behind her ears, and her cool, calculating gaze only hinted at the shrewd intelligence she possessed in abundance. The curve of her lips lifted as she gave him a suggestive smile that was an open invitation should he wish to partake. Mar Arden regarded her for a moment, and Kandra Rene patiently waited for him to give the reason he had summoned her here. The most rewarding challenges happened to be the ones filled with danger, and taking one such as Kandra Rene into his employ came with its own set of risks. Mar Arden's eyes slid down the black battle mesh that covered her perfectly proportioned body.

Kandra Rene's mouth opened slightly, revealing the sharp points of her teeth, but it was the fullness of her slightly swollen tongue that drew his gaze.

"Sion Shif will be along shortly," Kandra Rene said.

"Good," Mar Arden said. "I have a new project for you."

Kandra Rene's eyes widened hungrily in anticipation. "I wait to serve."

Mar Arden activated the holoscreen, which showed an image of a life-form lying unconscious in the room beyond them. "Have you reviewed the report I sent you?"

Kandra Rene nodded. "This is the new species?"

"Yes. Sion Shif captured this one before escaping the cruiser," Mar Arden said.

Kandra Rene studied the holoscreen. "And they were working with the Nershals and the Boxans?"

"Evidently. What I need from you is to find out all you can about this new species," Mar Arden said.

Kandra Rene glanced up at him in surprise.

"You're ready for this," Mar Arden said. He knew she would seize this opportunity to prove her worth, but he didn't want her efforts to be overzealous.

"Sion Shif brought him here. Why wouldn't you have him

interrogate the prisoner?" Kandra Rene asked.

"He will be occupied with me after we leave here. Sion Shif is more interested in the Boxans who sabotaged one of our cruisers," Mar Arden said.

Kandra Rene glanced at the being on the holoscreen. "Do you think the Nershals could have discovered a new species without our knowing about it?"

"Doubtful. While the Nershals are brilliant navigators, their focus is more primitive. And the Boxans' attempt to cultivate the Nershals as an ally against us has failed, so they wouldn't be withholding information," Mar Arden said.

"Or so we thought," Kandra Rene said. "Violent outbreaks from Nershals have been on the rise, and the cause is tied directly to the information leak from one of the research facility's sub levels."

"You're very well informed," Mar Arden said.

"You wouldn't keep me around if I weren't," Kandra Rene said.

The door chime sounded, and Sion Shif entered. The Xiiginn wore black armor, and his face always seemed moments away from scowling since the loss of his cruiser. Mar Arden weighed whether or not to replace him.

Sion Shif joined them by the holoscreen. "The Boxans have grown bolder. Their change in tactics exposed a blind spot on our ships—an oversight we will not fall victim to again."

"Their actions reveal much about their intentions," Mar Arden said. "Have you been able to recover anything we can use from the wreckage?"

"Tentran-level data was dumped to this facility," Sion Shif said.

"And the captured Boxan?" Mar Arden asked.

"Her whereabouts are unknown. The intruders came aboard to rescue Ma'jasalax, which means they had to have known she was there in the first place," Sion Shif said.

Mar Arden changed the output on the holoscreen to show the surveillance feeds from the research station that was attacked on Selebus. "We need to confirm my suspicions, but I believe the group of Boxans that attacked the research facility was also responsible for the cruiser's destruction. A bold move from them, considering the risks involved."

"The Boxans are adapting and taking more risks, it seems," Sion Shif said.

"This was Kladomaor. He was the one who attacked the research facility. He's managed to convince some Nershals to help him," Mar Arden said.

"They're using our own tactics against us. Should we expect more of these events in other star systems?" Sion Shif asked.

"The Nershals aren't as susceptible to our compulsion as the Boxans are. It's one of the reasons why they tried to cultivate the Nershals. We've driven the Boxans back on almost every front, but the presence of the Mardoxian priestess warrants some scrutiny," Mar Arden said, and glanced at Kandra Rene.

"She didn't follow protocol. The records indicate that she was alone when she was captured, so if she didn't follow the protocol herself that means her protector wasn't there to enforce the protocol," Kandra Rene said.

"That is correct," Sion Shif confirmed. "We've observed the

engagement of the protocol where the Boxan armor self-destructs, disintegrating all remains."

Kandra Rene nodded. "So if she didn't follow standard Boxan protocol, she must have been acting alone—a rogue faction acting independently of the Boxan High Council."

Sion Shif snapped his gaze in Mar Arden's direction. "A rogue faction!"

"Yes," Kandra Rene said. "The question that stands out in my mind is whether this Mardoxian priestess expected to be rescued. If she did, this implies that the events that occurred on Selebus and the events that occurred on the cruiser are related. The question remaining is how?"

Mar Arden smiled and enjoyed the realization that registered on Sion Shif's face.

"Is this your latest protégé to come from the Astra program?" Sion Shif asked.

"Yes, and pretty substantial proof of the program's effectiveness," Mar Arden said.

Kandra Rene kept her expression bland, and Mar Arden added another notch to his approval of her. The Astra program was the latest iteration in genetic modifications meant to further improve the perfection of the Xiiginns over the other species in the Confederation.

Mar Arden switched the holoscreen to show the unconscious form in the room beyond. "I think some of our answers lie with the being in the other room."

Sion Shif glanced at holoscreen and nodded. "I'm not sure what to think about rogue Boxan factions."

"We suspected something had to change," Mar Arden said. "For the Boxans to keep going as they have been would have all but assured our victory over them."

"They still represent our biggest threat," Sion Shif said.

"We have the Confederation to do our fighting for us, which effectively keeps the Boxans' hands tied," Mar Arden said.

"Giving us time to find their secret colony," Sion Shif said.

"Another interesting question is how the being in the other room came to be in this star system in the first place," Mar Arden said.

Sion Shif narrowed his gaze, taking a good look at the holoscreen. "It's doubtful they've developed anything like the Cherubian drive on their own. From what I've seen of their weapons capability, I'm not sure they're technologically advanced enough to make it here on their own."

"Well, they've obviously made it here somehow," Kandra Rene said.

"Or they were brought here," Mar Arden said.

"How?" Sion Shif asked.

"Before the Boxans fled this system there was a broadcast signal sent from the Mardoxian chamber at the listening station. We were keen on capturing the station to gain access into the Star Shroud network, but the station was destroyed. What if the signal that was sent out was received by the species in the next room and somehow they were brought here?" Mar Arden said.

Sion Shif's eyes widened, and Mar Arden nodded.

"That's right. There is an intact Boxan listening station out there somewhere, and that being in the next room is our key to it," Mar Arden said.

Chapter Four

Zack's mouth was dry and there was a slight ringing in his ears. He worked his mouth into a swallow and tried to push his eyes open, but he felt like there were tiny weights attached to his eyelids that prevented them from opening. A raspy breath left his mouth as he tried to move. He was lying on his back, and he couldn't get his muscles to cooperate.

Zack focused his will and forced his eyes to open. The room he was in was so dark that he could hardly see anything. He pushed the fogginess from his brain and began to wake up. The pain in his leg and side was gone. He tried to move again, but he was strapped against the table. A door on the far side of the room opened, and a soft amber glow streamed into the room. Zack squinted as he peered through the doorway. A large shape filled the area, and Zack noted the third appendage that hung to the floor behind it.

Xiiginn! The thought blazed through his mind like lightning, and his breath caught in his lungs. Zack struggled against his restraints, but they wouldn't budge.

"Don't try to move. You're being restrained for your own protection."

Zack stopped moving. He tried to access Athena through his implants, but there was no response. He flexed his wrists and realized that his PDA was gone.

"Where am I?" Zack asked.

"Safe," the Xiiginn said.

Zack followed its movements by the dim amber lighting engaged along the wall. The Xiiginn turned around, and Zack noticed stark white skin that seemed to give off its own glow. Icy cold fear settled in the pit of his stomach.

"I don't believe we've been properly introduced. I am Mar Arden."

Zack clamped his mouth shut, refusing to speak. He looked around, trying to find the nearest exit, and then his gaze settled back on Mar Arden.

"Surely members of your species have names," Mar Arden said.

"Zack," he said finally.

"Excellent," Mar Arden said. "A pleasure to meet you."

"Why can't I move?" Zack asked, refusing to let the Xiiginn dispel his suspicions.

"It was for your protection. You were wounded and were brought here for healing," Mar Arden said.

"Thank you. I'm feeling better now. Will you let me go?" Zack asked.

Mar Arden raised his chin while his dark eyes peered at Zack. "It's not that simple."

"Of course," Zack said. He wanted to get up off this bed, but he knew he couldn't. He was completely at the Xiiginn's mercy, and Mar Arden seemed to be waiting for Zack to arrive at that conclusion.

"We will let you go after we've had a chance to speak with you," Mar Arden said.

"Really," Zack said, fighting to keep himself from rolling his eyes.

"I will answer any questions you may have in return for your cooperation."

"Why is it so dark in here?" Zack asked.

"A necessary precaution," Mar Arden said.

"Against what?"

Mar Arden stepped closer to the bed, and the dim lighting cast long shadows over his features, distorting them. His green eyes reflected the light that made him look both menacing and perfectly sculpted. If Zack could have run away, he would have, but he couldn't be completely sure why he was so afraid in the first place.

"I think we've gotten off on the wrong foot. You've been misinformed about my race," Mar Arden said, the menacing shadows leaving his face only to be replaced by genuine impassiveness.

The Xiiginn raised his wrist and tapped a few commands into the controls, and Zack felt the pressure that was holding him in place lessen slightly. Then the straps holding him in place retracted. Zack tentatively tried to raise his hands and was able to do so. He sat up and then stood.

"There, that's better," Mar Arden said. "It took us a short while to figure out what treatment would heal your wounds. The tiredness you're feeling will pass. Now, will you answer some of my questions?"

Zack glanced at the doorway behind Mar Arden and knew his chances of getting past the Xiiginn were slim to none. "Sure," Zack said.

"Why did you attack the research facility on Selebus and then later attack one of our cruisers?" Mar Arden asked.

Zack pressed his lips together in thought. The snarky answer he wanted to give probably wasn't the smartest one. "We didn't attack the research facility."

Mar Arden stepped closer, and Zack became aware of the bulging muscles beneath the dark, mesh-like armor the Xiiginns wore. This Xiiginn was a good six inches taller than Zack. A switch clicked in his brain, and the overwhelming fear that had been building in him was pushed back.

"You mean the facility where you experimented on the Nershals? Is that the research facility you're talking about?" Zack asked.

Mar Arden's hand sprang up toward Zack's face with lightning speed, but the Xiiginn retracted it just as quickly.

"We know you were with the Boxans," Mar Arden said.

Zack remained silent.

Mar Arden roared as he snatched Zack by his neck and slammed him against the wall, holding him above the floor.

"I've tried being civil to you," Mar Arden said through clenched teeth, "but my patience is wearing thin. The attack on the cruiser cost many lives. I know you weren't alone."

"And I know you aren't concerned about the lives on the cruiser," Zack said between gasps.

He braced himself for another blow, but Mar Arden set him back on the floor. Zack collapsed to his knees, gasping, as Mar Arden stepped away and waited. With trembling hands, Zack slowly regained his feet.

"What makes you think the lives on the cruiser don't matter to me?" Mar Arden asked.

"I've seen the genetic experiments you've done on the Nershals. Anyone who could do that doesn't hold other people's lives in high regard," Zack said.

Mar Arden looked at him for a moment. "So I should just skip the formalities and do what I want to you?"

Zack's breath caught in his throat. He couldn't see a way out of this. He was alone.

"There were others with you. Why don't you tell me about them?" Mar Arden asked.

Zack opened his mouth to answer but stopped himself. Mar Arden's gaze intensified, and Zack felt as if there were something pressing in on his head. It made thinking difficult. The beginnings of a major headache formed, and Zack winced in pain.

"You can't control me," Zack said through clenched teeth. The pain grew to an excruciating level, and Zack collapsed to the floor, crying out.

Mar Arden squatted down and grabbed Zack by his hair, lifting his head up. "And yet you're the one on your knees."

Zack felt his consciousness begin to slip, and his field of vision became smaller and smaller.

Mar Arden smiled, and the pressure was gone. "In this you are mistaken. You'll find that we can control a great many things. What is your species called?"

Zack glared defiantly at the Xiiginn.

Mar Arden stood back up and went over to the wall, where he keyed in a security code, and a panel opened. He retrieved a silver rod and closed the panel.

"The physiology of every species is truly enlightening. One thing we've found across all species so far is the innate avoidance of pain," Mar Arden said. The Xiiginn crossed back over to Zack and held the silver rod in front of his face. "This has been configured for *your* physiology since we've had a small amount of time to study it. When I activate the field, it will cause your central nervous system to react. With a flip of a switch I can cause you to know pleasures you've never thought possible or pain you've never imagined."

Zack's eyes widened, and he tried to shuffle away across the floor.

Mar Arden crossed the distance in two strides. "Now, what is your species called? Where is your star system?"

Zack's eyes locked onto the rod, and he tried to brace himself.

Mar Arden's face twisted into a sneer, and the tip of the rod glowed blue.

In an instant Zack felt like his entire body were engulfed in flames. Every inch of his skin felt as if it were melting away. He screamed and rubbed his hands all over, trying to get the pain to stop. It hurt so much that tears streamed from his eyes. "Humans!" Zack shouted. "We call ourselves Humans."

The pain stopped, but it took a few moments for Zack to realize it.

"Humans, excellent. Now, how did you come to be in the Nershal star system?" Mar Arden asked and leaned in.

Zack felt the pressure intensify in his head. He squeezed his eyes shut. "No!" he growled and lashed out with his fist, catching Mar Arden by surprise.

The Xiiginn was knocked back, and Zack scrambled for the door, but something caught hold of his feet, and he went down. Zack struggled to move as he was pulled back into the room. Mar Arden had his back to him and Zack glanced at his bound feet, realizing that the Xiiginn had used his tail to capture him. Mar Arden pivoted with his hips, and Zack was swung through the air and slammed into the wall.

Mar Arden released him and waited for Zack to sit up.

"Now that the useless escape attempt has been gotten out of the way, are you ready to answer my questions?" Mar Arden asked.

Zack tasted copper in his mouth and spat blood onto the floor. "Go to hell," Zack said.

Mar Arden laughed. "Wrong answer," he said, and the rod in his hand glowed. It was the last thing Zack saw before he became engulfed in pain.

Zack woke up with his face on the floor. His body ached so badly that he didn't try to move. He just stared in front of him. The floor felt wet under his face.

"I don't have time for this," Mar Arden said.

Zack glanced up, and his heart thundered in his chest, but Mar Arden wasn't speaking to him.

"There is increasing unrest on Nerva. Your presence has been requested on the Nershal home world."

The two Xiiginn glanced toward him, and Zack shut his eyes, pretending to be unconscious.

"We need to release a statement about the information leak from the research facility that was attacked."

"Fine, Kandra can take over for me," Mar Arden said. "This species is highly resistant to compulsion. I think some time in the pit should soften his resolve."

"According to his vital signs, he's awake."

Zack opened his eyes and saw Mar Arden's sneering gaze.

"I know," Mar Arden said.

The stomping of boots came toward him and a Xiiginn roughly pulled Zack to his feet. Zack couldn't stand on his own, and his head sagged to his chest.

Mar Arden stepped closer to him. "You'll learn, Human. Trusting the Boxans is a fatal mistake."

CHAPTER FIVE

NEEDING TO GET some distance from the Boxans, Kaylan was back on the Athena for a few hours. Traversing between the two ships was significantly easier thanks to the Boxans. They had connected the two vessels by using an emergency docking tube that extended a hundred meters in length. The ends of the tubes were able to seal themselves around one of the Athena's airlocks. The dark gray material was both flexible and strong while maintaining a rigid structure once it was programmed in. Getting back and forth between the two ships took only minutes now.

Kaylan headed to the science lab where Emma waited for her, hunched over a microscope.

"Efren, I told you Kaylan was coming up here. The hydroponics lab will have to wait," Emma said.

Kaylan cleared her throat. "Efren come here often?" she asked.

Emma looked up from the microscope and grinned. Her short dark hair was pushed back behind her ears. "Just this morning. He's a little on edge. We all are. But how are you doing?" Emma asked.

"I'm fine," Kaylan said a little too quickly. "I'm sorry. It's almost automatic."

"No need to apologize to me. Still no luck finding anything in the wreckage?"

Kaylan shook her head. "Kladomaor says it's not safe to keep searching."

A soft chime sounded from the speaker near them. "The Boxan's risk assessment is correct. Significant potential of our presence being detected increases the longer we stay here," Athena's AI said.

Kaylan frowned at the speaker, but the ship's artificial intelligence was just speaking the facts. She had been encouraging the AI to share its insights with the crew more. "What about your own analysis, Athena?" Kaylan asked.

"The instrumentation available was insufficient to track all of the escape pods leaving the Xiiginn cruiser. There is a seventy percent probability that Zack Quick was taken to Selebus and a thirty percent chance of Zack Quick being moved to the Nershal home world," Athena said.

Kaylan frowned. "How did you arrive at these probabilities?"

"By leveraging my connection to the Boxan ship's computer. Before going to the Xiiginn cruiser, Zack had requested that an open connection between our two systems be allowed. Currently that connection is still authorized. According to the computer systems aboard the Boxan ship, the escape pods were brought to Selebus. However, ship traffic between the Nershal home world and Selebus has increased since the Xiiginn cruiser's destruction. I estimated that some of the crew members returned to the Nershal home world based upon the ship's capacity for additional passengers. I apologize that I cannot be of further assistance," the AI said.

Kaylan shared a glance with Emma. "No, you did a good job. I can find no fault with your reasoning," Kaylan said.

"Athena," Emma said. "Are you able to connect to Zack's PDA?"

"Not since the destruction of the Xiiginn cruiser. I am monitoring for it, and there are a number of reasons for lack of communication, ranging from a malfunction to the device simply being powered off," Athena said.

"Or the signal could just be blocked," Kaylan said.

"That is also a possibility," the AI answered.

Kaylan chewed the inside of her lip while she thought about their next move. Kladomaor had already confirmed that their Nershal allies on Selebus were looking for Zack and the Nershal called Etanu. Their search hadn't yielded any results either. Kaylan rubbed her eyes.

"When was the last time you slept?" Emma asked.

Kaylan shook her head. "I don't know. I don't need sleep right now. The more time that passes, the more I think we'll never find Zack."

The door to the lab opened and Katie Garcia walked in. Katie and Kaylan had more or less stayed by each other's side since Zack had been taken, both working toward finding a way to figure out where Zack was being held. Tiny seeds of doubt threatened to take root in each of them and, like a weed, they pulled one out only to have two more come up.

"I'm glad you're here for this as well, actually," Emma said to Katie.

"Hicks is with Redford on the Boxan ship. What can I do?" Katie asked.

Kaylan admired how Katie could be so focused, while Kaylan herself felt like more of an emotional wreck than she'd ever been before. In her mind's eye she saw Zack's face with that deep, penetrating gaze and the slight smile that had grazed his lips as he pressed his hand to the elevator door. He had sacrificed himself to save her. She wished she could go back to that moment and pull him into the elevator with her. Kaylan clenched her teeth and shoved her anger to the side, but it was getting harder to do.

"I've been thinking about the Xiiginn influence the Boxans are afraid of," Emma said.

"With good reason," Katie said. "I've never seen someone so completely taken over against their will. It goes beyond any brainwashing I've ever heard of."

Kaylan nodded. "Back on the cruiser, the Boxan who fell victim to it was aware of what he was doing but was unable to stop himself. He begged for the others to kill him even as he fired his weapon at them."

"It must have been horrifying," Emma said. "I want to better understand how it works so we can come up with a way to prevent it."

"Do you really think that's possible?" Katie asked.

Emma nodded. "I do. I realize we're not nearly as advanced as the Boxans, but the fundamentals of solving this problem are the same. If nothing else, it will give us something to report back to Earth when we make it there."

"The Boxans can only delay the effects, so they must have some understanding of how the compulsion works. I'm not sure how much they're willing to share with us at the moment," Kaylan said.

"That's because you're thinking about it all wrong," Katie said with a smile. "We need information, and the Boxans have it."

"Yeah, but Kladomaor won't share. Whenever I've brought up the subject, he deflects or acts as if the subject is too complex for us to understand," Kaylan said.

"Well, he *is* a victim of it. Remember when Gaarokk told us about when Kladomaor was taken captive by the Xiiginns? Mar Arden forced him to kill his own soldiers," Emma said.

Kaylan nodded and then her brows rose as she finally understood what Katie was implying. "Not Kladomaor, but Gaarokk. He's not a soldier, and I think with the right coaxing he would be willing to share the information they have about the Xiiginns and, in particular, how this compulsion of theirs works."

"Well I think I know a way we can get him to help," Emma said. "We invite him aboard the Athena. He's been wanting to see the ship. I say we give him a tour and get his opinion on the upgrades the AI had us implement."

"It would be a tight squeeze, but without their armor it could be done," Katie said.

"We need to be careful. We're not doing anything wrong by having him here, but I don't want to put Gaarokk in a position where he feels conflicted," Kaylan said.

"Yes, you do. We all do," Katie said. "The Xiiginns have Zack and at the very least are questioning him, but judging by what they did to the Nershals in the research lab, whatever they're doing to him could be much worse."

Kaylan looked away and shook her head. She wasn't ready for this. They were so far outside the Athena's mission parameters that she wasn't sure what they should do first. Kaylan looked back at the others. "I think Gaarokk will help us."

Kaylan's comms link chimed from her PDA, and she activated it.

"Greetings, Commander," Gaarokk said. "Ma'jasalax would like to see you on our ship if you have a moment. She wants to try to find Zack again and needs you with her."

"Of course. I'll be right over," Kaylan said. "Oh, and Gaarokk, we were wondering if you wouldn't mind coming over to the Athena for a quick tour. The AI had us perform several upgrades that we would like to get an outside opinion on, and you've mentioned in the past that you would like to see our ship."

A few seconds went by while they waited for his answer. "Thank you for inviting me. I would love to come see your ship."

The comms channel closed.

"Commander," the AI said.

"Yes, Athena?"

"The upgrades that were done to the ship have been tested and signed off by the crew. Having Gaarokk review these findings is counterproductive," the AI said.

"Well, it wouldn't hurt to have a second pair of eyes look at our systems, and we're also doing this to build trust with the Boxans, giving them a chance to learn more about us so we in turn can learn more about them," Kaylan said.

"I understand. Thank you for explaining," the AI said.

"Before you go, I had another thought," Emma said. "It would be helpful if we got a sample of Boxan blood from one who has been affected by the Xiiginn."

"I don't know how we can do that without them finding out what we're doing," Kaylan said.

"Leave it to me," Katie said.

Emma glanced at both of them.

"The only one affected was Kladomaor, and he was wounded during our escape from the cruiser. Perhaps I can find a sample of his blood in their med bay," Katie said.

"I didn't even think of that," Kaylan said.

"You have enough to worry about. We're all a team, and we do this together," Katie said.

Kaylan nodded and opened up a comms channel that would broadcast through their ship. "This is the commander. In a few minutes we'll be having a visitor from the Boxan ship. Gaarokk was nice enough to come over for a tour. Please extend him every courtesy while our guest is aboard. Katie and I are heading back to the Boxan ship."

*****

Kladomaor watched as Gaarokk rose from his console station and left the bridge. His curiosity was piqued, so he decided to follow as Gaarokk headed toward the airlock that connected them to the Athena.

"Going somewhere?" Kladomaor asked.

"Kaylan invited me to come see their ship," Gaarokk said. "Probably a good idea. Their partial AI has had them upgrading some of their ship's systems. They did their own checks, but it's probably not a bad idea that someone else takes a look."

"I remember Zack telling us about the AI. It was a partial construct from our listening station in their star system," Kladomaor said.

"He is quite clever—first figuring out how to access the Star Shroud Network and then helping the AI adapt to their computer systems," Gaarokk said, and turned to gather a few pieces of equipment to bring with him.

Kladomaor noted the somber tone from Gaarokk. "You don't approve of the course I wish to take?"

Gaarokk finished what he was doing and turned back toward Kladomaor. "It's difficult to say. I agree with Ma'jasalax that if we force the Humans to abandon one of their own, it may turn them against us. At the very least, they'll resent us for it."

"I don't want to force them to do anything. Leaving right now is the best course of action for them," Kladomaor said.

"No, in this you're wrong, my friend. Leaving now lowers the risk of the Humans falling into the Xiiginns' hands. Just because it might be safer for them to leave now doesn't mean it's what's best for them."

"He's just one member of their crew—" Kladomaor began.

"His name is Zack," Gaarokk said.

The sharp tone from the scientist surprised him.

"I know his name," Kladomaor said quietly.

"Then why don't you use it? Perhaps having the Humans with us will teach us something we've forgotten—the value of one life and that the bond across many individuals is enough to outweigh the risks for the safest course of action," Gaarokk said.

Kladomaor took a deep breath. "They could be an ally against the Xiiginns and be our salvation."

"That's just it. I understand where you're coming from. Seeing the big picture has its place, but only seeing the big picture isn't enough. That's not what inspires loyalty. Take a good look at the Humans. All of them want to find Zack, and I think if you'd just use his name, he may actually matter more to you. At least it would show the Humans that you understand how difficult this is for them, and that the burden is shared in some small way," Gaarokk said.

Kladomaor didn't say anything. It was for these moments that he had brought the scientist along. None of his soldiers would question him the way Gaarokk and Ma'jasalax had done. He nodded to his friend and headed back to the bridge, thinking about what had been said.

CHAPTER SIX

ZACK WAS DRAGGED away from Mar Arden. He tried to get a look at the Xiiginn soldiers who carried him, but he could barely lift his head. Wherever they took him, it was dark, with hardly any lighting at all. What had they done to him? Waves of exhaustion washed over him. He tried to get his feet under him so he could walk, but the brisk pace the soldiers set was too much for him. The soldiers came to a halt, and one of them keyed in a code. Zack glanced up at the pad and caught a glimpse of the sequence, but he couldn't read the alien symbols. One of the soldiers caught him looking and struck him on the side of his head. His ear stung from the blow.

The door retracted into the ceiling, opening the way, and amber lighting from the holoscreens drove the darkness back. There were other Xiiginns in the room. Some looked over in his direction as he was dragged inside. They were approached by another Xiiginn carrying a tablet computer. This one was covered head to toe in the black battle mesh all the Xiiginns seemed to be wearing. Zack couldn't see its face, but the tail was a dead giveaway as to what species it was.

"What's this?" the Xiiginn asked.

"Special projects. This one is heading to the pit," the soldier answered.

"We're already at capacity in the pit," the Xiiginn said, and took a better look at Zack. "I doubt he'll last long in there."

"My orders are from Mar Arden, and Kandra Rene will be overseeing. Here is the authorization," the soldier said.

The Xiiginn glanced at a new image on his tablet and nodded. He motioned to one of the techs standing by. "Tag him," the Xiiginn said.

Another Xiiginn approached, holding a chrome rod. One of the soldiers forced Zack to hold out his arm, and the Xiiginn jammed the rod against his forearm. Zack felt a pinch as something shot into his skin, but he didn't have time to give it much thought as he was dragged to the other side of the room. Dim amber lighting formed a circle in the darkened area. The soldiers deposited Zack in the middle of the circle and quickly moved away from him. Zack had just enough time to raise his head before the floor beneath gave way and he plunged downward into darkness.

Zack slid face-first down a dark tube. His body flopped to the side as he rounded a corner. He zipped past tiny globes of light, followed by another turn. Each time he saw a light in the distance, he braced himself for a turn in the small tunnel. He entered a long curve and the tunnel became steeper, increasing his speed. Zack gritted his teeth and tried to angle his body as best he could. He was flung around a sharp turn, the tunnel leveled off, and his body slowed down. A series of red flashing lights blazed up ahead, and a part of the wall fell away. Zack was thrust through the opening.

He tumbled down, and the night sky flashed into his field of vision as he was momentarily airborne, landing on the cold, wet ground and coming to a halt with his face in the mud. He lifted his head and spat the mud out in a half gag. It tasted like rotting garbage. He tried to push himself up, but his hands kept sliding away from him in the mud, and he decided to army-crawl toward what he hoped was drier ground. Zack reached ahead with one arm and drove his elbow down, moving slowly forward. He pushed with his legs as best he could until he was clear of the nasty mud pool.

Zack turned over on his back, gasping for breath, and lay there for a few minutes while his breathing eventually slowed. He looked up at the star-filled sky above him. Nothing looked familiar. He didn't know where he was. Zack rolled back over and pushed himself to his feet. He still had on the thin layer of underclothes he'd been wearing under his spacesuit. It was better than being naked but did little to warm him. He was drenched and covered in mud. He walked onto drier ground.

There were tall trees ahead of him that reminded him of the trees he'd seen in the valley on Selebus. He spun around and looked up the way he'd come. High above him was a towering structure that loomed in the night sky. A metallic wall stretched away in either direction, but not so far that he couldn't see where it curved around on itself. All the grogginess he had felt before his slide down the tube of horrors was gone. He wiped traces of mud and dirt from his mouth and face.

This must be the pit, Zack thought.

He lifted his forearm and ran his fingers across the spot where the Xiiginns had injected him, feeling something hard beneath his skin. It itched, and Zack held his arm up into the moonlight to get a better look. There was a dark spot beneath his skin. He poked at it, and whatever it was delved deeper. Zack tried to squeeze it, but it burrowed away from him. It didn't hurt, but he did feel a slight pressure.

Sounds of large footfalls stomping his way startled him, and Zack peered into the trees off to his right. He heard more stomping.

"Oh crap," Zack whispered and started backing away.

Zack had taken several more steps when he heard yipping sounds coming from the area he was moving away from. Several shadows detached themselves from the tree line and shuffled over to where he'd been. The creatures were hunched over, with their heads extended toward the ground. Zack quickened his pace as quietly as he could, but one of the creatures screeched out to the others and started coming after him. Zack turned around and fled.

He tried to activate his implants to enhance his vision, but they wouldn't respond. He glanced around him as he ran, looking for anything he could use as a weapon. Katie had drilled into him that even a simple stick could mean the difference between life and death. He wished she were here. Katie was among the strongest people he knew. He tried to think of what she'd do in a situation like this. Katie or Hicks, both in the military, would be able to handle the situation he was in.

Zack focused on where he was going, looking for higher ground to get a better vantage point, but the landscape was level in any direction he looked. He had eased his pace, trying to listen for sounds of pursuit, when another screech sounded into the night, but Zack knew he couldn't keep running. He felt a tiredness deep in his bones, and running away wasn't a long-term solution. He needed to get off the ground and hide, so Zack started looking for a tree he could climb. After a few minutes' searching he found a tree with branches thick enough to hold his weight. He sprinted straight toward the trunk of the tree and leaped. Using his forward momentum, he pushed off the trunk and reached for the lowest branch, pulling himself up and grunting while swinging his legs up, then getting into a crouching position and reaching for the next branch. Zack repeated this until he had gone as high as he could go. The creatures that chased him raced past the tree he was in, and the breath caught in his throat as they immediately circled back. He hoped they couldn't climb, but at least he'd have the high ground if they could.

It was difficult to see how big they were, but Zack guessed they were near the same size he was. They circled the tree he was in like a pack of hungry dogs. One of them let out a high-pitched growl and started to climb. The rest followed the first as they climbed straight up toward him, their claws biting into the tree.

Give me a break already, Zack thought. He glanced at the nearest tree and thought about leaping over. Then an image of plunging down to the ground and the pack of creatures swarming him knocked that idea out of his mind. He needed to fight. He reached for one of the smaller branches above him, trying to break it off. The branch was a little more than an inch in diameter, but it didn't break—just bent downward.

"Come on, damnit!" Zack shouted.

Sounds of the creatures' claws scraping the tree as they climbed made Zack double his efforts. Swinging the branch back and forth, he created breaks in it. He worked it as fast as he could, and the branch finally gave way as one of the creatures reached him, and Zack saw its face. It was a Nershal. Its pale green skin was horribly deformed, and its eyes were nothing but milky white orbs. The Nershal's nostrils flared, and it reached a clawed hand toward him. Zack swung his stick and hit the Nershal on the back. The creature howled in pain and lost its grip. Zack hit it again, and the Nershal crashed downward into another one, and they both went down. The Nershals landed roughly, and Zack could hear them crying out in pain.

More of the deformed Nershals were climbing up toward him. Zack climbed higher, trying to put more distance between himself and the mutant Nershals. He watched as they caught his scent and scrambled toward him. It was almost as if they came at him from instinct rather than a true intent to do him harm.

The next Nershal he hit with his stick was surprised by the blow.

"Stop!" Zack said. "Stay away."

The mutant Nershals stopped. At least they could hear him, even if they couldn't see him.

"I don't want to hurt you. Stay away," Zack said, and swung his stick so they could hear its sound.

The closest mutant Nershal cocked its head to the side and reached tentatively upward.

Zack swung the branch again and hit it against the side of the tree so hard that a large shaft broke off. The loud knock drew the mutant Nershal's attention, and several others climbed down to investigate the part of the branch that had broken away. Zack grabbed the end of another branch and snapped it off, thankful it was an older branch that easily broke from the tree. He flung the second branch away, and the sounds of it crashing to the ground could be heard. The remaining mutant Nershals climbed down and gathered around the area where the branch had landed. Zack heard several low growls and screeches, and two of the mutants abruptly turned away from the tree, their heads lifted while they listened.

Zack crouched with his back against the tree and faced the same direction, but the sound of a deep snarl caused him to jump back up, slamming his head into the small branch above him. The mutant Nershals began to scramble away, but several gathered around the two Nershals Zack had caused to fall from the tree and helped them up. One of the injured mutant Nershals looked up at Zack and screeched pleadingly. Zack's mouth hung open, but he had no idea what the creature was trying to tell him.

His internal HUD flickered to life.

Combat Mode Initiated.

He could see! The forest around him appeared in startling clarity as another deep snarl sounded, and Zack caught a glimpse of a massive creature as it pushed its way through the trees, heading straight for him. He squatted down and lowered himself to another branch, but his hands slipped and he tumbled toward the ground, banging into every branch on the way down. He felt as though the tree were beating him for daring to break off any of its limbs.

Finally, Zack crashed to the ground in a heap. He shook his head, trying to clear his vision while crawling away. A massive, clawed fist slammed the ground where he'd been just a moment before. Zack scrambled to his feet and stumbled around the tree. There was a loud whoosh and another massive fist slammed into the tree, causing some of its roots to snap as it grudgingly fell over. The creature roared, and just as its large head came around the bent tree, Zack's HUD flickered off. Zack gasped and turned, running as fast as he could.

The glimpse he'd caught of it put the creature at around twenty feet tall. Zack ran as fast as he could, darting around the trees, trying to keep them between him and the giant mutant now chasing him. The cadence of the creature's massive footfalls as it propelled itself forward reminded Zack of a gallop, and it was gaining on him. The mutant roared as it streaked out to the side, catching up to him. Zack changed course, and the terrain became rockier. The forest was thinning, with the gaps between the trees becoming more prevalent. He saw several large mounds and headed toward them. The giant mutant continued to gain on him, and Zack could hardly breathe. He couldn't go any faster.

As he rounded some brush, something grabbed him. Zack fell to the ground and was pulled into the brush. Whatever had hold of him kept pulling him deeper, and Zach realized the brush had covered the opening to a small cave. Zack struggled against whatever was holding him, and a hand clamped over his mouth.

"Quiet, Human," a voice said.

Sensing something familiar in the voice, Zack stopped struggling and tried to see who had spoken to him by the light of a wispy shaft of moonlight streaming into the cave from an opening above. He could still hear the large footfalls stomping around, and Zack tried to breathe as quietly as possible so he could listen. A loud roar seemed to rattle the stone walls around them. Zack couldn't tell where the creature was, but after a few moments it stalked away from the cave.

"I should have realized that only one such as you could cause all this noise."

Zack frowned. "Etanu?"

The Nershal stepped into the moonlight, stooping and favoring one side.

For a few moments the pain in his body was driven back. "How?" Zack gasped.

"They tossed me in here shortly after we arrived. I guess they figured I wasn't worth much compared to you. I did manage to get this though," Etanu said.

The Nershal withdrew Zack's PDA and wristband from the tattered remains of his uniform. Zack reached out and took it.

"Thank you," Zack said.

"I tried to get it to work, and it seemed to work for a few minutes, but then it just stopped," Etanu said.

"So that's why my HUD suddenly came on. Have you been able to contact the others? Is there a way out of here?" Zack asked.

Etanu sat down on a rock. "You saw the walls. This is a prison," he said and winced.

"Are you hurt?"

"I had a run-in with the blind mutants my first night here," Etanu said.

Zack took a good look at the Nershal. Etanu had been so strong, and he'd stayed with Zack on the Xiiginn cruiser and been captured. "Why didn't you just fly out of here?" Zack asked.

"I tried, but one of the Enforcers shot me down," Etanu said. "No lethal rounds."

Zack frowned. "I thought Enforcers were Nershals. Are you saying they're here too? I only saw Xiiginns up in the central building."

"They were Nershals," Etanu said, his orange eyes blazing with anger.

Zack didn't know what to say. How did one respond to the knowledge that their own species was betraying itself? "I don't know much about the Nershals. The only things I know, I learned from the ones I met on Selebus, but nothing I've seen so far would indicate that a Nershal would knowingly betray their own species."

Etanu looked away and shook his head. "We are immune to the Xiiginn compulsion," he said.

"They're experimenting on you. Perhaps the Xiiginns found some other way," Zack said.

His forearm itched, and he rubbed it.

"That's a tracer. I think they tag everyone they send down here," Etanu said.

The dryness in Zack's mouth reminded him of how thirsty he was. He glanced around the cave but didn't see anything in the way of supplies. Etanu followed his gaze.

"We'll need to stay here for a while, make sure the mutant is gone, and then we can get out of here," Etanu said.

"I don't suppose you have any water?" Zack asked.

"No," Etanu said. "There isn't much to be found either. The Xiiginns make sure all the food and water come from them."

"Do you know where we are?" Zack asked.

Etanu nodded. "We're on Selebus. At first I thought they might have moved us, but the length of this night has proven otherwise. Selebus's orbit around the gas giant gives it prolonged days and nights."

Zack was quiet for a few moments. "Thank you for saving my life. I think we're even now."

Etanu had sworn to protect Zack with his own life in return for Zack saving his life during a Nershal rite. That crazy life-and-death run through the valley to the Skybowl with a poisonous alien creature on his wrist seemed like it was so long ago now.

The Nershal looked over at him, considering his words. "I'm not sure it counts. We still need to get free of this place."

"Regardless, I appreciate it. That thing almost had me, and if you hadn't stepped in I would likely be dead right now," Zack said, his body shuddering at the realization of just how close he'd come to dying. How the hell were they going to get out of this place? Now that he wasn't running for his life, he felt his shoulders sag with exhaustion.

"Go ahead and rest. I'll keep watch," Etanu said, and looked as if he were about to say more but didn't.

"What is it?" Zack asked.

"I've explored some of the pit, but not all of it. This is the first time I've seen the large mutant hunt anything. I don't know why it was drawn to you in the first place," Etanu said.

"It wasn't the only one. The blind mutants were chasing me before that. I thought they wanted to . . . I'm not sure what the hell they wanted. I knocked one out of the tree I was in, and it seemed surprised that I hit it," Zack said.

"I was watching but wasn't close enough to help," Etanu said.

Zack settled down on the ground with his back against the cave wall. Every so often they heard the distant roar of the giant mutant. "I could be reading things into what the blind mutants were doing, but when that big mutant came, I would have sworn they were trying to get me to come with them."

Etanu blew out a breath and shook his head. "Do you really think they cared about you? They likely didn't even know what you were, let alone show concern that you would be killed by the giant mutant. They're mindless."

"They're not. They communicate with one another," Zack said.

"Fine, they communicate with one another," Etanu said. "They came after me, too, when I first got here."

"And?"

"And they left me alone after I killed a few of them," Etanu said.

Zack didn't say anything.

"You're too soft, Human. It's going to get you killed in here," Etanu said.

Zack clenched his teeth. He didn't need the Nershal to remind him just how out of his depth he was. He wasn't a survivalist or a soldier. He was a hacker, and he was trapped here on this moon in an alien star system. The others must have been trying to find him, but how long would they search for him before they assumed the worst? "How did you happen to be in the area?" Zack asked, deciding to change the subject.

"I've been here for a few days and made it a point to come back and check this area in case the Xiiginns dumped you in the pit. I guess they decided you were too much trouble," Etanu said.

Zack glanced at the Nershal, acknowledging his mild attempt at humor. "I think they ran out of time," Zack said, and swallowed hard. "Mar Arden questioned me, but he had to leave. Something about unrest on your home world."

"If you've met with Mar Arden, then you should count yourself lucky you survived the meeting. He's the same Xiiginn who held Kladomaor captive," Etanu said.

"Have you been able to find a way out of here?" Zack asked.

Etanu's eyes returned to the ground in front of him, and he shook his head. "Get some rest, Human. You're going to need it."

Zack had more questions but decided Etanu was right. Whatever they were going to do required that they rest for a bit before figuring out just how secure this pit really was.

CHAPTER SEVEN

KAYLAN WAS IN the room just outside the airlock. Despite assurances from the Boxans that the emergency transit shaft was perfectly safe, she wouldn't allow herself or any of the Athena's crew to use the shaft without an EVA suit. She glanced at Katie while they were getting their suits on. Kaylan could see why Zack liked her, beyond the generous curves of her body. Ever since Zack had gone missing, Katie Garcia had been quietly reserved with just about all of the crew, and Katie had hardly had any reaction at all when Kaylan had told her she loved Zack. All of Katie's attention had been focused on securing the Athena and searching for Zack.

Kaylan glanced at the airlock. Gaarokk would be on his way over to them soon.

"I think we need to talk," Kaylan said.

Katie stood up and was adjusting the EVA suit. "About what?" she asked.

"About Zack," Kaylan said.

Katie looked at her impassively and didn't say anything.

"I told you I loved him," Kaylan said.

Katie's arms came to rest at her sides, the top half of the EVA suit hanging down by her waist. "I don't see what there is to talk about."

Kaylan's brows arched in surprise. "Don't you have anything to say to that?"

Katie resumed donning her EVA suit by slipping an arm into the sleeve. "What would you like me to say?"

"I don't know. How about, 'Go to hell. Zack is with me,'" Kaylan said.

"No," Katie said. "I won't do that. My only concern is getting Zack back and the safety of the crew, just like you. If he decides he wants to be with you instead of me, that's between me and Zack."

"That's it?" Kaylan said.

Katie narrowed her gaze, and Kaylan caught a glimpse of Katie's emotions. "We need to work together," Katie said.

"Yeah, but if we don't get this stuff out in the open, it's going to affect how well we work together," Kaylan said.

Katie finished putting on the EVA suit and sighed. "Fine. I'm not sure you really love Zack, and I'm afraid it's going to hurt him in the long run, assuming we find him."

Kaylan's mouth hung open for a moment. "There is a history between us."

"I know. He told me," Katie said. She slipped her hands into her gloves, and they secured themselves to the suit.

"I just wanted to be honest with you," Kaylan said.

"What do you want me to say? That I love Zack too?"

"Do you?" Kaylan asked.

Katie closed her eyes.

The airlock door engaged. Gaarokk had arrived. Kaylan put on her helmet and inwardly cursed herself for a fool. She shouldn't have brought it up. It was stupid. She needed to focus on finding Zack, and whatever happened between them would happen.

The airlock door opened, and Gaarokk pulled himself inside. Despite how much bigger than a Human the Boxan was, he brought his feet under him, easily adjusting from a zero G environment to the artificial gravity field they had on the Athena. The Boxan's head was uncovered, but he did wear a form-fitting mesh suit Kaylan knew would help him survive in space. She'd seen the helmets on those suits retract to the neck area.

"Welcome aboard," Kaylan said.

The Boxan crouched lower and had to stoop. "Thank you for the invitation. One of my areas of study in the Confederation of species was spaceship designs. We've found it remarkably insightful to examine the spaceships a species builds."

"Well, I hope you share those insights with us," Kaylan said.

Katie stepped into the outer airlock area, and Kaylan followed. Efren had just arrived and gave them a wave.

"Kaylan," Gaarokk said. "We're doing everything we can to try and find Zack. I just wanted you to know that."

Kaylan nodded. "I appreciate it. We all do."

The airlock doors shut, and the outer doors opened. The gravity field diminished to zero gravity. They didn't speak while they went through the shaft that connected the two ships. Kaylan hoped Ma'jasalax would be able to help her find Zack. She didn't understand why she couldn't find him, and it gnawed at her. What good were her abilities if she couldn't use them to find Zack? She constantly tested herself by using her ability to see different parts of the ship and the Boxan ship, which still worked. She'd even used her abilities to help search through the wreckage of the Xiiginn cruiser, and that had worked fine, but she was unable to focus in on Zack like she'd been able to do when they'd escaped the cruiser.

They entered the airlock to the Boxan ship and transitioned back to an artificial gravity environment. Hicks greeted them in the corridor beyond. Kaylan had asked him to stay over on the Boxan ship to watch and listen to what Kladomaor was doing.

"Anything new?" Kaylan asked.

Hicks shook his head. "I would have contacted you if there were. The only thing I noticed was that Ezerah has been speaking with Ma'jasalax for the past hour. Ma'jasalax asked to see you, so it could be that they've come up with something."

Ezerah was a female Nershal who had known Kladomaor when she was a child. She had been serving the Xiiginn until Kladomaor got her to join them after the genetic experimentation at the hands of the Xiiginns was exposed. According to Kladomaor, the hierarchy of the Nershal government had roots in a caste system. Ezerah's family was powerful. To put it in Human terms, Ezerah was royalty, as was Etanu. Kaylan knew that at the very least the Nershals on Selebus were working hard to find out what happened to Etanu, and since Etanu had been with Zack, perhaps the two of them were together.

"Thank you," Kaylan said to Hicks.

"I wish there was more I could do," Hicks said, and looked at her, considering.

"What is it?" Kaylan asked.

"Nothing. I just need to speak with Katie for a few minutes," Hicks said.

Hicks waited until Kaylan was far enough away to be sure they wouldn't be overheard.

"Talk to me, Katie," Hicks said.

Katie leveled her gaze at him. "I'm doing everything I can to ensure we get Zack back."

"The Athena's shuttle has been on standby for the past three hours, all prepped and ready to launch," Hicks said with an arched brow.

"And your point is?"

"I know you. I think you intend to take the shuttle to Selebus to try to rescue Zack," Hicks said.

"You've found me out," Katie said dryly.

"Come on. Don't be like that. Why would you start taking steps for a solo mission and not include me?" Hicks asked.

Katie looked away from him. "I thought you'd try to stop me."

"Maybe. It depends, and we're not even sure if Zack is there," Hicks said.

"The Boxans are a half a step away from forcing us to leave with them, and I'm not going to just let that happen," Katie said.

"So what's the plan? Take the shuttle and search the entire planet for one person by yourself?" Hicks asked.

"If I have to, but I intended to find the Nershal who helped us before."

"Udonzari?"

"Yes," Katie said.

"Katie, we need to stick together. Not one of us is prepared for this.

You and I have dealt with high-stress situations, but the rest of them are relying on us to get them safely home."

"If it comes down to it, then come with me. Or would you trade Zack's life for our survival?" Katie asked.

Hicks frowned. "You know it's not that simple."

Katie's eyes flared in anger. "I'm done."

"Hold on a minute," Hicks said, quickly taking hold of her arm. "If we could find some credible information that Zack is alive and where he's being held, I would be the first one to volunteer to go get him. You know that. But we can't go charging off blindly." Hicks let go of Katie's arm. "Please," he said.

Hicks watched as Katie thought about what he'd said. They'd been friends for years, but he'd never seen her like this. If she closed herself off and began taking action on her own that would put them all in danger, it would be his responsibility to stop her.

"I can't promise you anything," Katie said. "And I'm not acting alone."

"Kaylan?" Hicks asked.

"She's starting to question whether we should stick with Kladomaor and the Boxans," Katie said.

Hicks's brows drew together in concern. "I think our best bet for finding Zack is to work with them."

"And if they won't help us?" Katie asked.

"They will," Hicks said.

"You're deflecting," Katie said.

"We'll cross that bridge when we come to it. There are too many variables to make this decision blindly. You saw what the Xiiginns were doing at the research facility. Genetic experimentation. If that's what the Xiiginns do to their supposed allies, then what's to stop them from doing that to us?" Hicks asked.

Katie bit her bottom lip but didn't say anything.

"I don't like it any more than you do, but if it comes down to saving Zack or warning Earth about the Xiiginn threat, then the decision becomes very clear," Hicks said.

Katie squared her shoulders. "Is that your final decision, sir?"

Hicks drew in a bitter breath. Katie going formal was a clear indication that the subject was closed. "We'll see, Lieutenant."

"They can court martial me if we get back," Katie said, and headed toward the bridge.

Hicks watched her go and hated every second of it. Zack was his friend too. The hacker had wormed his way into connecting with all of them. Hicks had hardly left Kladomaor's side so he would be there in case anything new was learned. He'd led enough operations to know that these things take time. Katie knew it too, despite her feelings for Zack. Deep down, she knew it too. Hicks believed that completely. The real question for him was what Kaylan would do if they had to leave Zack behind. Like it or not, Kladomaor was right to be concerned with the increased Xiiginn presence here. Essentially they were outgunned, and the resources they had available might not be enough to mount any type of rescue. What good would a rescue attempt be if it got them all killed? Or worse.

Hicks had headed back toward the bridge when he heard something behind him. Turning, he saw Dr. Redford coming from Engineering. Something about Redford of late had been making Hicks even more suspicious of the astrophysicist.

"Hello, Major," Redford said. "One of the Boxans was going over the sensor relay they have here. Truly brilliant. Some of the upgrades the AI had us do will open up a lot of doors for us."

"That's good," Hicks said. "Which Boxan were you with?"

Redford glanced back over his shoulder and then back at Hicks, his brows raised as if he'd just heard the question. "Oh, uh, Larx I believe his name was."

Well, that did make sense. Larx was an engineering specialist, but something was off about Redford, and Hicks couldn't figure out what it was.

Kaylan came around the corner adjacent to the bridge and waved over to them. Katie and the Nershal named Ezerah were close behind.

"We need to head back to the Athena," Kaylan said, walking toward him.

Hicks turned and walked next to Kaylan. "What's happening?"

"Ezerah has offered to help us with our navigation information, which will hopefully help us pinpoint where we are in relation to Earth," Kaylan said.

Hicks noted the slight elevation in her tone and came to a stop. The others filed past them, and Kaylan leaned closer to him.

"We have a way to find Zack," Kaylan said.

"That's great. Tell me what it is," Hicks said.

"No time. We need to get back to the Athena," Kaylan said, and walked to the airlock.

Hicks followed her and grabbed his helmet. The others were preparing to cross the emergency shaft that connected the two ships.

Hicks stood next to Kaylan. "I'm with you. I hope you know that," Hicks said.

Kaylan gave him a single nod. "Thank you. It means a lot to me. Come on, there's little time."

CHAPTER EIGHT

KLADOMAOR STOOD ON the bridge. Earlier, he'd ordered passive stealth protocols to be engaged, which would prevent both their ship and the Human ship from being detected by the lightweight scanning protocols used by the Xiiginns. Anything more aggressive from the Xiiginns would indicate that they knew they were still here in the Nershal star system. Remote scouts had been deployed that would report any Cherubian jump waves detected. The Cherubian drive was what allowed them to focus dark energy and fold space time to traverse the great expanse.

The increased Nershal space traffic didn't concern him as much as the two Xiiginn warships that had arrived a few hours before. The warships had headed straight toward the Nershal home world.

Kladomaor glanced toward the door to the bridge. He knew Kaylan had arrived a short while ago, and he had expected her to come for a status update.

"Battle Commander, I have an update," Devark said.

Kladomaor turned toward the battle strategist and nodded. "Go ahead."

"I have marked the list of known Nershal outposts and research facilities on Selebus," Devark said. An image of Selebus appeared on the main holodisplay, highlighted with the positions of the facilities. "I've positioned our scout pods in orbit around the moon, scanning for large power sources that would be indicative of rogue Xiiginn facilities."

"Excellent," Kladomaor said. "I want Udonzari and the Nershal rebels kept informed of anything we find."

"Understood, Battle Commander," Devark said. "But wouldn't it be premature at this point?"

"No, it's a show of good faith. I want the Nershals to know we mean to help them, and if the Xiiginns do have Etanu and Zack held prisoner down there, it would be at one of those facilities," Kladomaor said.

Ma'jasalax entered the bridge, and Kladomaor noticed that Kaylan wasn't with her.

"The Humans have returned to their ship," Ma'jasalax said in response to his unasked question. The Mardoxian priestess noted the holodisplay but didn't say anything else.

"Were you successful in locating Zack this time?" Kladomaor asked.

"No, the Xiiginns are taking steps to cover their tracks. It's preventing either of us from locating the Human," Ma'jasalax said.

"That would mean they know you're alive," Kladomaor said.

"The Xiiginns are being cautious. They must realize your presence here signifies a change in tactics," Ma'jasalax said.

"We've had reports that some Nershal provinces are in open rebellion," Kladomaor said.

"Your efforts brought about their break from the Xiiginns faster,"

Ma'jasalax said.

"They have a long way to go," Kladomaor said.

Alarms blared on the bridge.

"Battle stations," Kladomaor said.

"We've detected three Cherubian drive waves," Devark said.

Kladomaor's brows furrowed, and he went to his command couch. He glanced at the report on his console and looked at Ma'jasalax. "The Xiiginns are coming here in force."

"To be expected," Ma'jasalax said.

"We're out of time. We need to convince the Humans that we must leave this system. Stealth systems cannot be engaged indefinitely. Start jump prep for the away coordinates," Kladomaor said.

"What do you intend to do?" Ma'jasalax said.

"I intend to get us out of here," Kladomaor said.

"Are you planning to inform the Humans?" Ma'jasalax asked.

Kladomaor clamped his mouth shut and then gave a frustrated nod. "Open a comms channel to the Athena."

"Comms channel open, Battle Commander," Devark said.

"This is the Athena, go ahead," Kaylan said.

"We've detected the gravity waves of a recent wormhole entering this system. The Xiiginns are coming in force. We cannot evade their detection for long. We must leave," Kladomaor said.

There were a few moments of silence while Kladomaor waited for Kaylan's reply.

"We're not leaving," Kaylan said.

Kladomaor's fist slammed down on the console. "You'll be captured, and we'll all be killed."

"I'm sorry, Kladomaor, but I'm not leaving one of my crew in the hands of the Xiiginns," Kaylan said.

Kladomaor muted the comms channel and growled. "Be ready to expand our artificial gravity field to keep the Athena tethered to us," he said, and then opened the comms channel again. "Kaylan, please listen to reason. Zack is gone. He sacrificed himself so you would live. If you won't listen to reason, then you leave me no choice."

"Battle Commander, the Athena's engines are coming online."

"Engage the gravity tether," Kladomaor said.

He left the comms channel open and waited for them to realize they weren't going anywhere. The Athena's engines fired, but the ship remained firmly in place, held by the gravity tether.

"They've closed the comms channel," Devark said.

"Understood," Kladomaor said, and glanced at Ma'jasalax.

"Your actions may be our undoing," Ma'jasalax said.

Kladomaor didn't reply. He turned his attention to the countdown for leaving this system. They had no choice. He couldn't take on three Xiiginn warships and protect the Humans. They had to leave. It was their only option.

CHAPTER NINE

WARNING ALARMS BLARED throughout the Athena. Kaylan took in the readings from her console. The engines were engaged, but they weren't going anywhere. A shimmy began to run through the walls and floor.

"Warning, hull stress up by eighty percent," the AI said.

Kaylan frowned. "Cut power to the engines," she said.

"Engines are off," Hicks replied.

Kaylan glanced at Ezerah. "Do you know how they're holding us here?"

The Nershal shook her head. "I'm not sure. The Boxans were never ones to share their technology."

Kaylan opened a comms channel to Engineering. "Efren, is Gaarokk with you?"

"Yes, Commander, he's right here," Efren said.

"Gaarokk, we need your help. We have a way to find Zack, but it requires us going to the Nershal home world. Ma'jasalax believes the Xiiginns are masking Zack's presence somehow, and that's why we've been unable to find him," Kaylan said.

"What's happening up there?" Gaarokk asked.

"We're trying to leave, but Kladomaor won't let us. He's controlling the ship somehow. Can you help us leave?" Kaylan asked.

"Kladomaor would never do such a thing without good reason. I'm going to open a comms channel to—"

"Don't," Kaylan said. "Kladomaor is trying to make us leave because three Xiiginn warships have entered the system. He says he can't protect us and hide from them."

"Gaarokk," Ezerah said, "everything the Human has told you is true. Ma'jasalax knew something like this was going to happen, and she believed you would help us when we needed it most."

Kaylan allowed the silence to drag on but kept a careful watch on the countdown timer on the main holoscreen.

"What's on the Nershal home world that you think will help you locate Zack?" Gaarokk asked.

"A Mardoxian chamber," Kaylan said.

Gaarokk sucked in a breath. "The only one in this system was destroyed during the Nershal uprising. We never built any on their home world," Gaarokk said.

"There was one other that was kept secret and is located in the province of my family's abode," Ezerah said.

"To the best of my knowledge that area was quarantined," Gaarokk said.

This is taking too long, Kaylan thought. The countdown timer was running out.

"Gaarokk, please, this is the only chance we have of finding Zack," Kaylan pleaded.

"You must choose, Boxan," Ezerah said. "The Cherubian drive is charging, and we're moments away from being pulled into the wormhole that follows. Can you break the tether that holds the ship in place?"

The silence that followed drained away any hope Kaylan clung to. Her hands balled into fists.

"Gaarokk," Hicks said, "we just need more time. Kladomaor said he can't protect us and face the Xiiginn warships. If we leave and head for the Nershal home world, then Kladomaor will be free to distract the Xiiginns for a while."

Gaarokk cleared his throat. "That . . . could work."

"Where are you going?" They heard Efren ask over comms. Gaarokk was in Engineering.

"Kaylan," Hicks said, "open a channel to Kladomaor. Let's tell him what we intend."

Kaylan nodded and opened a comms channel to the Boxan ship. "Kladomaor, we've found another option," she said. There was a sharp power spike showing on the main holodisplay. The lighting on the bridge dimmed. Kaylan felt the artificial gravity on the Athena increase, pressing her into her seat. Those who were standing on the bridge were driven to their knees. Kaylan grunted with the effort just to stay awake. Then the pressure was gone.

"We're free. Go!" Gaarokk's shout came through comms.

Kaylan engaged the Athena's engines, and they sped away from the Boxan ship.

"Warning," the AI said. "Fusion reactor power levels will be detected if we maintain this speed."

Kaylan's eyes were fixed on the console that showed their current position in the Nershal star system.

"Kaylan," Hicks said quietly. "Stealth is our best defense now."

Kaylan glanced at Hicks. He smiled, and his clear blue eyes conveyed his earnest intentions. She nodded and reduced the engines to ten percent. "Athena," Kaylan said, "will this speed keep us from being detected?"

"Affirmative, Commander."

Kaylan blew out a breath and rechecked their coordinates. She climbed out of the pilot's seat and turned to face the others on the bridge.

"We're with you, Commander," Hicks said.

"Thank you," Kaylan said.

The door to the bridge opened, and Gaarokk's hunched form came through. Kaylan walked over to the Boxan.

"Thank you for helping us. I know it couldn't have been easy," Kaylan said.

Gaarokk's large golden eyes held a shocked expression, as if the Boxan couldn't quite believe what he'd done.

"How did you free us?" Hicks asked.

Gaarokk blinked a few times as he came to grips with the moment. "Kladomaor used a gravity tether that kept this ship attached. The basis for the tether relies on maintaining a strong magnetic field. I increased the artificial gravity as much as I dared here and momentarily reversed the field. The disruption was enough to get us free. Kladomaor is smart. He will not be fooled a second time."

"Let's hope there won't be a need to do this again," Kaylan said.

Gaarokk glanced at Ezerah. "I just checked our records, and there is no reference of a Mardoxian chamber ever being built on Nerva."

"I've never seen it," Ezerah said, "but Ma'jasalax assures us it's there. She said it was built in secret to test for the Mardoxian potential in my species."

"You were a child when we were forced from this system, so I wouldn't expect you to have seen it, but how are we supposed to find it?" Gaarokk asked.

"We have the coordinates," Kaylan said. "And Ezerah should be able to get us through any security that's still in place. Given the state of unrest between the Xiiginns and the Nershals, I'm hoping we can sneak down there and use the chamber without anyone being the wiser. The trip there will take longer than it normally would, but we can use the time to prepare."

Gaarokk frowned. "How long have you been planning this?"

"When we last went aboard your ship," Kaylan said, "Ma'jasalax warned us that Kladomaor would try to force us to leave with them to keep all of us safe. I know he's doing what he thinks is right, and so am I."

"What's done is done. I'll see what I can do to help prepare against quarantine," Gaarokk said.

Kaylan felt the tension drain away from her shoulders.

Hicks came to her side. "How do you feel?"

"Like we're finally doing something constructive," Kaylan said. Katie nodded as she came over to them.

"And if what you intend with the Mardoxian chamber doesn't work?" Hicks asked.

Kaylan shared a glance with Katie and swallowed hard. "Then we'll need to accept that Zack is gone."

*****

Kladomaor growled. "Stop the jump clock and figure out what happened. How were they able to break free from the tether?" he said, and turned toward Ma'jasalax.

"It's time to see if you can live up to the legend," Ma'jasalax said.

"What's that supposed to mean?" Kladomaor asked.

"You said you couldn't face the Xiiginn warships and protect the Humans. Well, now they've gone on their way to Nerva," Ma'jasalax said.

"Not for long," Kladomaor said. "Execute an intercept course with the Athena."

"Don't do that," Ma'jasalax warned.

"You're just buying them time to get away," Kladomaor said.

"Perhaps, or you're too stubborn to admit you've been outmaneuvered," Ma'jasalax said.

"With your help," Kladomaor said.

"I may have pointed them in the right direction, but they were already withdrawing from us before this. You should have realized that when Kaylan had all the Humans report back to their ship. Now, instead of racing off after them, let's try helping them," Ma'jasalax said.

Kladomaor glared at the main holoscreen that showed the Athena moving away from them.

"Let them go," Ma'jasalax urged. "Give them the time they need to try and find their missing crew member."

"What would you have me do?" Kladomaor said.

Ma'jasalax's gaze swept past all the Boxans on the bridge. "Remind the Xiiginns that they are not unopposed. This is a stealth ship. Make the Xiiginns fear the shadows. Make their strength their weakness."

Kladomaor felt a burning in his chest and an eagerness to enact retribution against those who had made their race suffer—made *him* suffer. As Kladomaor glanced at his fellow Boxan soldiers, he could see the same yearning reflected in each of their eyes. One by one the Boxans on the bridge rose to their feet, grasping their elbows with each of their hands, and bowed their heads.

"Battle Commander," the Boxans murmured.

Kladomaor looked back at Ma'jasalax, who also brought her arms up and clasped her elbows, bowing her head. It was an ancient form of salute that the Boxans reserved for their most revered leaders.

"Return to your stations," Kladomaor said. "We have Xiiginns to hunt."

Chapter Ten

Zack and Etanu left the safe confines of the cave. Zack had slept for hours and had awakened bruised and stiff. He didn't feel like moving all that much, but Etanu said they couldn't stay in the cave, so Zack grudgingly got up and tried to work out some of the stiffness that had set in from sleeping all night in a damp cave.

Etanu told him that it would be dawn soon, and Zack wondered how the Nershal could tell the time. He was hungry and couldn't remember the last time he'd eaten. Etanu had no food, and they'd only been able to find small amounts of water. The forest around them was deserted.

"Are you sure there isn't anything dangerous around?" Zack asked and glanced around.

The darkness of the night sky was fading to a pale gray with hints of red.

The Nershal glanced back at him. His fierce orange eyes under his furrowed brow clearly conveyed his thoughts about Zack's question.

"I get it," Zack said. "We're never not in danger as long as we're held captive here. But where did everything go?"

Etanu continued walking and Zack followed. "They're gathering on the far side of the pit. To the place where they feed us," Etanu said.

Hearing there was food got Zack's attention; however, Etanu's ominous tone didn't fill Zack with a lot of hope. Zack had strapped his PDA to his wrist, even though it wasn't working. He didn't have time to look at it, and it didn't appear that Etanu was willing to give the time.

"Is there any way you can contact other Nershals nearby?" Zack asked.

"There aren't any nearby. At least not that I can tell," Etanu said.

Zack had to believe the others were looking for them. They needed to send some sort of signal that would let them know they were alive. *How long will they keep looking before they believe we're dead?* Zack wondered.

"What can you tell me about this place?" Zack asked.

"There are walls that surround the entire perimeter. Go far enough in any direction and you're bound to find the wall. We can't fly out of here. At least I can't fly out of here. I've seen different kinds of mutants that have banded together. You've already met the blind mutants. They're pretty good at tracking but won't throw themselves at you if you fight back," Etanu said.

Zack frowned. "What do you mean?"

"What I mean is that if you kill a few of them, they'll leave you alone," Etanu said.

Zack took a deep breath. Last night when he'd been chased by the blind mutants he had thought they wanted to kill him, but the more he thought about it the more he was convinced he could have been wrong about them. "What else?" Zack asked, preferring not to press the issue.

"There are the silent hunters. They will kill anything that wanders into their territory, with the only exception being the giant mutant, although I've seen them trade blows with it," Etanu said.

This place just gets better and better, Zack thought. "What do the silent hunters look like? And this may seem obvious to you, but why do you call them silent hunters?" Zack asked.

Etanu came to a stop and surveyed the area in front of them. They were leaving the hilly area. Zack glanced above the trees, trying to catch a glimpse of the tower he'd seen last night.

"They are all Nershals," Etanu said. "All the mutants I've seen so far have the traits of my species, with the exception of the giant. The silent hunters never speak. They don't make a sound, not even when they're wounded. I'm not sure if they're *able* to make a sound. Sometimes they communicate with each other with gestures, but I think they might be connected with neural implants. The ones I've been able to see up close have extensive scarring," Etanu said, and brought his hand to the side of his head.

"So they might have been enhanced somehow," Zack said.

Etanu considered this for a moment and nodded. "Enhanced? Yes, this is correct," the Nershal said, and his gaze hardened.

"What is it?" Zack asked.

"What the Xiiginns have done is unnatural. They are exploiting my species," Etanu said.

"I'm sorry," Zack said.

Etanu glanced at him. "Why would you say this? You're not the one doing this to us."

Zack shrugged, feeling uncomfortable. "It's just what we do. If someone we're with is in pain and we're not able to do anything immediate to help, then saying 'I'm sorry' shows the other person that you sympathize with their pain—their loss."

Etanu glanced at him, and Zack had the feeling that the Nershal didn't understand.

"It's called compassion," Zack said.

Etanu straightened himself to his full height. "I understand the meaning. You may feel it is well placed, but it encourages weakness."

Zack blew out a breath. He certainly knew about being weak. "Fine, it won't happen again," he said, and started walking.

Etanu caught up to him. "You're angry?"

Zack shook his head. "I really don't understand your species at all. It's like you're hardwired against emotion. What's the difference between feeling a certain way about what the Xiiginns are doing to your species and me saying I'm sorry about it? I mean, how does your species make any friends if you're always so preoccupied with whether it makes you look weak or not?"

Etanu gave him a long look. "The bonds my species share with one another are strong and are never given lightly."

"That's good to know. I guess I thought that since we're stuck in this place there would be some sort of bond between us. At least until we got out of here," Zack said.

"I'm required to protect you until I have saved your life," Etanu said.

"Got it. Crystal clear now," Zack said.

Etanu took the lead and Zack followed. He wasn't sure if he just didn't understand the Nershals or if it was just Etanu. Zack recalled how Etanu had come to stand with him against the Xiiginns on their ship. He'd stayed behind and was captured with him. Was Etanu really saying he did all those things because of some oath about protecting him? They needed to work together if they were going to get out of this alive. Zack pressed his lips together. He needed to stick with Etanu if he had any hope of surviving.

"Does your species use implants?" Zack asked and tapped the side of his head.

"Of course," Etanu said.

"Then what do you suppose the scars on the silent hunters' heads are for?" Zack asked.

"Some type of enhancement. They are quite strong but seem to stick to only one area of the pit," Etanu said, and glanced over at Zack. "We use implants, but we do not enhance ourselves beyond the confines of what is natural."

"So the fact that the Xiiginns are doing this to you is an even more serious offense," Zack said.

"Of course," Etanu said. "Do Humans manipulate their genetics to make them into something they're not?"

Zack shook his head. "No—well I'm not sure. If someone is sick or hurt and we fix what's broken with an artificial part so the person can stay alive, then technically we're changing them."

"I don't mean healing. I'm referring to crossbreeding between species to create something that nature wouldn't have created on its own," Etanu said.

Zack wished Emma were here. He was sure the xenobiologist would be able to have a more meaningful conversation about this subject than Zack ever could.

"What do you know about the giant mutant?" Zack asked.

"Enough to stay away from it. It has a lair, and in the time I've been here, I've only seen it leave it to feed, but something drew the creature out last night," Etanu said, giving him a sideways glance.

Zack felt a chill zip down his back. "What could it possibly want with me?"

"I don't know, but if we see it, we do what everything else does in this place—run," Etanu said.

They continued on and within the hour they saw the walls of the pit. The gray walls appeared to be smooth, and Zack doubted they could climb their way out.

Zack had hoped Etanu would be able to find something for them to eat, but the Nershal said nothing was safe. This place was a prison, and the Xiiginns were the ones in control. "When you tried to fly out of here, do you remember how many guards they had on the walls?" Zack asked.

"Not many, there were more automated turrets. They're meant to keep us in. One of the other mutants must have seen me, because a number of them tried to climb the walls. Their claws were able to pierce the wall material. Some actually made it over," Etanu said.

Zack's eyes widened, and he glanced back at the walls. Could they climb it somehow? He felt an itch on his arm where the Xiiginns had placed their tracker.

"They didn't escape," Etanu said. "There were several loud pops, and after that the mutants on this side of the wall stopped trying to climb over. They knew the ones who got over the wall had all died."

Zack kept scanning the walls, trying to force a solution into his mind, but he couldn't think of anything. "We need more information about this place."

"What do you mean?" Etanu asked.

A wave of hunger gathered in the pit of his stomach. He wished he were in the mess hall aboard the Athena, joking and eating with his friends. Katie would be laughing with the others while Efren tried to get her to forget about the geek she was with. Sometimes Kaylan would be with them, but he had often found her on the bridge or in one of the observatories, working away—always working. Zack closed his eyes and thought about the last time he'd seen Kaylan. He had pushed her onto the elevator and locked out the controls. She had slammed her fists on the doors and screamed at him, her beautiful honey-brown eyes wide with shock at what he'd done, but he couldn't hear here. He thought he was going to die, and he hadn't wanted her to die with him. She had to live. He knew she would be furious with him for what he'd done, but it was worth it. He remembered the tender feel of her lips when he kissed her, and a small pang settled into his chest.

"Zack?" Etanu asked.

Zack swallowed hard. "Sorry, I just got a bit distracted. What I mean is that if we're going to get out of here, we need to learn all we can about this place. Including all the inhabitants, what they do, when the Xiiginns feed us—anything we could use."

Etanu glanced at the walls. "Do you think there's a way for us to escape?"

"That's what I want to find out. One thing I've learned over the years is that no place is totally secure. There has to be a way for us to get out of here," Zack said.

Etanu regarded him for a moment. "Strength is highly valued among my species."

"I'm not strong—" Zack started to say.

Etanu reached out and grabbed his arm. "I mean up here," Etanu said, and tapped his head. "I know how to fight, how to survive. Most Nershals can't see beyond their own strengths, but you're different. I begin to understand how you survived the rite."

A loud gong rang throughout the pit, catching Zack by surprise.

"We must move quickly, or there will be nothing left for us," Etanu said, and began to run.

Zack caught up with the Nershal and matched his pace, but he suspected Etanu was taking it easy on him. The closer they got to where the gong had sounded, the more Zack could hear the other creatures in the pit moving in the same direction. He flinched as the sounds of the mutants came closer to them. Zack saw the edge of the tree line, and Etanu slowed down. They were close to the towering wall of the pit. The edge of the trees was less than fifty yards away, and Etanu signaled for him to stop.

Another gong sounded.

Large shafts of metal rods burst from the wall, extending outward and forming a large tunnel. Bolts of lightning crackled along the rods, leaping from each one. Zack tried to see what was in the tunnel, but the glare from the lightning bolts kept blocking his vision. Closer to the tunnel entrance, a group of mutants exited the trees across from where he and Etanu were hiding. Some cocked their heads to the side while others sniffed the air.

Zack stepped closer to get a better look. As Zack moved, the lead mutant snapped its head in his direction, peering into the brush. The other mutants fanned out on either side of the leader. Each had a long, jagged scar that went from the temple to the base of the skull. Zack froze in place and hardly dared to breathe. The snarling sounds of more mutants grew in intensity until a large roar heralded from deeper in the pit. The silent hunters swung their formation around to face the direction of the roar.

Etanu eased into place by Zack's side. "Quiet," he whispered. "Follow my lead."

Zack bobbed his head that he understood.

Loud thumps of something large stomping through the forest came closer. The treetops shook violently as the giant mutant burst through. The giant leaped from the tree line and closed the distance to the silent hunters guarding the makeshift tunnel. The breath caught in Zack's throat as he got his first glimpse of the creature that had almost killed him the previous night. He couldn't tell what it was. The mutant was easily twice as tall as any Nershal he'd ever seen. It had a long dark tail that ended in a large stinger. Zack recognized the stinger from the protokars he'd seen. The mutant was bipedal, like the Nershals, and its skin appeared dark green, with deep crags across its massive torso that reached up its neck like armor. The giant mutant roared, swinging its head from side to side. It had the blazing orange eyes of the Nershals, with three blue glowing points forming a triangle on its forehead. The shape of the head was significantly wider above the jawline, which was both alien and familiar.

"Oh my god," Zack gasped. "That mutant looks like it's part Boxan."

Etanu leaned forward to get a better look, then turned back toward Zack with wide eyes, as if he didn't quite believe what he was seeing.

The silent hunters stood between the giant mutant and the makeshift tunnel, and something shimmered in each of their hands when it caught the sunlight. Zack squinted and saw that the silent hunters had elongated claws.

Other mutants gathered behind the giant and began to press forward. The giant spun around and grabbed hold of the nearest mutant while the others scrambled to get out of reach. The giant flung its victim into the silent hunters, who scattered out of the way. With the way cleared, the giant mutant leaped forward and slammed its massive fists onto the shafts. Bolts of lightning lashed out from the shafts at the behemoth, but the electric current only seemed to enrage the creature as it kept slamming its fists onto the metal shafts. A deafening gong sounded, and the metallic shafts withdrew back into the wall. A huge supply cache was left in their place, and every living thing nearby sprinted forward.

Zack stood rooted in place while the chaos before him unfolded. Mutants large and small darted in, trying to claim some tiny portion of the foodstuffs that would keep them alive until the next feeding. Next to the supply cache was a large basin of water. The water sloshed and soaked the ground as the frenzied mutants fought around it. The giant mutant tore into the supply cache, dumping small canisters on the ground. Zack watched in silent horror at what the Xiiginns had reduced intelligent creatures to. Even though they were genetic experiments, there was still something of their old selves buried beneath the madness.

Etanu raced forward and fought his way to some of the canisters that had been flung away. Several dead mutants littered the ground. Zack glanced up at the tower where he knew the Xiiginns were watching and swallowed hard.

The giant mutant howled, grasping a large green canister. The creature slammed the canister onto the ground and then pried the lid open. Several mutants got too close to the giant and were swatted back by a massive fist. The giant tossed the lid to the side and emptied the canister's contents into its mouth. Zack couldn't get a good look at what it was. Without a backward glance, the giant mutant returned to the woods from which it had come. Smaller groups of mutants rushed in to snatch whatever was left. The dead were carefully avoided, as if the mutants couldn't bear to face the victims of the chaos. Zack took several steps toward the remnants of the supply cache. Etanu was heading toward him with several canisters clutched against his chest.

"Why didn't you follow?" Etanu asked.

The feeding grounds were quiet but for a few small mutant scavengers. Zack didn't answer the Nershal.

"Don't go over there. It's not safe," Etanu said.

Zack continued on, ignoring him and trying to walk without drawing too much attention to himself. The scavengers quickly worked their way through the area while keeping a wary eye on Zack. He hoped they wouldn't bother him if he stayed clear of them. He came to the body of the first dead mutant and simply stared at it for a moment. Its body was broken and its limbs stuck out at odd angles. Some of the dead had large gashes from the fighting, but most were just trampled. Their faces were frozen in permanent agony. Zack didn't consider himself an overly religious person, but he couldn't stand idly by while the dead rotted on the ground. They deserved to be buried or, at the very least, not left lying on the ground like garbage.

Zack squatted down and grabbed beneath the arms of the Nershal mutant, then dragged the body a short distance away. He straightened the limbs as best he could and tried to arrange the arms and hands so they rested across the body. Zack retrieved two more bodies and repeated the process. He returned for a fourth Nershal mutant and noted its large size. He wasn't sure if he could move it by himself. Some of the mutants wore some type of leathery mesh that hadn't torn as he thought it might when he'd dragged the other two bodies away. He took a firm hold of the shoulders and strained to lift the large body. Sweat blurred his vision, and when he wiped it from his eyes he saw several of the blind mutants he had encountered the night before. Zack gasped, but the blind mutants slowly approached and came to a stop at the dead mutant's feet. They each grabbed hold of a leg, and Zack gritted his teeth while lifting the shoulders. Together they carried the dead mutant away to where Zack had taken the others. His muscles ached from the exertion of moving the bodies, but he felt better in the depths of his core. More of the blind mutants joined them and carried the bodies of the dead until they were all lined up and arranged as neatly as possible.

Zack took a quick look around. There were no more dead to be moved, and the large basin of water nearby was destroyed, so he didn't understand why the mutants were still with him. One of the blind mutants came toward him, and Zack wasn't sure what to do. He thought about running and immediately dismissed the idea. He was too tired to run. Zack glanced behind him and saw Etanu start to approach, but Zack motioned for him to stop. If the blind mutants wanted to hurt him, they would have already done so. The creature came to within a few feet of Zack and held out a metal canister that it must have gotten from the supply cache. Zack slowly reached out and took the canister. The creature's milky white eyes seemed to stare off in the distance for a moment.

Zack couldn't read the blind mutant's expression. He had a hard enough time trying to discern what Etanu was thinking. The blind mutant's facial features closely resembled the Nershals he'd seen— enough to know they had once been the same.

"Thank you," Zack said.

One of the other mutants grunted, and the blind mutant who stood in front of Zack turned around and joined the others.

Etanu walked over to him. "I don't believe it. I've never seen them do anything like this before."

Zack frowned. "Like what?" he asked while twisting the lid to the canister open. Inside was a yellowish liquid that had the consistency of oatmeal. Zack leaned in and sniffed. Putrid smells slithered up his nostrils, and he almost gagged from the stench. He glanced over at Etanu, who gave him a nod. Grimacing, Zack raised the canister to his lips and gulped down its contents. His stomach clenched as the gruel made its way down, and Zack clamped his mouth shut to stop himself from throwing up. It tasted awful. He hoped whatever it was wouldn't kill him. After a few moments, the nausea eased up enough for Zack to stop dry heaving. At least his hunger diminished while his body figured out whether it would accept what he'd swallowed.

"That was disgusting," Zack said.

"But necessary. What you've just consumed was likely one of their daily rations," Etanu said, and handed Zack a small serving of water from one of the canisters he'd captured. "I've never seen the blind mutants so calm. I saw them approach you. They seemed to be drawn to what you were doing. It didn't appear as though they were going to attack, so I stayed away. I didn't want to provoke them."

"There's still a part of them that remembers being a Nershal," Zack said.

Etanu regarded Zack for a moment before speaking. "Why did you do this?" he asked and gestured to the line of neatly arranged dead mutants. They seemed oddly more at peace than before.

"It didn't seem right to just leave them like they were. Back home we would have buried them in the ground and given them their last rites, depending on what they believed," Zack said.

"You surprise me, Human. Our customs for how we deal with our dead is similar to yours, but I would caution you against such actions in the future," Etanu said.

"Why?" Zack asked.

"While the blind mutants were receptive to this practice even though the dead weren't all one of theirs, there are others who would kill you on the spot for disturbing their fallen," Etanu said.

"I don't understand," Zack said.

"The creatures in this pit aren't true Nershals. They've been reduced to our primal instincts. Your intentions are good, but they could also get you killed in a place like this," Etanu said.

Zack pressed his lips together. "So we should only look out for each other and ignore the rest?"

Etanu nodded. "If you wish to survive this place."

The area around them had become serenely quiet, almost peaceful. A gentle breeze blew through the area.

"What will happen to them?" Zack asked, gesturing toward the line of dead mutants.

"They will be collected," Etanu said.

Zack's stomach clenched, and the nausea faded away completely. "Do you think the stuff I just ate is safe?"

"Yes," Etanu said. "While it may not appeal to your palate, it's just a basic ration with proteins and other nutrients that will keep you alive. Your body will be able to process it."

Zack glanced over at the wall where the metal shafts had opened. He walked over and touched it. The gray surface was mostly smooth, but Zack saw the indentations of where the shafts had exited. He traced his fingers to the central area.

"What are you doing?" Etanu asked.

"I think there's a door here. It must be how they send the supplies in. So if there's a door to get in . . ." Zack said.

"Then we can use it to get out," Etanu finished.

Zack frowned while tracing his fingers across the surface. He wished he had access to his PDA. At least then he could use his implants to try and detect any signals. Zack glanced at Etanu. "Do your implants work?"

"Partially. Otherwise we wouldn't be able to understand each other," Etanu said.

The same applied to Zack, but the higher functions of his own implants were only available in conjunction with his PDA. "Are you able to use your implants to connect to the systems that control the doors?" Zack asked.

Etanu looked at the wall. His furrowed brow pushed forward in concentration. "No, they must have me blocked."

Zack continued to feel his way along the wall, certain there must be some sort of access panel. As he did so, he heard Etanu take a few steps away from him. He noticed a slight indentation and pressed his fingers in. Nothing happened. Zack tried to pull on it, but he couldn't get a firm enough grip. He sank to his knees and started digging where the wall came to the ground. After he cleared some of the dirt away he noticed that there were thick cables surrounded by smaller wires that fed into the wall.

"Hurry, Human," Etanu called over to him.

Zack glanced behind him. Etanu was facing the tree line.

"What is it?" Zack asked.

"The hunters are returning," Etanu said.

"Help me," Zack said.

Etanu came to his side.

"Do you know what these wires do?" Zack asked.

Etanu examined the wires and cables that Zack had exposed and shook his head.

"Damn," Zack said. He glanced down at them and knew better than to start pulling the wires without understanding exactly what they were. They could be high-powered lines that would fry him in an instant. He kept clearing away the dirt, but Etanu grabbed him by his shirt and pulled him to his feet.

"What the—" Zack began and stopped.

Somehow a large group of the silent hunters had closed in on their position. The scarring on their heads looked even more horrifying than before. Oozing pink skin was sewn together along the mutants' scalps. Their clawed hands dripped with a bright greenish liquid, and their blazing orange eyes burned with a primal savagery that froze Zack in place.

The lead hunter raced forward, with the others howling as they came. Zack flinched and stumbled to the side as Etanu pushed him away. An ear-piercing siren sent a lance of pain through Zack's head. He collapsed to his knees while holding his hands to his ears in a feeble attempt to block the sound. He forced his eyes open and saw that the mutants were suffering as he was. The siren stopped and the mutants backed away from them. A large doorway opened from the wall, and Xiiginn guards poured out. They held some type of short rifle and leveled the sights on the mutants, along with Zack and Etanu. Zack held up his hands. The mutants cowered low to the ground as they backed away from the Xiiginns, submitting to their jailers without so much as a challenge.

The guards came over to Zack, seized him by the arms and dragged him away. He glanced at Etanu, but there was nothing the Nershal could do. The Xiiginns shoved Zack to the ground, and when he moved to get up the guards pointed their rifles at him, so he stayed on his knees.

A deep, sultry laugh came from the dark opening in the wall. Zack watched as a female Xiiginn sauntered over. Thin black clothing reminiscent of leather stretched over her skin, leaving nothing to the imagination.

"I see you've experienced some of our hospitality," Kandra Rene said.

Zack glanced at the Xiiginn guards. They wore dark mesh armor with helmets, so he couldn't see their faces.

"If that's what you want to call it," Zack said.

Kandra Rene came over to him and ran her smooth fingertips along Zack's face. Her claws were smaller than the ones he'd seen on other Xiiginns, but Zack believed that had she wanted to, she could have killed him right then and there.

Kandra Rene squatted down, her pale skin showing in stark contrast against her clothing. Zack saw flecks of purple in her eyes. Her long platinum hair draped like a shimmering curtain. She seemed different than she had moments before. It was as if her face had become a combination of human and alien qualities.

"Things could be so much easier for you," Kandra Rene said.

"You could let me and my friend go," Zack replied.

"I could also leave you to them," Kandra Rene said, and glanced over at the prostrating mutants that had been moments from killing them before.

Zack looked over at the hunters. Their submissiveness made him clench his teeth. "You're a monster," Zack said.

Kandra Rene narrowed her gaze, losing the soft quality she'd had before. "Do you not have animals on your home world? Your species could never advance without becoming masters of your own environment."

Zack's lips lifted in a half snarl. "Is that what you call this? They're not animals. They were once Nershals."

"And what is the life of a Nershal to you?" Kandra Rene asked.

"What the hell kind of question is that?" Zack said while rising to his feet.

Kandra Rene waved the guards back and waited for Zack to speak.

"No species should be treated like this—rounded up, stuck in a pit and treated like animals," Zack said, clenching his teeth at the last word.

"We're doing scientific research here. Their sacrifice will benefit many more," Kandra Rene said.

"You'll have to forgive me if I don't take your word for it," Zack said.

"Tell me about your home world. Where is it?"

"I'd rather not," Zack said.

Kandra Rene's eyes narrowed in anger, and Zack felt as if something were pressing in on his mind.

Zack squinted his eyes against the pain. "You've tried this before. What makes you think it's going to work now?"

Kandra Rene spun, her tail taking out Zack's feet. She was on him in an instant, her claws at his throat. "Because it *has* worked," she said.

Zack's arms were pinned down, and he felt a trickle of warm liquid drip across his neck. This was it. She was going to rip his throat out. Kandra Rene screamed, and Zack waited for his inevitable demise.

The Xiiginn pushed herself off of him and regained her composure. "I see you need more time in the pit," Kandra Rene said, and glanced over at Etanu. "We'll take this one with us for questioning."

The Xiiginn guards rushed over to Etanu. Zack opened his mouth to speak, but Etanu shook his head.

The Xiiginns retreated back through the door, and Kandra Rene lingered there for a moment, watching Zack.

"I'll give you a head start. It should make it more sporting for the very creatures you believe are still intelligent," Kandra Rene said, and gestured with her chin behind him.

Zack turned around and saw that the hunters had risen from the ground. All the submissiveness from earlier was gone, and in its place was what he'd seen before. He had to run. Zack blew out a breath, and without another thought he sprinted for the trees, running as fast as he could.

CHAPTER ELEVEN

IT HAD BEEN an entire cycle since the Athena had left them. Not wanting to draw attention to the Human ship, Kladomaor hadn't sent any communication. The fact that they hadn't pursued the Human ship should be communication enough for them. At least they had Gaarokk there to guide them. But the fact that Ezerah had also joined the Humans had surprised him.

Ma'jasalax filled him in on the details now that he agreed with this foolish plan. Kladomaor frowned. "Agreed" was too strong a word. Now that he had calmed down, he could see the wisdom in Ma'jasalax's actions. If anything, the Mardoxian priestess had greater insight into dealing with the Humans than he did. The Humans were stubborn—all of them. Like most of the intelligent races he'd come across, they needed to learn some of the harsher truths about the galaxy for themselves. He just hoped they could avoid some of the painful lessons the Boxans had learned about the Xiiginns—lessons that had left their home planet, Sethion, in chaos. The star system defenses kept Sethion in quarantine until they could come up with a permanent solution. At least their secret colony hadn't become compromised. Neither the Xiiginns nor the Confederation knew where it was, and it had given them some much needed breathing room to recover.

Ma'jasalax came onto the bridge and walked over to his side. "The Athena is nearing their final approach to Nerva."

"You've been in contact with them?" Kladomaor asked.

"Not directly. I've been monitoring their progress," Ma'jasalax answered.

Kladomaor arched a brow. "The likelihood that the Mardoxian chamber is still intact on Nerva is remote at best."

"I think the odds are better than that," Ma'jasalax said.

"Time will tell," Kladomaor said.

"Indeed it will," Ma'jasalax said. "I know you still have reservations about this whole endeavor, but showing our support will go a long way toward earning cooperation from the Humans."

"I'm well aware of why we're doing this. One thing I don't understand is how a Mardoxian chamber came to be built on Nerva. We already tested the Nershals to see if the Mardoxian potential was present, and there were no indications that it was," Kladomaor said.

"That is correct. The standard tests did not reveal that the Nershals had the Mardoxian potential. However, nothing we did with the Nershals was standard. We kept them secret from the Confederation in hopes that they would become our allies. They were the only species that could resist the Xiiginn influence. Direct control from a Xiiginn wasn't possible with the Nershals," Ma'jasalax said.

"And yet they allied with the Xiiginns anyway. At least now some of the Nershals are challenging that alliance, but this doesn't explain how a chamber was built on Nerva," Kladomaor said.

"Like the other species, the Nershals felt betrayed by us and the use of the Star Shroud on their star system. A small group of Boxans from the Mardoxian sect—some of the more open-minded scientists, such as Gaarokk and myself—built a test chamber on Nerva. Since the Nershals could resist the Xiiginn influence, we thought we'd try and cultivate the Mardoxian potential in their species," Ma'jasalax said.

"How? I thought the potential was either there or it wasn't at all," Kladomaor said.

"We mapped their genetic markers and looked for similarities with ours. No changes were made to their genetics. The Nershals were quite adamant about that, and we wouldn't have done anything without their knowledge or consent regardless. We invited some of the Nershals to observe connections within the chamber," Ma'jasalax said.

Kladomaor frowned. "I thought that was forbidden, that it was too dangerous because of the amplified connection the chamber helps create for traversing the higher planes?"

Ma'jasalax eyed him for a moment. "I had no idea you knew so much about the chambers," she said.

"I've considered every potential asset in our war with the Xiiginns," Kladomaor said.

"I have no doubt you have, and so have we, which is why we built the chamber on Nerva in the first place," Ma'jasalax said.

"Were you successful?" Kladomaor asked.

Ma'jasalax shook her head. "The Nershals we tested could only detect faint traces of the energies and connections the chamber was capable of. Nothing like the Humans. Kaylan was able to use the

Mardoxian chamber on her own the first time she tried," Ma'jasalax said.

"That's what makes the Humans different. Even though Kaylan and the others assert that what Kaylan is able to do is rare among Humans, the potential exists. This makes them both valuable and dangerous," Kladomaor said.

"The Human potential goes beyond whether they can use the Mardoxian chamber. I've reviewed some of the data their AI construct gathered on our listening station from their star system," Ma'jasalax said.

"It's our artificial intelligence construct they copied," Kladomaor said.

"Perhaps at one time, but they've adapted it to their ship. The AI is loyal to them, just as it would be to us. I believe Zack is largely responsible for that," Ma'jasalax said.

"He is quite clever, that one, but even if they do find him, he will never be the same. You know what the Xiiginns will do to him," Kladomaor said.

"Based on your report, the Humans are also resistant to the Xiiginn influence," Ma'jasalax said.

"I believe I said it is highly probable that some of the Humans can resist the compulsion of the Xiiginn. I didn't actually see any of the Xiiginns attempt to control one of the Humans. We were too busy staying alive and rescuing you," Kladomaor said.

"For which I'm grateful. Even if they are only partially resistant, they can make a much better stand against the Xiiginns than we can alone," Ma'jasalax said.

"We've fought the Xiiginns long enough to know they have other ways of making species do as they command. They are ruthless," Kladomaor said.

"Don't you see? That's why even if Zack becomes lost to the Humans, they must learn what is at stake so they can take that lesson back to their home," Ma'jasalax said.

"Their planet will need more than just the account of nine Humans to invoke change. They don't even have a unified global government," Kladomaor said.

"We must do everything in our power to ensure the Humans survive here. They will be as a pebble cast into a pond that will evoke a time of great change for their species," Ma'jasalax said.

A silent alarm flashed on the main holoscreen. They were running in stealth mode, and given what they were about to do, they couldn't risk their alarms being overheard by the enemy.

"One of the Xiiginn warships broke off from the rest to investigate our decoy," Triflan said.

"Acknowledged," Kladomaor said. "Stand by for the other decoys to engage."

Kladomaor had wondered if he could entice one of the warships to break formation. He had raced their ship to the outer star system, leveraging the strength of his ship, which was in speed and stealth. He would loiter and coordinate their decoys to distract the Xiiginn warships for a while. By now they must have received a report of the Boxan presence in the Nershal star system. He would entice them to give chase, and the Xiiginns would be restricted in their response to the threat he represented. They were in an occupied star system and couldn't exactly unleash the full measure of their arsenal here, but the Xiiginn's alliance with the Nershals was growing more fragile. If it came to open conflict, Kladomaor had given Udonzari a way to send communication to the Boxan fleet.

"Are you just deploying decoys?" Ma'jasalax asked.

"You mean there's something you aren't able to foresee?" Kladomaor said, baiting Ma'jasalax. "The decoys we've deployed will put their warships on a path of our choosing, forcing them to fly through whatever we have lying in wait for them."

"You mean to only wound them?" Ma'jasalax asked.

"I only need to wound them. We don't have the arsenal to destroy all of them. We'll ratchet up the pressure and see how they respond," Kladomaor said.

*****

Mar Arden disembarked from the transport ship that had taken him from Selebus to Nerva. It seemed his agents had been unable to silence the vid of the research facility on Selebus that exposed the truth of the Xiiginn activity there. He was surprised by how fast Nershal unrest was spreading. Perhaps the Nershals weren't as weak as he had originally thought. The younger generation clamored for the chance to use more advanced technology by serving aboard some of the Xiiginn ships. Initially it had been the elder Nershals who had posed the greatest risk to the Xiiginn interests here, but like any species, they had just needed the right push.

A comms signal was relayed to him from Selebus that had Kandra

Rene's identification associated with it. Mar Arden accepted the signal. "What's the status with the Human?" Mar Arden asked.

"He continues to resist us. I've sent him to the pit to soften his resolve," Kandra Rene said.

Mar Arden frowned. "If he dies, that will reflect poorly on you."

"I'm operating from within the restrictions you put in place. You've forbidden me to attempt our more aggressive interrogation techniques, and he seems to be able to resist compulsion," Kandra Rene said.

"Understood. I will remove you from the project then—" Mar Arden began.

"Don't do that. I allowed the Human to reconnect with his Nershal companion in the pit, and then I took the Nershal back into custody. Since there are no restrictions on what I can do to the Nershal, I should have more information about the Human shortly. There is a bond between the Nershal and the Human, which I plan to exploit," Kandra Rene said.

Mar Arden rubbed his fingers together in thought. "Interesting. Keep me informed of your progress," he said, and closed the connection.

The right amount of pressure always yielded results. That was why he was here at Nerva. When properly motivated, he had no doubt that Kandra Rene was up to the task of extracting the information they needed from the Human.

He crossed the landing pad to a vehicle that would take him to Nerva's global congress. He was scheduled to address the allegations brought forth in light of the investigation being conducted against the Xiiginns. Mar Arden climbed into the Nershal vehicle specially marked for him as the ranking ambassador for the Xiiginns. He would make them listen. The Nershals weren't as independent as they had once been, and it would be time for them to face that fact sooner rather than later. Mar Arden nodded for the pilot to leave.

In addition to dealing with the Nershal unrest, Mar Arden had to keep in mind that the Humans were important to the Boxans and therefore also warranted his full attention. He would find the Boxans in this system. It was only a matter of time.

CHAPTER TWELVE

Zack fled the feeding area. The Xiiginns had taken Etanu because of him. What were they going to do to him? He and the Nershal weren't the best of friends, and sometimes he suspected Etanu didn't like him very much, but he didn't want anything bad to happen to the Nershal. They needed to work together.

Zack sprinted toward the middle of the pit, and after a few moments the sounds of the hunters' pursuit faded. Like most of the planet Selebus, the pit was actually in the middle of a forest. The Xiiginns must have chosen this area for its remote location, but the only way he could know for sure was to get beyond the walls. Zack glanced around, trying to decide which way to go. He couldn't go back the way he'd come or the hunters would get him. The giant mutant had gone in the direction Zack was heading, and he definitely wanted to avoid that creature. He glanced at the PDA strapped to his wrist. He needed to fix it, and in order to do that, he needed to find someplace safe to work on it.

Whenever he thought of being stuck out in the pit alone, he felt his chest tighten with the constant need to look over his shoulder. How was he going to survive in this place without Etanu? He had no survival skills to speak of. Once again he found himself stuck in a situation that would be better handled by someone like Dale Hicks. The Air Force Major was accomplished in all of this stuff. Zack tried to think of what Hicks or Katie would do if they were in his shoes.

Zack slowed down to a walk, thinking he wanted to avoid blundering into another group of bloodthirsty mutants, for starters. *That isn't right,* Zack corrected himself. *The mutants are prisoners here just as much as I am.*

Some of the mutants were severely deformed, leaving Zack to wonder why the Xiiginns were doing any of this. Kladomaor had said the Xiiginns were always looking to advance themselves beyond any other species they came across. At the time Zack had thought the Boxan was only referring to technological advancement, but given what he'd witnessed, perhaps the Xiiginns' obsession with advancement extended to biological endeavors as well. He didn't have Emma's expertise in biology, but why else would the Xiiginns be genetically altering the Nershals if it didn't serve them in some way?

Zack glanced over at some fallen trees and damaged brush—results of the giant mutant smashing its way through. Thoughts of the giant reminded Zack that the Xiiginns weren't only researching Nershal genetics but the Boxans as well. If they were orchestrating those practices here, then what were they doing elsewhere? Zack was beginning to get a better understanding of why Kladomaor had been so driven to get the Athena out of there. If the Xiiginns made it to Earth, what would stop them from doing anything they wanted? Sure, Earth's military would fight, but could they stand against the Xiiginns? Zack wasn't sure, and he'd rather not be the one who told the Xiiginns about Earth. So far he'd been able to resist their attempts, but what would Etanu tell them? Zack pressed his lips together, thinking about all the conversations Etanu had been a part of, trying to gain some insight into what the Nershal knew about the crew of the Athena. Etanu didn't know the location of Earth—hell, the Athena crew didn't even know where they were in relation to Earth. Zack suspected the Boxans knew but hadn't shared that information yet. But Etanu could be forced to tell the Xiiginns about the Athena's crew.

Kaylan! Zack thought. A surge of panic blazed through his core. Kladomaor was keen to keep her away from the Xiiginns because she had the Mardoxian potential. Even the Boxan AI that resided on the Athena had conveyed the importance of such a discovery. If Etanu revealed anything about Kaylan to the Xiiginns, they would know how important finding Earth was. The Xiiginns might even get it into their heads to use Zack as bait to draw the others here.

Zack glanced over at the tower. He was a good distance away from it. He swallowed and glanced up at the sky. It had been a few days. Was the crew even looking for him anymore?

Zack closed his eyes. He wanted his friends to come rescue him, and at the same time he felt guilty about it. He kicked at a fallen branch and glanced over at part of the gray walls that surrounded the pit. He couldn't get out of here by himself, and he didn't want his friends to risk coming to rescue him.

He tried to imagine what Katie Garcia was doing. Her thick, dark hair was likely tied back while she focused on whatever she was doing with rigid intensity. She had intended to protect him on the Xiiginn cruiser. He'd seen her fight on the spaceship with practiced efficiency. But when the catwalk had started to come down, he'd thrown himself at Kaylan to keep her from falling. It had all happened so fast. Then he'd kissed Kaylan when he thought he was dying. He hadn't planned it. He had just acted without thinking. He cared about them both, and he didn't want anything bad to happen to either of them.

During the time the Xiiginns had sedated him, he had periodically regained consciousness, and he'd thought he felt Kaylan there with him—not in the room, but somewhere close by. He'd had the same feeling when he'd been forced to participate in the Nershal rite, which involved racing across a valley while being chased by feral protokars.

If Kaylan was trying to find him using her abilities, she could already be on her way here. Zack pressed his lips together and dismissed the thought. He hadn't felt like she was watching him since he'd been dumped into the pit, but still the thought gnawed away at him. Kaylan was among the stubbornest people he'd ever met. He could easily imagine her arguing with Kladomaor about not leaving without him.

Zack shook his head. He needed to find a way out of here. Like Commander Hunsicker had said on more than one occasion, he needed to work the problem. Solve enough problems and he might be able to get out of here, but there was no way he could do it without Etanu. Since there was no way he could rescue the Nershal, Zack set his mind on what he could do to help them both escape. He didn't want to think about never seeing Etanu again. The Xiiginn, Kandra Rene, had taken Etanu to get to Zack, so they had at least some motivation to keep him alive.

Zack decided to explore the areas nearest the wall. He needed more information about this place if he was going to come up with a plan to escape. He had a sneaking suspicion that there had to be other ways of getting in and out of the pit. The hunters guarded the feeding areas, and the giant mutant had likely claimed some other part of the pit. There could be some correlation there. It would be strategic for the Xiiginns to place the most dangerous and territorial mutants in the most vulnerable areas. He made a mental note to further explore this line of thinking.

Zack headed toward the wall, stopping every now and then to climb a tree for a better vantage point to spot any potential threats. Hicks would have been proud of him. He spotted a small group of mutants gathered near some sort of shelter that looked barely more than a shack. They appeared to be smaller versions of the Nershals, but he didn't see any of them unfurl their wings. He wondered if they could fly. Zack lowered himself to the ground and slowly approached the group to get a better look. Whatever clothing they had was in tatters, hardly more than rags. Other than their small stature—perhaps four or five feet tall—they closely resembled the Nershals—smooth, pale green skin with darker swaths on their faces. Zack looked at the shack, where one of the females was coming out.

Children! Zack gasped when he saw that she was carrying a small Nershal child. Some of the mutants glanced his way, but Zack wasn't sure if they'd seen him. He backed away, and the last thing he saw was the mutants ushering the mother and her child back into the shack. Zack moved as quietly as he could. When he was far enough away, he blew out a breath. The only other mutants he'd seen so far had been adults.

He glared over at the tower for a moment, then moved on and darted toward the wall in intervals. He tried to get close enough to see the area just above the ground, looking for signs of a door or the power lines he surmised must be beneath the walls. Since he had nothing to write with, he made mental notes about the different groups he encountered. He guessed the diameter of the pit to be around five miles—quite large. He was happy to learn that not all of the pit's occupants appeared menacing or dangerous. As long as he kept his distance, the mutants he encountered hardly paid him any mind, and Zack wondered how often a new captive was introduced to the population here.

Zack opened the lid to a canister of water he'd been carrying and took only a sip, intending to make his water supply last because he wasn't sure when he would be able to get more. He sat, resting his back up against the trunk of an old, gnarled tree. He was at the edge of the tree line before an open area, thinking this position would at least allow him to see if anyone or anything was approaching. He needed to take a break, so he removed his PDA and started examining it. He tried to power it on, but it was unresponsive. There was a small clasp on the side where it could be opened. He gently pulled on the clasp and the PDA opened, revealing the mechanism inside. Since the PDA wouldn't power on, he checked the connections to the power supply and reseated the connections where he could, but there was so much more he could check and fix if he had some tools.

A large shape flew overhead, catching Zack's attention. He glanced toward the open field and heard the distinct whine of engines that powered a Nershal sled. They must be tracking him. Zack looked down at the red spot on his forearm where the tracking device had been inserted. He thought of trying to dig it out and then run but dismissed the idea as foolish. Zack hastily put his PDA back together and rose to his feet.

The Nershal sled landed around twenty yards from his position, so they must have come for him. Zack walked out into the field and saw a heavily armored sled hovering over the ground. The sled was equipped with heavy gun turrets, and a large group of Xiiginn soldiers had gathered on the deck. Kandra Rene stepped off the craft and walked purposefully over to him. Her dark clothing clung to her shapely figure, the plunging neckline revealing her firm, ample breasts beneath. Her eyes were locked onto him, and her lips lifted in a half smile. She must have been able to get some information from Etanu. Zack glanced over to the sled, looking for some sign of the Nershal, but he wasn't there.

The soldiers accompanying Kandra Rene kept their weapons pointed at him, and Zack raised his hands.

"You didn't run," Kandra Rene said.

"I didn't see much point since you can track my every move," Zack said, and raised the forearm the tracking device was in.

"I have more questions for you," Kandra Rene said. She raised her wrist and activated a holoprojector. "We've collected some data from the cruiser you and your companions destroyed. The images were quite informative."

A holoimage appeared, hovering over the ground, showing Zack kneeling outside the elevator doors with his hand pressed on the glass.

Zack knew that if they zoomed in on the elevator they would see Kaylan.

"And this," Kandra Rene said, stepping closer to him.

The image rewound to where it showed Zack kissing Kaylan before locking her in the elevator. Zack's throat thickened, and he tried to keep his face impassive.

Kandra Rene watched him intently. "I'm not familiar with this practice, but judging from your pheromone levels I'd say there was a strong attraction between the two of you. This begs the question of who you were protecting. Who is so important that you would sacrifice your own life to protect theirs?"

Zack clamped his jaw shut and refused to answer.

Kandra Rene circled around him until she came to stand right in front of him. The Xiiginn's tail slinked behind her. Zack glanced at the Xiiginn solders that had surrounded him, then forced himself to look Kandra Rene in her alien eyes. The deep purple irises seemed oddly dilated. She stepped closer to him.

"Does this form not please you?" Kandra Rene asked.

Zack felt a slight buzz begin to build in the back of his mind. As the Xiiginn spoke, he kept focusing on the fullness of her lips, then slid his eyes down her revealing outfit. Zack's mind felt as if it had become muddled, and he forced himself to look away.

Kandra Rene reached out and gently raised Zack's chin so he had to look back at her. The buzzing in the back of his mind increased to a level where it became hard for him to think. Zack became aware of his rapid breathing.

Kandra Rene rested her gloved hands on his shoulders, and Zack felt her tail slink around his waist. "See how easy this could be? I could show you pleasures undreamed of if you just tell me what I need to know," she said.

Zack glanced at the holoimage behind her. It was still on a loop showing him kissing Kaylan and then pushing her into the elevator. He focused on his hand pressed against the glass door of the elevator and Kaylan's silent screams coming from inside. Zack closed his eyes and replayed the memory over and over in his mind. Suddenly, he felt like someone had poured an icy bucket of water over his head. The buzzing in his mind instantly ceased, and Zack's eyes snapped open.

Kandra Rene was leaning in, and Zack roughly pushed her away.

"Get away from me, psycho!" Zack said.

Kandra Rene barely stumbled and came at Zack in full force. Her fist snapped against his chest, and Zack was knocked off his feet by the force of the blow. His chest burned as if an electric charge had been unleashed. She leaped atop of him, howling in rage and pummeling his face. Zack tried his best to block her, but she was too strong.

Grabbing his hair, Kandra Rene pulled Zack's head off the ground. "You will tell me what I want to know," she hissed and struck him again.

Later on, Zack woke up lying on the ground. He didn't know how long he'd been unconscious, but his head was throbbing with pain. His face and jaw hurt from where Kandra Rene had beat him. When he tried to sit up, his vision swam, and he almost passed out again. He just lay there on the ground and looked up at the sky. The sun was still up, but that didn't really help him figure out what time it was because the days were longer here. He shook his head and clenched his teeth, only to be painfully reminded of how tender his jaw was. Catching a flicker of movement off to the side, he tried to look over.

Zack heard soft footfalls near his head, but he didn't have the strength to look over at the source. Someone placed a damp cloth over his face and immediately the burning and aching lessened considerably. Part of him reeled with worry about what manner of creature was with him, but the damp cloth felt so good on his face that he just didn't care. There wasn't anything he could do about it, so he just lay there on the ground and drifted back to sleep. When next he woke, the cloth that had been on his face was gone. His mind felt clearer, and there was much less pain. Someone groaned next to him.

"Don't you do anything the easy way, Human?" Etanu said.

Zack glanced over and saw the Nershal lying on the ground near him. Etanu didn't look any better than Zack felt.

"They let you go?" Zack asked.

Etanu rolled onto his side and glanced at Zack tiredly. "We were interrupted. After she got done with you, she returned to the sled where I was. Thankfully, a proximity alert was triggered, and they dumped me near you," Etanu said.

Zack frowned. "There was someone else here before. I think they helped. They placed a damp cloth over my face, and it took the sting out of the wounds."

"Healing," Etanu said.

"Who would heal us?" Zack asked.

"Not us—you—and I'm not sure who they were. The Xiiginns knocked me out with one of their stunners," Etanu said.

"What happened to you?" Zack asked.

Etanu looked away. "They questioned me about you and the others."

"What did you tell them?" Zack asked and braced himself.

Etanu closed his eyes, and his mouth became a grim line. He forced his eyes open and looked at Zack. "I told them everything. They did something to me, and it was like I couldn't stop myself. I tried. Please believe that I tried."

Zack's stomach clenched, and he felt weighed down. "I believe you," Zack said and looked away. His lips lifted in a half snarl. "I really hate her."

"Kandra Rene?" Etanu asked. "Me too."

Zack felt his blood begin to boil. "Yes. Are all Xiiginn like her? Cruel and manipulative?"

Etanu glanced away again. "We didn't always think so. They were admired as an ideal to strive for. The Boxans tried to warn us. It wasn't until much later that my father started to question the Xiiginns' motives. He began to teach us to question their motives as well, but it's difficult. At least it used to be."

"Well they seem to be showing their true colors now," Zack said. He stood up and clenched his fists. There was a fire blazing inside him, and he couldn't clench his fists tight enough. He pictured Kandra Rene here with him and imagined his hands wrapped around her throat, choking the life out of her. The anger in his heart purred at the thought, but other parts of him were silent—the silence one experienced when being judged—and it made him push away such dark thoughts.

"We need to focus on getting out of here," Zack said.

"You'll get no arguments from me," Etanu said. "I saw what might be a way for us to cross over the wall."

Zack shook his head. "I mean all of us," he said.

Etanu frowned. "What are you saying?"

"I'm saying we need to find a way to free every living thing trapped in this pit. It has to be all of us or none of us," Zack said.

Etanu regarded Zack for a moment. "The strong will rise," he said.

Zack's eyes widened. "I'm not strong. I just had my ass handed to me, and you think I'm strong?"

"Strength comes in many forms. Tell me what you have in mind for escaping this place," Etanu said.

Zack scanned the area, looking for possible threats. Sitting out in the open around twenty yards away was one of the blind mutants. The creature was alone, rocking back and forth. There was a pile of rags with dried blood in front of him. The creature's milky white eyes stared off into space, but its hands were working on something in its lap. Zack took a few steps closer, trying to get a better look.

"It has my PDA," Zack said.

Etanu came to his side.

The blind mutant cocked its head slightly when they spoke but otherwise kept working. Pieces of Zack's PDA were spread out on a piece of tan cloth that matched the remnant robes the creature wore.

"It's in pieces," Zack said, and started to walk toward it.

Etanu grabbed his arm and stopped him. "Wait. Look at the rags at its feet. This is the one that healed you."

"Yeah, but I need my PDA. I was trying to fix it before Kandra

Rene decided to pay me a visit," Zack said. He tried to move, and Etanu held him back.

"Just wait," Etanu said.

The blind mutant lifted up one of the components of Zack's PDA and examined it. The tips of its fingers traced the component. After a moment the mutant placed it back into the PDA's housing. Next it ripped out the small battery pack.

Zack pulled his arm free. "It's tearing it apart. If I don't get it now, I may never be able to fix it."

Zack walked over and stood in front of the blind mutant. The creature's fingers were still fiddling with the battery. It ripped the cord that connected it to the pack and threw the actual battery onto the ground.

"Stop," Zack said, squatting down and picking up the battery pack. It was a tiny thing, no more than an inch square.

Zack saw the spread of the PDA's components on the mutant's lap and groaned. He wanted to reach out and snatch it away. He'd never fix it now.

"I'm going to need that stuff back," Zack said.

The blind mutant ignored him. It grabbed another piece and placed it into the PDA's housing. The creature repeated this process until all the pieces were put back into place, with the exception of the battery. The blind mutant reached inside its robes, withdrew a small circular crystal, and pushed it into the spot where the battery was supposed to be. The mutant then reconnected the wiring, with one end being absorbed into the crystal. The mutant held the PDA up so the crystal captured the sun's rays, and it immediately began to glow. It brought the PDA back down, attached the cover, and handed it toward Zack.

Zack reached out and took his PDA. He thumbed the power button and gasped as it powered on. A brief status check flashed on Zack's internal HUD.

::Available power increased by five hundred percent. Personal Digital Assistant ID 11757, primary user Zackary Quick,:: Athena said.

"Yes!" Zack shouted. "It works," he said more quietly to Etanu.

He strapped the PDA to his wrist and ran a few more system checks to be sure it was fully operational.

Zack glanced over at the mutant. "I'm not sure if you can understand me, but thank you," he said.

The blind mutant stood up and waited.

Zack's implants came fully back online, and a threat assessment appeared on his HUD. He didn't need a computer to tell him that the blind mutant was a benign entity.

::Athena, can you reach the ship?:: Zack asked.

::Negative, the ship is out of range,:: the AI answered.

Zack relayed the information to Etanu. Zack tried to speak to the blind mutant again, but he didn't get a response. He offered the mutant his canister of water, which it accepted and drank.

"I'm not sure he can speak," Zack said.

Etanu glanced at the mutant. "There is scarring in the throat area."

Zack tried to see what Etanu was referring to but couldn't see anything that looked like scarring. Instead of the smooth, pale green skin of the Nershals, the mutant's skin was much looser, as if it were older.

"What do we do?" Zack asked.

"About him? Nothing. I want to hear more about this plan of yours. I'm assuming with your PDA working you can do more with your implants?" Etanu asked.

"Yes, but we should move and talk at the same time. There's something we need to check out," Zack said.

Etanu frowned. "Why do I get the feeling we're heading back into trouble?"

Zack smiled. "When are we not in trouble?" he said, and got his bearings.

Zack began walking and glanced behind them to see if the blind mutant was going to follow them. The creature was already moving, and it was surprising how quiet it was.

"You do realize what lies in this direction?" Etanu asked.

"The giant mutant," Zack said, "but I need to check out the area."

Zack told Etanu about his theory for the placement of the mutants that were highly territorial. It would be extremely dangerous to try and sneak into the area with the giant mutant, but he had to know if there were power lines and a hidden doorway in that area. Now that he had his PDA and access to the AI, he would be able to scan for ways to open those doors, if there were any. And, of course, assuming the giant mutant didn't mutilate them in the process.

CHAPTER THIRTEEN

KAYLAN SAT IN the pilot's seat on the Athena's bridge. They couldn't burn their engines all the way to Nerva; the risk of detection was too great. They did strategic burns and put Sir Isaac Newton in the driver's seat. They needed to get within shuttle range of Nerva and sneak onto the planet without alerting anyone. Ezerah would help them with the Nershals, but they had to avoid contact with the Xiiginns. The Athena wasn't equipped to deal with conflict. It was strictly a passenger ship for scientific research. Kaylan supposed that if it came to it, they could try to run if they were detected, but she didn't place their odds for getting away very high. She was glad Kladomaor hadn't pursued them and had instead worked to give them the time they needed to find Zack. Despite Ma'jasalax's assurances that Kladomaor would change his mind when the situation changed, Kaylan hadn't been sure he would. The Boxan was extremely self-assured, but she supposed Kladomaor's opinion of her was similar. Kaylan's lips curved into a smile.

She climbed out of the pilot's seat and stretched her arms overhead. At Brenda's insistence she'd gotten eight hours of sleep, and she felt much better. She could probably use more rest, but that would have to wait.

The door to the bridge opened and Ezerah walked in. The Nershal wore a dark, formfitting suit made of smart mesh fibers that could readjust for a variety of conditions—anything from the vacuum of space to the atmosphere maintained on the Athena. Ezerah had commented that the suit was extremely comfortable. The squarish pack on the back allowed the Nershal to safely fold away her wings.

The Nershals were a beautiful alien race and not at all what Kaylan expected to find in the galaxy. Truth be told, she hadn't known what to expect. Ezerah's features were quite alien yet familiar at the same time. Nershals had two eyes at the front of their heads and were generally humanoid in shape—bipedal with two arms. They had hardly any hair to speak of. Their skin was a pale green with darker swaths that adorned their face and, Kaylan assumed, other areas as well. Their eyes were larger than any Humans' and were several shades of orange. The Nershals also had twin sets of translucent wings. Zack had commented that they reminded him of dragonfly wings. Emma had noted that the similarity in the wing design was actually quite profound. Each wing functioned on its own. The wings didn't flap per se, but rotated around, which allowed lift to be achieved. This wing design enabled the Nershals to fly with a level of precision that went beyond an ordinary bird.

After a few moments, Gaarokk squeezed his way through the doorway. Boxans were very different from the Nershals, although they shared their bipedal stance. They had two large flaxen eyes about the diameter of a teacup. Their brown, roughened skin was reminiscent of the bark of a tree, and their triangular-shaped heads had a full mane of thick hair. And the Boxans were extremely tall, with an average height of eight to ten feet. Gaarokk, being only eight feet tall, was on the shorter side for a Boxan, but he was still quite thick and muscular. His voice sounded deeply cavernous when he spoke. Gaarokk was extremely open-minded, and Kaylan detected none of the superiority complex she got from Kladomaor.

The rest of the Athena crew joined them on the bridge. Hicks and Katie were armed with pulsar pistols.

Redford glanced at them. "Expecting trouble?" he asked.

Hicks shrugged. "Better to have them and not need them than need them and not have them."

Redford turned his gaze to Kaylan. "I've been monitoring the comms channel and scanning on the frequencies Gaarokk provided, and so far we've remained undetected."

Kaylan nodded. "That confirms what we suspected; however, I'm still concerned about being detected when we take the shuttle down to Nerva."

"There's no avoiding it," Ezerah said. "Our orbital installations will detect anything coming toward the planet. When we're challenged, I can provide my identification and tell them this is a survey ship."

"Won't they be able to determine that our shuttle is different from a Nershal vessel?" Kaylan asked.

"We'll need to transmit ship specs to them, and I will have your AI send the necessary information," Ezerah said.

"Commander," Gaarokk said. "They won't perceive this ship as a threat at all. They will scan the ship for weapons of a greater magnitude than you have available, so we shouldn't have any problems getting down to the surface."

"I'll need to upload the protocols to your AI," Ezerah said.

"Athena," Kaylan said, "allow Ezerah to upload comms protocols."

"Confirmed," the AI said. "Upload can commence at any time."

Ezerah tapped a few commands on her suit computer.

"Thank you for your help with all this. I don't think we would have gotten this far without it," Kaylan said, looking at Ezerah and Gaarokk.

"The Xiiginns have much to answer for," Ezerah said. "We've been blinded by their lies for far too long. I'm also curious about the Mardoxian chamber that's located at my family's residence."

"I'm sure you are," Gaarokk said. "We were quite surprised we couldn't find evidence of the Mardoxian potential in your species, given your abilities."

"What abilities?" Kaylan asked.

"Calculating space jumps for one," Gaarokk said. "The Nershals make superb navigators. Their brains are made up of three lobes, which allows for superior mathematical calculations. Combine that with an implant link to a ship's computer and you have a much more agile force at your command. It's one of the reasons the Xiiginns were so keen to align with them and bring them into the Confederation."

"And according to the research data from the facility we raided, it's one of the things the Xiiginns are trying to steal from us," Ezerah said.

Gaarokk didn't reply, which Kaylan thought was for the best. It was quite disconcerting for Ezerah to find out that at least some of their leadership had known about the experimentation and had essentially given the Xiiginns permission to genetically experiment on their species. What the Nershals got in return was access to advanced technology that expedited their rise as a spacefaring race. Kaylan frowned. She could easily see a similar course of events happening on Earth if they didn't get back in time to warn them. The idealist in her didn't want to believe her own species would sell each other out for access to advanced technology, but she wasn't convinced they wouldn't. She glanced at Vitomir. The cosmonaut had sabotaged Titus Station in the asteroid belt, killing four people, including his wife, all for the chance to gain access to advanced alien technology. How would the government leaders on Earth react to such an offer?

"What is it?" Hicks asked.

"I keep thinking about how our own species would react to the Xiiginns," Kaylan said. "I don't know the history of all the interspecies relations here, but I can see certain similarities to how our own people would react."

This drew several ominous glances from the crew of the Athena.

"This is one of the things the Star Shroud program sought to avoid," Gaarokk said. "It wasn't a perfect program, and I don't want to drag us down into a philosophical discussion about it, but one of our guiding principles was to limit our interference in the development of a less advanced species—something the Xiiginns have gotten the Confederation to change."

"Is the Confederation something we can appeal to?" Kaylan asked.

"No," Ezerah said. "Your species isn't even registered—" She broke off and looked at Gaarokk.

"The Boxans aren't exactly welcome in the Confederation anymore,"

Gaarokk said.

Kaylan frowned. "How are new species admitted into the Confederation then?" she asked.

"The Nershals were the last species to be admitted," Gaarokk said.

Kaylan glanced at Ezerah and then back at Gaarokk. "Kladomaor said there were other species being observed. Wouldn't the Confederation reach out to those species?"

"The Confederation is aware of the fact that more species exist in the galaxy, but they remain ignorant of their exact locations," Gaarokk said.

Hicks cleared his throat. "I think I get it. The Confederation wanted the Boxans to relinquish control of the Star Shroud program so they would have access to their star-system data. The Boxans refused, so they cast you out of your own creation."

"Partially," Gaarokk said. "We took the Star Shroud networks offline. Though the request came through the Confederation, it was really the Xiiginns pushing for this information."

"What about the other members of the Confederation?" Kaylan asked.

Gaarokk's jaws clenched. "Those allied with the Xiiginns form a majority. There were some species that spoke out against the Xiiginns but not many. Most agreed that the Star Shroud program should be under control of the Confederation."

"Who are essentially controlled by the Xiiginns," Hicks said.

"So to prevent a species like ours from falling to the mercy of the Xiiginns, you've been keeping the information about star systems with intelligent life secret from them," Kaylan said.

"That is correct," Gaarokk said.

"But Zack and I were able to access the Star Shroud network from our solar system," Redford said.

"Zack is an exceedingly clever Human," Gaarokk said. "You were able to access information about your own system, and if you'd had more time you might have figured out where the information went from there. But you wouldn't have been able to access the master copy, which lists all the known star systems in the Shroud program."

Redford looked at Kaylan. "It makes sense, and I think if Zack were here, he would agree."

Kaylan nodded and looked at Gaarokk. "You never told us how the Boxans learned the truth about the Xiiginns. How did this conflict start?" she asked.

"We discovered that the Xiiginns were actively looking for undiscovered life forms. They were given limited access into the Star Shroud program. At the time we'd envisioned bringing them and the rest of the Confederation into that role. The short version is that they were caught exploiting the resources of a star system we'd been observing. The star system was rich in materials used for building ships, among other things," Gaarokk said.

"You don't take any materials from the star systems you learn of?" Redford asked.

Gaarokk shook his head. "No. We note whether a system is rich in particular types of resources, but we'd never take them. We note it so when they are brought into the Confederation other species could trade for those materials."

"You said among other things," Kaylan said.

"Yes. There was a primitive life form in this star system. They were hundreds of cycles from being able to reach into the great expanse, or space, as you Humans like to call it. One of the defining characteristics of that race of beings was their ability to quickly heal themselves. They had redundant nervous systems—something worth studying in concert with that species. However, the Xiiginns didn't see it that way. In secret, they shared advanced technology with them in exchange for permission to experiment on their species. They were looking to enhance themselves by taking advantage of millions of years of evolution. Because the species then had access to technology they weren't ready for, they wiped themselves out. Their planet became a wasteland," Gaarokk said.

"Why didn't you stop them?" Kaylan asked.

"We didn't learn about it until it was too late. It was after this that we started to deploy a specially constructed artificial intelligence to assist in monitoring the star systems in the Star Shroud program. It would have alerted us if such a thing had happened again," Gaarokk said.

"What happened with the Xiiginns after that?" Kaylan asked.

"We kept a closer eye on them, but we didn't fully understand their ability to control other species. It wasn't until we locked them out of the Star Shroud program that we started to see their true colors. That conflict with the Xiiginns divided our species," Gaarokk said and looked at Ezerah. "That's why it pains me to see the same conflict beginning here with the Nershals."

Ezerah returned the Boxan's gaze. "We are responsible for what happens to our species. We decided to ally with the Xiiginns, and the

Nershals will feel the weight of those decisions for generations to come," Ezerah said.

"Commander," the AI said. "We're receiving a signal from the Nerva Space Command."

"Acknowledged, stand by," Kaylan said and glanced at Ezerah. "I thought they wouldn't contact us until we were closer to Nerva?"

"They're likely on high alert since the Xiiginn cruiser was destroyed near Selebus," Ezerah said.

"How close are they to the ship?" Hicks asked.

Gaarokk shook his head. "Ezerah's right, this is just standard protocol. The Nershals are tracking all objects that have the potential to come to Nerva."

"Are they able to detect that this is a ship and not something else?" Redford asked.

Jonah did make a good point, Kaylan thought. If they answered right away they confirmed that they were out here, but if the Nershals weren't sure what the Athena actually was, it might be best not to answer them.

"I'm not sure," Ezerah said. "I would suggest we answer them so as not to draw attention to ourselves later."

Kaylan nodded. "I agree. If they continue to monitor us and we don't answer them, then once we change course they'll know right away we're not some benign piece of space junk. And the fact that we didn't answer them would raise an alarm in those who are watching."

No one else offered any comment.

"Athena," Kaylan said. "Send the information Ezerah uploaded earlier."

"Sending," the AI said.

Silence settled on the bridge while they waited for a response. They had to get onto the surface of Nerva. It was their only chance to find Zack; otherwise, they would have to leave the Nershal star system. Kaylan watched the holoscreen over the conference table, which showed the blue and green planet they were approaching. It was strange to look at, considering the only other living planet they'd seen was Earth. Nerva was similar in size to Earth but with smaller oceans, and there were different weather systems swirling their way across the planet. A deep pang settled in Kaylan's chest. She glanced at the other Athena crew members, who were watching the same thing. Seeing Nerva this way was a reminder of just how far from home they'd come.

"Nerva Space Command cleared us to approach the planet," the AI said.

Kaylan released the breath she'd been holding and smiled. "Thank you, Athena."

Kaylan hadn't realized how tense she'd been until that moment, but this was the easy part. They still needed to get down to the surface and find the hidden Mardoxian chamber.

"Since they know we're here, we can shave some time off our approach," Kaylan said.

"Are you sure that's a good idea?" Redford asked.

"Ezerah," Kaylan said. "If we increased our velocity, would it appear to be suspicious?"

"A slight increase in speed isn't unreasonable once clearance has been granted," Ezerah said.

Kaylan increased the Athena's velocity by twenty percent, which meant they would hit their objective thirty minutes earlier than previously expected. Every second counted.

"Commander," Hicks said. "We need to finalize the away team."

Kaylan had given this some thought on their journey here, but she took a moment to consider whether she wanted to make any changes. She looked around at all of them while they waited for her to speak. "Here's the long and short of it. I can't ask any of you to come down to Nerva's surface. It could potentially be very dangerous. As it stands right now, the away team is comprised of myself, Katie, Ezerah, and Gaarokk. I can't make any assumptions for the rest of you. In other words, if you want to come down to the surface of the planet you'll need to volunteer. I want to be clear on one thing: there will be no repercussions if you feel you cannot do this. So take a moment and think about it. I'll be waiting in the shuttle prep area."

"Hold on, Commander," Hicks said. "I volunteer to go to Nerva with you."

One by one each crew member repeated the same. Redford glanced at the others. "I'm in," he said.

Every one of them had volunteered. "Thank you," Kaylan said, "but with Ezerah and Gaarokk joining us, we can't all fit into the shuttle."

"What is it that you propose?" Redford asked.

"Efren and Vitomir will stay on the ship. The rest of you are coming to the surface," Kaylan said.

She had expected some protest from Vitomir, but he seemed determined not to be any trouble.

"I'd like a moment to speak with them alone before we leave,"

Kaylan said.

The rest of the Athena crew, along with Ezerah and Gaarokk, headed to the shuttle prep area.

Kaylan looked at Vitomir and Efren. "I just wanted you to know that if I could fit everyone on the shuttle, I would bring you. Efren, I need you to keep the Athena ready in case we need to leave quickly."

Efren nodded and glanced sideways at Vitomir. "Why is Vitomir staying?"

It was no secret that Efren didn't trust the cosmonaut, and with good reason. Vitomir's actions on Pluto were on everyone's mind.

"Two reasons. One, if we run into trouble on Nerva we need to be focused on the situation down there," Kaylan said.

"And the second?" Vitomir asked.

"If something happens to us on Nerva, Efren will need help with the ship. Hicks is my second in command, but I need him with me. I have no choice but to make use of you and your experience as commander," Kaylan said.

Vitomir winced. "I will help in any way I can," he said.

"I doubt you'd put the Athena in jeopardy, but as a precaution, both Efren and the AI will have the ability to lock you out of the systems and isolate you wherever you happen to be on the ship," Kaylan said.

"Quite understandable given the circumstances, Commander," Vitomir said.

"I want you to man the bridge while we're away," Kaylan said.

Vitomir nodded. "Godspeed, Commander. I do hope you find what you're looking for down there," he said.

Kaylan nodded and left the bridge. Hicks was right. You went into war with the army you had whether you liked it or not.

Kaylan quickly made her way to the shuttle prep area. Gaarokk and Ezerah were ready to go because their suits easily adapted to multiple environments, including space. Kaylan donned her spacesuit and methodically checked to be sure it was in good working order. She got on the shuttle and headed for the pilot's seat next to Hicks. Kaylan glanced behind her. Gaarokk's stooped form barely squeezed through the doors, and he settled onto the floor. Kaylan didn't like that he wouldn't be able to strap in. Even seated on the floor of the shuttle, the Boxan's head reached the height of those sitting in one of the shuttle's seats.

Kaylan shut the airlock doors, closing them off from the Athena, and the shuttle's HUD came online. She released the docking clamps and eased the shuttle away. A few minutes later Vitomir fired the breaking thrusters and they left the Athena behind. Ezerah sat directly behind Kaylan. The Nershal had fed the coordinates into the nav computer, so all Kaylan had to do was follow the flight path.

The star in this system shined with a deeper yellow that was quite different from their own sun, and the surface temperature near Nerva's equator was a few degrees warmer than that of Earth. Kaylan gripped the stick, ready to take control if they ran into any trouble. The nav computer adjusted the angle of their approach to the Nershal home world.

"Okay, then. Here we go," Kaylan said, and gritted her teeth.

"Approach is nominal," Hicks said while keeping his eyes fixed on the readouts in front of him.

The shuttle's handling changed as its surfaces bit into the thickening air. A faint orange glow built as they plunged through the upper atmosphere. As they broke through, the shuttle's flight smoothed out. They descended through a layer of wispy, white, vertically trailing tendrils. Layers of storm clouds from a weather system gathered farther away. Kaylan tightened her fingers on the stick. She just had to follow the flight path. They broke through more clouds, and the air around the shuttle grew misty. This was to be expected, but no pilot was ever comfortable when visibility was reduced to practically nothing.

The mist dissipated and they got their first glimpse of Nerva's surface. The land area in their direct path showed remnants of impact craters that had since become overgrown. Vegetation also grew over the ruins of what appeared to be a city.

"Looks like this place was populated at one point," Hicks said.

"This place was among the first to suffer from a Boxan bombardment," Ezerah said. "We'd thought they attacked us because we decided to break our alliance with them."

"The Boxan battle commander was under the Xiiginn influence," Gaarokk said, his eyes drawing downward. "It was our failure that brought this destruction upon your world."

Kaylan watched as Ezerah tore her eyes away from the HUD.

"There were a lot of failures that day, on all sides," Ezerah said.

"This is where it all began for us," Kaylan said.

Ezerah frowned. "I'm not sure I understand."

"What I mean is that when this was happening here, Ma'jasalax was sending a signal to Earth through the Mardoxian chamber from the monitoring station in this star system," Kaylan said.

"I suppose that's true," Ezerah said.

"It *is* true," Gaarokk said. "Kladomaor and I were with her. Given how things have turned out, I wonder if she foresaw it."

"The Mardoxian priestess is very wise," Ezerah said. "Even when we severed ties from the Boxans, we remembered the keen insights from those of the Mardoxian sect."

"How could she have known?" Redford asked. "She sent that first signal to Earth, which brought us here, but how could she have known we would come at this moment?"

"Those with the Mardoxian potential are given a heightened insight into more far-reaching events than most. The same could be true of your species, should you explore this potential," Gaarokk said.

Kaylan frowned. It seemed that Dux Corporation did continue to explore abilities like Kaylan's, but it was hardly common back on Earth. She'd tried to convey that to the Boxans, but they weren't convinced that what their species was quite comfortable with as a societal norm was still an outlier on Earth.

Their flight plan had them circle around the ruins. The skies were clear. "Why didn't they rebuild the city?" Kaylan asked.

"This place has become a living monument for those who died," Ezerah said. "Things may change now that the actions of the Xiiginns are coming into question."

"I hope so," Kaylan said. "How do you think your species will react?"

Ezerah glanced at Gaarokk and then turned back to Kaylan. "They will deny it. They won't want to believe such a thing could be possible. I know I didn't want to believe it. Even when the proof was there before my own eyes I wanted to find some reason to explain away the atrocities. The Boxans were the enemy."

"What do you think will happen after this? Will your species help the Boxans?" Kaylan asked.

Gaarokk coughed. "It's too soon for that. Kladomaor's mission was to expose the Xiiginns. We don't expect anything in return. It was our hope that the Nershals would break their alliance with the Xiiginns and tell the other members of the Confederation to do the same."

"I do not speak for the Nershals," Ezerah said. "I will help you find your missing crew member, but after that I'm not sure what I'll do."

Kaylan nodded. "We appreciate your help."

A proximity warning flashed on the HUD as they approached their destination. The experimental Mardoxian chamber was supposed to be hidden somewhere close by. They flew across a boundary to what must have been a vast estate. Ezerah had called it something else, but the AI that handled the translation for them had found the closest word they could understand.

Nershal architecture was one that worked to coexist with the local flora. Bronze oval buildings sat atop wide circular planes, and the supporting structure appeared to merge with thick vines. Some of the oval buildings were flanked by tall spires that were thicker at the base. In the deep, yellow sunlight, the bronze colors were soothing to Kaylan's eyes. "It's beautiful," she said.

The rest of the crew craned their necks to get a better view, and she heard Brenda echo her sentiments. Kaylan turned to look at Ezerah. The Nershal's brows tugged forward, and her eyes were a mix of emotion.

"When was the last time you were here?" Kaylan asked.

Ezerah blinked, and she glanced at Kaylan. "Not since I was a child. This place was quarantined for a number of cycles."

Kaylan's eyes widened. "Emma, can you—"

"I'm on it," Emma said.

"What's she doing?" Hicks asked.

"She's going to scan for anything that might be harmful to us," Kaylan said.

Hicks nodded.

"So far, we're clear," Emma said. "I'll continue to monitor and let you know if I find anything. Otherwise our suit computers will warn us of environmental dangers such as radiation."

"You should be able to set us down on that landing pad," Ezerah said.

Kaylan nodded and slowly decreased their speed as they approached the landing pad. She had to navigate the shuttle through the dense vine overgrowth, which slapped against the wings as she approached the landing pad. Kaylan maneuvered the shuttle into a hover over the landing site.

"Landing gear is deployed," Hicks said.

Kaylan lowered the shuttle, and the alert on the HUD showed that they'd touched down. She blew out a breath, and Hicks gave her a pat on the shoulder.

"Nice work," Hicks said.

"Thanks," Kaylan said, and looked toward Emma. "Are we clear?"

Emma nodded. "We're good to go."

Gaarokk was the first to exit the shuttle and was followed by Hicks and Katie. When they gave the all clear, the rest of them came out.

An alarm blared from the far side of the landing pad, and a console rose from the ground.

"They want your authorization," Gaarokk said.

Ezerah went over to the console and navigated through the interface.

Hicks came to Kaylan's side. "I'm not sure how we're supposed to get around here. There don't appear to be any staircases."

Ezerah rejoined them. "It seems I still have access. Apparently heirs of the estate are allowed to bypass the quarantine lockout," she said.

"Ma'jasalax said the chamber is located from within the main enclave. Do you know where that is?" Kaylan asked.

"The entrances are up there," Ezerah said and frowned. "Apologies, but I take for granted that we are a winged species. I should be able to summon a transport that will get us up there," Ezerah said.

The Nershal brought up the holo-interface for their version of a PDA. After a few moments she closed it. "It's not working. I can't summon it from down here. I'm going to try going up to the main enclave and send transport down to you," Ezerah said.

"Are you sure you should go alone?" Hicks asked.

Ezerah glanced at him and Hicks shrugged. Translucent wings unfurled and Ezerah leaped into the air. Kaylan watched as the Nershal zoomed away from them.

"They're truly a remarkable species," Emma said.

The minutes dripped by and Kaylan glanced at Gaarokk. The Boxan didn't appear to be worried, so Kaylan decided to take a look around. The air was humid, but the heat wasn't oppressive. The vast estate stretched up and away from their position.

"Ezerah comes from an ancient line of Nershal leaders," Gaarokk said. "Before the capital was moved and the many factions formed a single global entity, this place was a seat of power for the Nershals."

A strange-looking animal crowed from above. The creature appeared to be a much larger version of Earth's flying squirrel. It leaped from different vines and used its body to provide enough lift so it glided to where it wanted to go. The heart-shaped head reminded Kaylan more of a house cat.

From high above them, a shimmering bronze shape detached itself from the main structure and headed in their direction.

"Here we go," Gaarokk said. "That's the transport the Nershals use for species that can't fly."

The floating platform descended and came to a hover several inches over the ground. Ezerah waved them aboard.

"This was the only one with power enough for the trip. The power cores in the others were all depleted," Ezerah said.

"Will we be able to get back down?" Kaylan asked.

"We might need to find another way, but once we get up there we can set it up to be recharged," Ezerah said.

The others climbed aboard, and Kaylan almost expected the platform to lower under Gaarokk's weight, but it didn't budge at all. Ezerah keyed in several commands and a railing rose along the edges. Kaylan gripped the railing, grateful for it. The platform lifted them up into the air, and the landing pad fell away. Redford kept looking above them, and Kaylan encouraged Emma to do the same. Soon they came to the main enclave.

The platform landed, and Ezerah led them toward the entrance. The immense oval building loomed in front of them, and Kaylan wondered how it had escaped the destruction they'd seen on their way here. As they approached the massive, ornately carved glass doors that adorned the entrance, a small column rose from the ground, and Ezerah placed her palm on it. After a wide red laser beam scanned Ezerah's face, a high tone chimed from the interface and the doors pulled themselves open. As they crossed the threshold, they saw that the area beyond was carpeted, and a thick layer of dust covered everything, swirling up into the air as they passed. Ezerah led them to the enclave's interior. The air inside smelled stale and old, and the sparse furnishings were overturned, as if whoever had been there had left in a hurry.

The vastness of the atrium reminded Kaylan of a cathedral, and she realized the others must have felt the same because they spoke to each other in hushed tones.

"Do you know where the chamber could be?" Kaylan asked.

"I didn't even know it was here," Gaarokk replied. "But Ezerah should have clearance to find it."

Ezerah walked over to a console. "The links to the neural net are down," she said. After a few moments working on the console, the Nershal looked up at them. "I'm not sure how to search for this."

Kaylan frowned and her mind raced to find an answer. They glanced at Gaarokk, who had a concerned, puzzled look on his face. They'd been so focused on getting here that none of them had considered how they were going to actually find the chamber.

"Okay, hold on a minute," Kaylan said. "Let's think this through logically."

"How much time do we have before someone figures out we're here?" Hicks asked.

"No one should be monitoring this place," Ezerah said.

"Let's assume they are," Katie said. "How long before someone comes to check on things?"

Ezerah frowned in thought. "The nearest installation of any kind is more than an hour away."

"So we have an hour then," Redford said.

Hicks and Katie shared a glance. "No, we have much less than that," he said.

Kaylan cursed inwardly. "Whoever is monitoring would have detected our approach in the shuttle, so the clock would have started after we first landed. We've been here for about twenty minutes, so that leaves us forty minutes to find the chamber and use it."

Gaarokk headed for the console. "Let's see if I can speed this up."

Hicks and Katie walked over to Kaylan. "I can't believe we didn't think of this," Kaylan said.

"Give them a chance. They should be able to find it," Hicks said.

Kaylan nodded and couldn't help thinking that the best person to find the proverbial needle in a haystack of data was the very one they were trying to find. She shared a glance with Katie, who seemed to be thinking the same thing.

"What would Zack do to find it?" Katie said.

"He was always practical about these things," Kaylan said. "He'd start at the top and work his way down. So the top would be the layout of this place and perhaps the function of each building or area.

But the project was a secret."

Ezerah came over to them and listened in.

Katie nodded. "If it was hidden, then only certain people knew about it," she said, and glanced at Ezerah.

The Nershal nodded and headed back to the console. "Show me the access logs from the day of the attack," Ezerah said.

Gaarokk activated the wall screen so they could all see. A long list of access logs appeared.

"This is going to take too long," Redford said.

Kaylan had to agree with the astrophysicist. "How would Boxans appear on this list? If we can we isolate them, it might give us a much smaller list."

Ezerah nodded and her fingers flew through the interface. A much smaller list appeared. Kaylan was about to speak, but Ezerah cut her off. "I'm already looking for Ma'jasalax and where she went."

The log entries dwindled down even further.

"Try filtering out known locations, like living quarters," Gaarokk advised.

A few minutes passed. "There it is," Ezerah said. "It has to be in one of the spires."

"How do you know?" Kaylan asked.

"Because that's the only place that fits with the frequency of Ma'jasalax's visits, but the logs only show that she was on this level. They don't show which spire she went to. We need to choose," Ezerah said.

Gaarokk killed the holoprojection, and the rest of them followed Ezerah farther inside the enclave. The Nershal led them down a long corridor with high ceilings. The corridor opened to a landing, where they came to a stop. There were two further corridors that went off in opposite directions.

Ezerah looked at Kaylan. "Which way?" she asked.

Kaylan swallowed hard as the others all waited for her to answer. She glanced at both corridors and closed her eyes, pushing out with her senses and trying to focus on the chamber. In her mind, she raced down one corridor and up to the top of the spire. There was nothing there. Kaylan backtracked and headed down the other one. It had to be there. She went to where the chamber should be, and all was dark.

Kaylan opened her eyes and pointed down one of the corridors. Ezerah led the way.

Hicks walked next to Kaylan and leaned in. "Are you sure?" he asked quietly.

"No," Kaylan replied, but it was her best guess.

They came to an open landing with wide doors, and Ezerah dusted off a wall panel, which lit up at her touch.

"We're at the southernmost spire, and if Kaylan's right, the chamber should be near the top," Ezerah said.

"Why would they build it near the top?" Redford asked.

"Access to these spires is restricted, and since they're out of the way, they would have been able to bring Nershals here without alerting anyone," Ezerah said.

Kaylan closed her eyes and hoped she'd guessed right as the elevator doors opened and they got inside. The ride seemed to take forever, and when they finally came to a stop, the doors opened onto darkness. As they stepped out of the elevator into what felt like a large space, motion-sensor lighting along the walls progressively engaged, revealing dark, octagonal plating that lined the chamber they found themselves in. Multiple glowing cyan lights raced along the walls and came to a central point on the ceiling high above them.

Hicks glanced at Kaylan. "This is it," he said.

Steel-colored blocks formed a pyramid in the center of the room, and crimson lines pulsed to life, outlining the structure. Mesmerized by the pulsing light as they approached, no one had a chance to speak before the door to the pyramid sank into the floor, showing an inner chamber beyond. The others fanned out into the room and Kaylan headed for the door.

Gaarokk came to her side. "Remember, the chamber will amplify your abilities. Focus is absolutely paramount."

Kaylan nodded and felt herself go cold. "The last time I was in there, Ma'jasalax guided me back. What if I get lost?" she asked.

"This chamber isn't fully powered like the one you were in. This is only for testing viable subjects. You should be able to find Zack, much like how you focused on finding our listening station in your star system," Gaarokk said.

Kaylan nodded.

"We'll be right out here waiting for you," Hicks said.

Kaylan turned toward the others, and Katie gave her a nod. This is what they had come for. Kaylan turned around and entered the chamber.

CHAPTER FOURTEEN

IT TOOK THEM longer to find the giant mutant's lair than Zack thought it would. Etanu insisted that they move cautiously, which slowed their pace. This gave Zack time to note the small orange pods growing on shrubs close to the ground. The pods were a lighter color in the center, making them appear as miniature suns, and there were tiny protrusions along the pods, reminding Zack of the valley with the Skybowl. He'd seen orange pods like this there.

As Zack followed Etanu along the path, he was careful to walk as quietly as possible. When they had first set out, Etanu informed him that—vow or not—he wasn't going near the giant mutant if Zack wouldn't at least try to mask their presence here. Zack realized he'd been lucky during the time he'd spent exploring the pit that nothing had heard him plodding along—either that or they hadn't cared. Regardless, paying attention to every little footfall was hard work and required all of his focus. In contrast to his intense effort, the blind mutant followed silently while maintaining his distance.

The area around them seemed quiet enough, but they still had to travel a bit before they closed in on the giant mutant's lair. Zack really hoped they could confirm his theory that there were other doors in and out of the pit. If he was right, they just had to figure out how to open one of the doors and avoid being recaptured. But if they could entice all the mutants in the pit to escape at once, they stood a far greater chance at avoiding capture. At least that was what he hoped.

Never in a million years had he thought he'd be in some alien prison. Try as he might to focus strictly on getting out of the pit, he sometimes found himself yielding to hopelessness. What if they did get free somehow and then immediately got recaptured? All their efforts would have been worthless, and there was no way their plan would work a second time. He felt like Kandra Rene always had her eyes on him, and she could take his life at any moment. He'd seen his own death in her alien eyes while she beat him. How long would she hold out before she killed him?

A rough hand grabbed Zack's arm, and he found himself looking into the eyes of the blind mutant, who was pointing at the sky. Zack glanced up and, along with a few clouds, they had a typical view of the encroaching gas giant. He looked back at the blind mutant. "I don't understand," Zack said.

The blind mutant pressed its fingertip onto Zack's forehead and then back up at the sky.

"I got nothing," Zack said, and looked at Etanu. "Any idea what he's doing?"

Etanu shook his head. The blind mutant walked off.

"I'm not sure they're completely blind," Zack said.

"So now you think he can see?" Etanu asked.

"A little bit. How else would he be able to walk around in a forest?" Zack said.

"At least he's quieter than you, and presumably you can see just fine," Etanu said.

"I didn't have any problems before," Zack said.

"And you weren't purposefully going near one of the deadliest creatures in this place," Etanu answered. "Speaking of which, what's your plan for luring the creature away so we can check out its lair?"

"I thought you had something in mind," Zack said.

Etanu glared at him. "No, I thought *you* had a plan for this."

"I thought you would distract it for a while, and I would take a closer look," Zack said.

Etanu's eyes bored into him. "You want to use me as live bait?"

The Nershal's hard tone gave him pause. "It's just an idea. You're the soldier. Do you have a better idea for luring him away?" Zack said, and scratched his forearm where the tracker had been placed.

Etanu looked away for a moment. "Well, you're right about one thing. We do need to distract it for a while. Let's scout the area and see what we're dealing with. And why are you scratching your arm so hard?"

Zack grimaced. "It's the tracker they put in there. It itches really bad sometimes," he said, and glanced down at his arm. He'd scratched it so hard that he was bleeding.

"You need to stop scratching. Wounds like that can fester," Etanu said.

Zack wanted to stop, but he couldn't. It itched so badly, and scratching it gave him a momentary reprieve from it.

"Stop!" Etanu said, and grabbed Zack's arm to make him stop.

Zack struggled against the Nershal's vice-like grip. He knew he should listen to Etanu, but he could feel the tracker crawling against his skin.

"If you don't stop, you'll trigger the detonator and you'll die," Etanu said.

Zack ceased struggling and felt his face go pale. Then he shook his head. *What just came over me?* Zack thought. "I'm alright. It just comes in waves. Don't you have one?"

Etanu shook his head. "I don't think they're too concerned about me. Remember when I told you about the mutants that tried to escape over the wall?"

Zack nodded.

"It was the detonator in the tracker that killed them," Etanu said.

"Great," Zack said and sighed.

"Focus. I need you to focus on something else. Tell me about your companions," Etanu said.

Zack's mouth hung open. "We don't have time for this. You've already met—"

"Just tell me about them," Etanu insisted.

The blind mutant came over and squatted down, facing in their direction.

"Well, there are ten of us," Zack began. His hand started to head for his forearm again, and he stopped.

"That recording Kandra Rene kept showing you—who was that? I didn't get a good look at it," Etanu said.

Zack brought his hand to his side and swallowed. "That was our commander, Kaylan."

"This is the one you care for? The one you would form a bond with?" Etanu asked.

"Depends on what you mean by bond."

"I assume your species mates in order to procreate. So, is Kaylan the one you want to bond with?" Etanu asked.

Zack felt his cheeks flush. "Yes—no—I don't know. Katie and I were just starting to get to know each other."

"Can you not have more than one partner?"

Zack snorted. "No, the women of my species tend not to like it when men are intimate with more than one of them at the same time. The same works both ways."

Etanu frowned. "But you have strong feelings for both of them?"

"Well, yeah I do, and for the rest of the crew. I wouldn't want anything bad to happen to them," Zack said.

"But this is different. With Nershals we bond for a time and can have as many partners as we choose. When you bond, is the pairing meant for life?" Etanu said.

Zack swallowed. "Sometimes," he said.

"The Boxans have similar practices. So, if you would bond for life, who would you choose?" Etanu asked.

Zack's mouth opened, but no words would come out. He shook his head. "I have no idea. What would you do if you were me?" he asked.

"I would know which I had stronger feelings for and who I was most compatible with. How does your arm feel?" Etanu asked.

Zack frowned and glanced at his arm. It was red and still bleeding in a couple of spots. "The itchiness is gone."

Etanu nodded. "Good. If it comes back, think about your companions. It will help shield you against the itch."

"How'd you know that would work?" Zack asked.

"At some point a new soldier runs the risk of giving into irrational behavior. It's standard practice to reorient their attention to clear their mind," Etanu said.

"Do you know how I can get this thing out of me without tripping the detonator?" Zack asked.

"It is unknown to me," Etanu said.

"Athena, is this something you can help with?" Zack asked, speaking into his PDA.

"I can monitor the device. One moment," the AI said.

Zack glanced at his forearm while he waited.

"Confirmed. There is a signal coming from the tracker. If the prime directive of the device is to report on your position and there are fail-safes in it that account for unsanctioned removal, then removal isn't recommended," the AI said.

"You're right. That would be the safest course of action, but if we're going to escape from here, I need to get this tracker out of me," Zack said. "Safely," he added.

Etanu narrowed his gaze. "Do you have a portable AI contained in that device?"

"Yes, it's part of our ship," Zack said.

"But your ship isn't anywhere near here," Etanu said.

"The PDA links with my implants, so it's a portable version," Zack said.

"And you rely on it for advice?" Etanu asked.

"Well, yes, it's helped us in the past. I copied it from the Boxan station and it adapted to our ship's systems," Zack said, and wondered why Etanu looked so alarmed.

"You cannot trust an AI. You should power off that device immediately," Etanu said.

"I can't power it off. That AI is our best chance at getting out of here," Zack said.

"AIs can become corrupt and highly irrational. You would be wise to expunge such an entity from your ship," Etanu said.

"I don't understand what the problem is," Zack said.

"We've used artificial intelligence constructs in the past and have since stopped using them because they become unreliable. Besides, if the Xiiginns learn of its existence, they'll use it against us," Etanu said.

Zack sucked in his bottom lip. "Maybe this one is different. This AI was part of the Boxan monitoring station in our star system. It maintained that facility for over sixty years without an incident. I don't think it could do that if it were unreliable."

Etanu frowned but still had that alarmed expression. "That's something at least, but how would you know if the Xiiginns corrupted that AI to work for them?"

"I understand your concern," the AI said, "but I am not completely autonomous. There are restrictions within my core programming that prevent unauthorized access."

Zack arched a brow.

"There, you see," Etanu said. "If the Xiiginns bypassed your AI's defenses, it could be disastrous."

Zack's stomach clenched. Athena knew about Earth, but how much of that data actually resided on his PDA?

"Athena," Zack said, "for the time being, I want to be notified of any outside contact prior to your giving a response."

"Understood," the AI said. "Would you prefer an audible notification or an alert on your internal HUD?"

"The HUD will be fine," Zack said.

As Etanu led them onward, Zack wondered at the vehemence of the Nershal's alarm about using the AI. He glanced up through the canopy of trees, trying to catch a glimpse of the wall, and it seemed they were far enough away that he should be able to ask a couple of questions without Etanu getting too upset about making noise.

"What happened that made you so mistrustful of artificial intelligence?" Zack asked.

"When they work as expected, there are great advantages to using them, but they also make you vulnerable. We still use them, but not without heavy restrictions. The AI you have would be considered unshackled. Extremely dangerous," Etanu said.

"What do you mean by unshackled? This AI does have limitations," Zack said.

"Your AI has the ability to access a multitude of systems, and in doing so you've allowed all those systems to become vulnerable. Think about all the ship's systems that could be affected, like life support or the main engines," Etanu said.

"So your solution was to just stop using them altogether?" Zack asked.

Etanu glared at him.

"What good did that do?" Zack pressed.

"Better that than the alternative," Etanu said.

"Fixing problems is how we improve. It's how we survive—"

"Survive!" Etanu shouted. "You wouldn't last one day if it weren't for me. Are all Humans so blindingly stupid?"

Zack's nostrils flared. "I suppose if we took the Nershal approach, we'd just give up and accept that perhaps we're not up for the challenge, that there are some things beyond our comprehension," Zack said. He was sick and tired of all these aliens thinking they knew better about everything—the Boxans with their superiority, the Nershals with their rigid honor codes that involved contests to the death, and the Xiiginns who were only concerned with their own gains. "It's no wonder the Xiiginns were able to control your species so easily. They handed you advanced technology and you fumbled with it, then just set it aside because it was too dangerous, never following through on why it failed and questioning who provided said technology in the first place. But," Zack shouted, not caring about being quiet, "come across a new species that unknowingly violates one of your precious laws or traditions and it's a contest to the death."

Etanu sneered, and his eyes blazed with anger.

A deep growl came from the other side of a large mound, and Zack glanced up, realizing they were already at the wall. A loud blast of air made him jump back. A large, clawed hand gripped a tree and the giant mutant pulled itself around. Its blazing orange eyes narrowed as it caught sight of them, and the three glowing points on its forehead flared. The triangular-shaped head and roughened skin left little doubt that the Xiiginns had somehow created a Boxan hybrid.

"Run, Human!" Etanu said, shoving Zack and then screaming for the creature's attention.

Zack stumbled back. The Nershal unfurled his wings and leaped away, momentarily drawing the creature's attention. Zack knew Etanu couldn't fly for long with one of his wings damaged, but the other three wings enabled him to make long jumps.

The giant mutant emerged from its hiding spot, its eyes locked on Etanu, but then it cocked its head to the side, sniffing the air. It blew out a breath and circled around to face Zack, the soft ground giving way beneath its massive feet.

Oh crap, Zack thought and backed away. The mutant followed, its massive chest heaving. Etanu tried to get its attention by crossing in front of it. The mutant hissed in his direction but kept coming for Zack.

What the hell does it want me for?

Zack turned and ran, the massive stomps of the giant mutant trailing in his wake. The gray wall loomed just ahead, and as he got closer he looked for any sign of a hidden door. Zack skidded to a halt. A chasm more than twenty feet across separated the land from the wall. There were no power cables visible, just a deep fissure. The giant mutant closed in with Etanu shouting behind it. Zack turned around, his heels inches from the edge. The giant slowed down when Zack didn't run away.

"What do you want from me?" Zack shouted.

The creature came to halt just a dozen feet away. Narrowing its gaze as if it didn't quite know what to make of Zack, it dropped down to one knee and leaned on its fist. The mutant sucked in some air through its nostrils and extended its head closer to Zack, and Zack noted that its labored breathing had a slight whistle near the end.

With the creature this close he hoped Etanu didn't do anything to antagonize it.

Zack glanced at the claws that had mercilessly ended the life of the other mutants at the feeding area, and he hardly dared to breathe. He had to work to keep his legs from shaking. But the creature closed its eyes, the blue glowing dots on its forehead pulsing. The creature's long tail stretched lazily behind it. Even if Zack sprinted away as fast as he could, he doubted he could get away fast enough.

The creature opened its eyes as if sensing Zack's thoughts. It reached out with a clawed hand and then snatched it back. The giant mutant surged to its feet, howling as it backed away. Zack moved away from both the edge of the chasm and the creature. He saw Etanu standing farther away, looking shocked. Etanu gestured for him to keep moving, but the mutant wasn't even looking at them. It brought its hands to its head and spun around as if it were trying to block something out. Zack heard ragged breathing that was a mixture of growl and gasp. It was suffering.

Someone grabbed Zack's arm and pulled him back. He turned and saw the blind mutant guiding him away. How the hell could it guide him if it was blind? Zack patted its hand, and the blind mutant let him go. Zack could still hear the giant mutant growling and thrashing, though the trees blocked his view. Etanu had circled around and caught up to them, but before he could speak, a loud gong rang, echoing throughout the pit.

There was a flurry of activity as if all the creatures trapped in the pit had responded to the gong. The giant mutant howled again, but it had stopped thrashing.

"We have to move," Zack said, and started heading toward the feeding area.

Etanu caught up to him. "Why?"

"Don't you think it's a bit coincidental that the gong would just happen to go off now? The Xiiginns are up to something," Zack said.

"What do you intend to do? You've seen what happens at the feeding area. It's chaos," Etanu said.

"It's another way for them to control everything that goes on in this place," Zack said.

"And it works. They are the ones in control," Etanu said.

"Not entirely. There are things we can influence," Zack said.

"I think this place is starting to get to you," Etanu said.

Zack ignored the Nershal and kept moving. His mind kept going over his encounter with the giant mutant. Why hadn't it attacked him? It had first showed signs of being curious, and then it started acting crazy.

"Slow down, Human," Etanu said. "Zack, wait."

Zack glanced back at the Nershal, slowing his pace.

"I just want to know what you have in mind. If there is a way I can help you, I will," Etanu said.

"Save it. You already saved my life the other night. Your vow has been fulfilled. If we survive this place, I'll even tell Udonzari the same thing," Zack said.

"You think I've stayed by your side because of a vow?" Etanu said. "We haven't encountered as many species as the Xiiginns or the Boxans have, but one behavior persists regardless of the species. The smart ones follow strength."

Zack shook his head. "I'm not strong."

"I don't mean physical strength or even that of martial skills. What you did back there with the hybrid was extremely brave," Etanu said.

"Or stupid. I was lucky. That thing could easily have killed me," Zack said.

"All true, but a smart fool knows when to take a risk and when to run. It is for that reason that I continue to help you," Etanu said.

"Then let's hope my luck doesn't run out, because I'm about to do something even more foolish than what I just did," Zack said.

He quickened his pace, and Etanu and the blind mutant followed him. He couldn't understand why Etanu kept going on about his being strong. Zack considered himself to have a few choice character traits, and strength wasn't one of them. Smart and clever on occasion, he would acknowledge. He couldn't have hacked all those corporate networks without being able to outsmart them and their security firms. But trapped in this alien world he hadn't been able to use any of those skills. He just wanted to stay alive.

Before stumbling into this whole mess and getting recruited for the Athena mission, he hadn't been living. It had been a half-life, and now that he realized this he wanted more than anything to get back to the others. He pictured Kaylan's face in his mind, immediately followed by Katie's. He made a promise to himself that if he survived the next few minutes, he would come clean and tell them both how he felt.

Another gong rang through the pit, louder this time, and they arrived at the feeding area a lot quicker than they had expected.

Zack glanced at the blind mutant. "Can you help? Will others like you help?" he asked.

The blind mutant turned his milky white eyes toward him for a moment and then headed away. Zack hoped that was a yes.

They came to the tree line, and the silent hunters were fanned out in front of the makeshift tunnel, where the supply caches were being unloaded.

Zack stepped forward and Etanu grabbed his arm.

"They will kill you without a moment's hesitation," Etanu said.

Zack nodded. "I know. I just hope that blind mutant brings some help."

Etanu reached for the short sticks he had tucked inside his belt. "Any weapon is better than no weapon."

"Hopefully, we won't need them," Zack said.

A guttural howl sounded a short distance behind them. The giant mutant would be there in a few minutes.

"Here goes nothing," Zack said, and headed directly toward the mutants guarding the supply cache.

The hunters bunched together as Zack got closer. Some hissed out a warning. Zack glanced at the elongated claws and the long surgical scars on the sides of their heads.

::Foreign signal detected transmitting to the Nershal mutants directly ahead.:: The AI's words appeared on his HUD.

::Are you able to decode it?:: Zack asked.

::Analyzing,:: the AI replied.

Zack kept moving forward at an even pace. ::I don't have a lot of time, so if you've got something for me that will help, now would be a good time to share it,:: Zack said.

The AI didn't respond, and the hunters grew more restless the closer Zack got. Some charged forward, only to stop after a few steps and return to their position in front of the makeshift tunnel. Zack saw the supply cache slowly creep into view in the darkened tunnel. His internal HUD was enhancing his own vision.

The hunters hissed and bared their teeth.

A series of tones sounded from his PDA, catching them all off guard. The hunters glanced around, looking for the source of the sound, and then back at Zack. Another series of tones spewed forth from the speaker in his PDA, and the hunters retreated a few steps.

::It's working,:: Zack said.

::Foreign signal strength is increasing. I'm not sure how long this will work. Recommend retreating to a safe distance,:: the AI said.

Some of the hunters brought a hand to the side of their head that had the scar, and Zack engaged his implants to see if he could somehow block the foreign signal they were receiving, but the transmitter on his PDA was nowhere near strong enough. He heard a number of soft footsteps gathering behind him and risked a glance over his shoulder. A wave of relief washed over him as he saw a group of blind Nershal mutants, their tan, tattered clothing hanging off them. They swiftly moved forward, interweaving themselves among the hunters. The hunters, disoriented by the tones coming from Zack's PDA, didn't attack, but allowed themselves to be corralled back away from the entrance to the tunnel.

Zack seized the opportunity and moved inside.

CHAPTER FIFTEEN

THE MARDOXIAN CHAMBER was smaller than the one on Pluto, but that didn't keep Kaylan's hands from shaking as the chamber door hissed shut behind her. A dark blue beam shot down from the ceiling to a crystal sphere rising from the central point in the chamber. The glowing sphere rose until it was eye level with her. Kaylan braced herself for what was to come, but nothing happened. The sphere continued to hover there in front of her. She glanced around. The chamber was silent, as if all outside noise were blocked. Remembering what Ma'jasalax had had her do on the Boxan ship, Kaylan closed her eyes. She focused on Zack—from his deep, penetrating eyes to the last press of his lips on hers. In her mind she saw him kiss the tips of his fingers and place them on the clear elevator door. Her throat thickened, and she wanted to hold him in her arms. She wished she'd told him how she truly felt.

Memories of their time on the Athena played through her mind—both the times when they'd laughed and when they'd argued. She eagerly sought all memories, strengthening her image of Zack. She remembered him first coming into the room at Dux Corp's secret base in the mountains of North Carolina. He had aged beyond the boy she'd known at MIT. A deep warmth spread within her, and her beating heart sounded in her ears as the images crowded into her awareness. She strained, reaching deeper inside. Kaylan held her breath, and in that moment she heard a slight gasp. Daylight shone from the end of a tunnel, and she saw a figure move, shadowed by the light from behind. Kaylan inched closer, trying to get a better view. The figure was hunched over a large crate. Then daylight raced toward them and the tunnel disappeared.

Kaylan turned and her mouth opened in astonishment. Zack was right there in front of her! Alive! His face was a mask of concentration while he fiddled with a large crate. His hair was caked with mud and his clothing was torn and bloodied. Shadows moved along her field of vision, but she wouldn't take her eyes from him. She wanted to tell him she was there, that they were trying to find him, but she didn't know how. The large crate opened and Zack glanced fearfully behind him. Kaylan pulled back and tore her eyes away. He was alive, and she didn't have time to cling to a fleeting memory. She needed to figure out where the hell he was.

She shifted her gaze. Zack was surrounded by—she didn't know what. Some of them looked like Nershals, but they were horribly deformed. There was fighting going on all around. Several dead bodies littered the ground. A large shadow loomed in, and the fighting Nershals scrambled out of the way. Kaylan turned toward Zack. He reached inside the crate and pulled out a large green capsule. Leaping down, he held the capsule above his head.

Kaylan shifted her perspective once again. A creature easily twenty feet tall was heading directly toward Zack. It looked different than the others. Its wide, triangular head reminded her of a Boxan, but the creature's large orange eyes were that of a Nershal. A long tail dragged behind it, ending in a large black stinger that looked to have come from a protokar. *Oh god,* Kaylan thought. The Xiiginns' cross-species genetic experiments included races from other worlds. Zack was trapped in a place full of genetic experiments beyond what they'd found at the research facility on Selebus.

Zack walked toward the giant mutant and stopped in front of the crates. He placed the large green capsule on the ground and stepped back. The giant mutant's face twisted in a ferocious sneer, and then it charged directly at Zack.

"No!" Kaylan cried out. The giant mutant came to a sudden halt. There were three glowing blue gems in its forehead. The mutant looked directly at her, its head tilted to the side. Could it hear her? Zack glanced up, following the creature's gaze, but his eyes swept past her.

"Here, take it," Zack said, gesturing with his hands toward the capsule. "It's yours."

The other mutants waited to see what the giant among them would do. Kaylan watched as Zack turned his back on the giant and went back to the crates. He opened them and began tossing out the contents to the mutants. She watched as small metal canisters tumbled to the ground and then, one by one, they were snatched up by the closest mutant.

Kaylan turned back toward the giant mutant, who was still watching her. The mutant seemed oddly peaceful as it reached one of its hands toward her. She didn't understand how the creature could possibly detect her presence since she wasn't physically there. Then it hit her. The mutant was part Boxan and might possess some part of the Mardoxian trait they revered so much. Seeking out the Mardoxian potential in other species was a genetic imperative for the Boxans that clearly transcended lessons taught by their culture.

Kaylan looked toward Zack and the creature followed her gaze. She wanted to find some way to tell the giant not to harm Zack, but glancing at all the other mutants surrounding him, she got a better idea. She shifted closer to Zack, who was busy emptying the crates and distributing their contents. A Nershal joined him, and it took Kaylan a moment to realize it was Etanu.

Protect. Kaylan pushed the word and the meaning across to the creature. She couldn't know if it understood, but she had to figure out where Zack was being held. With one last look at him, she reluctantly pulled away.

There was a tower and a large wall cutting the area off from the surrounding forest. Kaylan couldn't see much else in the way of structures, so the Xiiginns must have kept this place remote. She didn't see any Nershals on the walls and assumed there were only Xiiginns in this place. She pulled back further, rising high into the air. The presence of the gas giant told her Zack was being held on Selebus. She noted the landmass and the exact position of where he was being held. She built a map in her mind so she could recall it later on. Zack was alive. All they had to do now was get to him.

Kaylan resisted the urge to go back and take one last look at Zack. Time was of the essence, and Zack would be better served if she went back to the others and told them where he was, so Kaylan allowed her mind to relax as she released her hold on her memories of Zack. She felt the tension drain away and opened her eyes. The crystal sphere lowered itself to the floor, and the chamber went dark.

The door hissed open and Hicks was the first one through. His eyes shone with relief as she came over to him.

"Are you alright?" Hicks asked.

Kaylan nodded. "I found him," she said.

They left the chamber and joined the others, who were eagerly waiting. Katie was nearest her.

"I found him. He's alive on Selebus," Kaylan said.

Katie's eyes softened and she nodded.

"Remarkable," Redford said. "What did you see?"

Kaylan explained what she'd seen as best she could. She was still processing everything. Gaarokk brought up a miniaturized holoprojection of Selebus, and Kaylan marked the position.

"The area is quite remote," Ezerah noted. "And it's not a place I'm familiar with. It's not registered with our colonial charter. Another thing the Xiiginns kept from us."

"There's more," Kaylan said. "There are genetic hybrids being held there. One of them definitely had Boxan traits."

Gaarokk's large flaxen eyes widened at this.

"It seemed to be able to detect my presence there," Kaylan said.

The rest of them looked at Gaarokk to see what he had to say.

"That can only mean one thing. The Xiiginns must have captured genetic samples of a Boxan who is a member of the Mardoxian sect," Gaarokk said.

"Ma'jasalax?" Kaylan asked.

Gaarokk shook his head. "No, there wouldn't have been enough time for them to grow a mutant while they held her. They must have been working on this for a while."

"What are they after?" Emma said. "What does splicing multiple species together actually gain the Xiiginns?"

"Can you think of no reasons?" Gaarokk asked.

Emma frowned. "We study mutations of organisms to better understand how they work. If it's a disease, we try to find a way to cure it or prevent it from spreading."

"This is more than simply trying to make themselves more powerful," Hicks said. "They're trying to create an army. If they've lumped all these different mutants together, they could be testing methods of control on a larger scale. They could be trying to get them to work together."

"But they were fighting," Kaylan said.

"Makes sense. They are competing for limited resources, like food and water. Controlling resources and forcing them to compete creates a hierarchy," Hicks said.

"Zack was trying to distribute the contents of the supply crates," Kaylan said.

"He must have been trying to get them to stop fighting," Katie said, speaking up and drawing everyone's attention to her.

"Why would he do that?" Redford asked. "If I were him, I would focus on trying to get out of there."

"Maybe he can't. The reason doesn't matter; he can't get out of there without help," Katie said.

Kaylan looked at Ezerah. "Zack wasn't alone. Etanu was there with him."

"Udonzari should be informed at once," Ezerah said.

"We're not going to figure this out here," Kaylan said. "Let's get back to the ship and start heading back to Selebus. And also send an update to Kladomaor."

Gaarokk powered off the holoprojector and watched Kaylan for a moment.

"What is it?" Kaylan asked.

"I'm just glad you haven't cut yourself off from Kladomaor," Gaarokk said.

"We need to work together," Kaylan said.

They made their way back through the tower. Kaylan glanced at Emma and noticed she was recording them as they made their way through the Nershal building.

"We need to document our journey. Otherwise, NASA is never going to believe we were actually here," Emma said, holding a palm-sized recorder in her hand.

Kaylan smiled and nodded. Hicks walked next to them, keeping careful watch on the dark corners and the area ahead.

"Do you really think the Xiiginns are trying to create some type of mutant army?" Kaylan asked.

"It could be one of the things they're doing. Given their actions and the testimony of the Boxans, I don't think creating a mutant hybrid army would be beyond them," Hicks said.

"I guess I don't think like that," Kaylan said.

"That's what you have me for—to help balance out all that logic with some good old-fashioned military suspicion. I'm sure Redford would say something about how I only see things from a militaristic perspective," Hicks said.

Kaylan snorted. "Probably."

"How do you feel?" Hicks asked.

"I feel fine," Kaylan answered.

"It's just the last time you went into one of those chambers you passed out for almost a whole day," Hicks said.

Kaylan nodded. "Not this time. It could be that it was only a test chamber, but Brenda told me that sometimes the brain just needs time to adapt," she said.

"One day we're going to have to sit down with them and get a better understanding of how all this Mardoxian business works. Is it safe? And what are the risks? That type of stuff," Hicks said.

They came to the atrium, where sunlight streamed in, with prisms of light forming rainbows on the floor and ceiling. But the massive, ornately carved glass doors wouldn't open. Gaarokk positioned himself on one door, while Hicks, Redford, and Nikolai grabbed the other door. They grunted with effort, and the doors started to open. Once they were open enough, the others moved in to help push them the rest of the way.

"Looks like this place is running low on power. We're lucky we didn't get stuck in the elevator shaft," Redford said.

They returned to the transport platform, and Ezerah checked it.

"The power cores are almost depleted. Is it possible for you to pilot the shuttle here?" Ezerah asked.

Kaylan shook her head. "It's not designed to maneuver through an area like this. Tight quarters."

"We'll have to chance using the platform then," Gaarokk said.

Ezerah unfurled her wings and hovered nearby while the rest of them got onto the platform.

Gaarokk stood at the controls and looked to make sure everyone was aboard. "This might turn into a rough descent. Make sure you hold on."

The crew of the Athena spread out and grabbed hold of the railing. Kaylan glanced at the bronze platform and tried to ignore the aging state it was in. She couldn't see an alternate method of getting down, so she held her breath as the platform lurched up and over the edge. They hovered for barely a second before the platform began hurtling toward the ground. The wind blasted her long brown hair back as she clutched the railing and looked over at Gaarokk. The Boxan was frantically trying to get the control console to respond. Kaylan gritted her teeth and held on. They needed to stop or they were all going to die.

Gaarokk's hands slipped off the console, and the Boxan lunged for the railing. Kaylan inched over to the console and pulled herself up. She glanced down at the interface and couldn't read any of the Nershal symbols. The status on her internal HUD showed that it was working on a translation.

"What do I press?" Kaylan shouted.

The ground was rushing up to meet them.

Gaarokk said something, but Kaylan couldn't make it out.

Kaylan looked back at the console, and her HUD flashed the translation. Kaylan immediately slammed her palm on the symbol for stop, and the platform pushed up against her feet as it slowed down and then slammed into the ground in a bone-jarring halt. Kaylan was thrown back, but Gaarokk grabbed hold of her hand, keeping her close to him. Sparks spewed forth from the console. Kaylan gasped for breath and regained her feet, glancing around at the rest of them. They appeared shaken, but no one was hurt. The platform must have had some type of emergency repulsors to keep it stabilized.

Brenda came over to her and gave her a quick check. "We were lucky, but you more so. If Gaarokk hadn't gotten to you . . ."

"What happened?" Redford asked.

"The control console became unresponsive," Gaarokk said. "I think it shorted out."

Redford frowned. "If it shorted out, how did it come back on?"

Ezerah flew down to them. "I shouldn't have let you take such a risk. I should have gone and found another transport for you to use."

"You couldn't have known," Kaylan said. "We're fine."

"I tried to reach you, but I couldn't catch up," Ezerah said.

Hicks and Katie came over to them. "We should get to the shuttle," Hicks said.

Kaylan nodded. The shuttle was only a few hundred yards from where they were standing, but before she moved toward it, Kaylan glanced up at the dizzying heights they'd fallen from. Suppressing a shudder, she returned her gaze to the others and noticed Gaarokk watching her.

"Are you injured?" Kaylan asked.

"No," Gaarokk answered and seemed to be considering something.

"What is it? The platform malfunction wasn't your fault," Kaylan said.

"I just don't understand how you got it to stop. The console was dead," Gaarokk said.

"No it wasn't. When I crawled over to it, the screen was on. I just couldn't read the symbols," Kaylan said.

Gaarokk looked as if he were going to say something else but then reconsidered as the group started moving toward the shuttle.

They closed in on the shuttle, and the AI opened a comms channel to Kaylan.

"Commander, the Athena is picking up a planet-wide broadcast," the AI said.

"Okay, I'll let the others know," Kaylan said. She glanced at Gaarokk, who had moved on ahead. "Athena, did you experience any comms issues with us?" she asked.

"Comms blackout occurred approximately thirty minutes ago and was reacquired fifteen seconds ago," the AI said.

Kaylan frowned. "Are you sure? Didn't you just help translate a Nershal control console?"

"Negative, Commander. I've been trying to re-initiate communications since you went offline and have only reestablished comms just now," the AI said.

Kaylan's eyes widened and she glanced back at the platform wreckage. If the AI hadn't helped her with the control console, how was she able to get the platform to slow down enough for them to survive the fall? She looked at Gaarokk. The Boxan knew *something* had happened, but she got the impression he wasn't sure exactly what.

Kaylan climbed aboard the shuttle and went to the pilot's seat. She told the others about the planetary broadcast, but they wouldn't be able to watch it until they returned to the Athena.

Kaylan engaged the shuttle's engines and they lifted off. Hicks retracted the landing gear, and flight status indicators became green across the board. She engaged the main thrusters, propelling the shuttle forward. Kaylan increased their speed and angle of ascent. They quickly made it to the upper atmosphere, and the shuttle achieved breakaway velocity. They continued to climb until they broke through Nerva's thermosphere and entered outer space. A comms signal alert showed on the shuttle's HUD, and Kaylan opened it.

"Commander, we have your signal," Vitomir said.

"Acknowledged, Athena," Kaylan said.

"Were you successful?" Vitomir asked.

Kaylan smiled. "We know where he is," she said. Her mind flashed back to where she'd last seen Zack, surrounded by mutants, and she hoped he was okay. "We'll debrief when we get back. Shuttle out," Kaylan said.

Hicks looked back at Ezerah. "Are planetary broadcasts common occurrences on Nerva?"

"It depends, but given the current state of unrest, perhaps this broadcast is more important than others," Ezerah said.

Hicks nodded and turned back around.

Kaylan guided the shuttle toward the Athena. "Well, this confirms that the engine upgrades for the shuttle work as expected," she said.

"Please don't tell me you had doubts," Hicks said.

"This was the first field test on a planet that has gravity comparable to Earth's. All the preliminary tests in the world can't replace an actual field test," Kaylan said.

Within the hour the shuttle was docked with the Athena. Emma Roberson and Brenda Goodwin headed directly to the science lab. Kaylan knew Emma had a number of samples they'd gathered from Nerva to work through, in addition to their work on the Boxan samples. The rest of them gathered on the Athena's bridge.

"Commander, ship traffic around Nerva has increased by thirty percent. Nershal military vessels are starting to launch inspections," the AI warned.

"We don't want that," Hicks said.

"Agreed," Kaylan said, heading to the commander's chair on the bridge. She laid in a course for Selebus.

"Commander," Gaarokk said. "I would advise taking it slow at first. It would be best to put some distance between us and Nerva before increasing speed."

Kaylan stopped what she was doing and glanced at Hicks, who gave her a nod. "Okay, I'll gun the engines when we're far enough away."

Gaarokk frowned. "I'm not sure I understand."

"She means we're going to go really fast," Katie said.

Kaylan double-checked her calculations. "Estimated time to Selebus is about three hours. We need to figure out a way to inform Kladomaor."

"I think I can help with that," Gaarokk said.

*****

Kladomaor had hardly left the bridge during the past cycle, but

Boxans could go cycles without rest if they needed to. In this case, he stayed because they were on the offensive for once, fighting their true enemy. It was an opportunity he shared with his loyal crew.

The armament for his stealth ship was largely passive in nature. He'd deployed drones that wouldn't activate until the Xiiginn warships came near. Thanks to Ma'jasalax's efforts, their intel on the precise location of the Xiiginn warships was as accurate as if they'd used their own active scanners; however, using their scanners would also alert the Xiiginns to their presence. The Xiiginns strongly suspected they were in the Nershal star system, but until he showed his presence they couldn't declare it to the Nershals. For this reason, he wanted to avoid confronting any Nershal ships.

"Sir, the Nershals are consolidating their ships near Nerva and Selebus," Triflan said.

Kladomaor glanced at his tactical officer and nodded. He turned toward Ma'jasalax. "Still think letting the Humans go off to Nerva was a good idea?" he asked.

The Mardoxian priestess gave him a placating look. "You already know it is."

"They need to flee Nerva now before the Nershals start a blockade," Kladomaor said.

Kladomaor watched as Ma'jasalax closed her eyes for a moment.

"You have the Xiiginns chasing ghosts, but I would advise that we start withdrawing our position further in this system," Ma'jasalax said.

"What have you seen?" Kladomaor asked

"I don't see the Athena," Ma'jasalax said.

"Then what would the purpose of withdrawing into the system be?" Kladomaor asked.

"If we're going to lend tactical support to the Athena, we need to be closer to them," Ma'jasalax said.

Kladomaor pressed his lips together, taking a moment to consider. "Navigation, plot a course further into the system. Tactical, activate beacon 46B suite."

Kladomaor glanced at Ma'jasalax, and she smoothly returned his gaze. They'd been doing this mental Shar match for a while. Shar was a game of strategy, and he had to admit that she was an effective player.

"Course laid in, Commander," Varek said.

"Execute," Kladomaor responded.

"Beacon suite 46B has been activated. Confirm broadcast," Triflan said.

Kladomaor turned back toward Ma'jasalax and waited.

"They haven't changed course or heading," Ma'jasalax said.

Kladomaor nodded. "It appears the Xiiginns grow tired of this game. Passive scan broadcast from suite 46B."

The broadcast would limit the beacon's operational efficiency, but it would present a more enticing target.

"Engage our passive scanners," Kladomaor said.

The main holoscreen switched on and showed three Xiiginn warships in the outer system. The other one was currently at Nerva. Too bad Mar Arden wasn't on one of these ships. Kladomaor might have been tempted to take it out.

"Confirm, single Xiiginn warship breaking off to investigate the beacon," Triflan said.

"Acknowledged. Set suite to detonate payloads the moment they're within range," Kladomaor said.

Ma'jasalax moved over to be next to his command couch.

Kladomaor rose out of his seat. "Please sit," he said.

Ma'jasalax started to protest.

"You yield nothing by taking your ease for a few moments. Please, it's an honor for me to have one of the Mardoxian sect sit in my chair," Kladomaor said.

"Flattery will get you nowhere," Ma'jasalax said.

"Fine, then would you just allow me to do something courteous to show my appreciation for all you've done to assist me and my crew?" Kladomaor said.

Ma'jasalax considered this for a moment and then sat down. Kladomaor didn't know if it was just Ma'jasalax or others of the Mardoxian sect, but they were a stubborn group. Ironically, he was positive Ma'jasalax had the same opinion about him.

"Commander, two Xiiginn warships have changed their headings. Designation for the warships are Zeda-2 and Zeda-3," Varek said, and updated their flight paths on the main holoscreen.

Kladomaor narrowed his gaze. The new heading put them almost on an intercept course. "Ready course update on my mark," Kladomaor said.

"Waiting orders, Commander," Varek said.

"Tactical, activate beacon suites 48 through 52," Kladomaor said. The status for those beacons updated on the main holoscreen.

The Boxan crew waited in silence to see what the Xiiginn warships would do.

"One Xiiginn warship changing course. Zeda-3 is maintaining heading," Varek reported.

"Acknowledged," Kladomaor said.

Kladomaor waited. If the Xiiginns truly knew where he was, they wouldn't have gone to investigate the other beacons, but the fact that one was inbound confirmed for him that the commander was experienced. The Xiiginn warship drew steadily closer to their position, and he could sense the growing tension on the bridge. Kladomaor calmly watched the holoscreen.

"Commander, confirm detonation of beacon suite 46B," Triflan said.

"Acknowledged," Kladomaor said.

Ma'jasalax rose from the command couch and stood at his side.

"Wait for it," Kladomaor said.

"Only if the warship has taken damage," Ma'jasalax said.

"They did," Kladomaor said.

"Commander, Xiiginn warship, designation Zeda-3, is slowing down. It looks like they're turning around and heading toward Zeda-1," Triflan said.

The tension drained from the bridge.

"Execute course update," Kladomaor said. "Let's bloody them some more. Configure remaining beacons to detonate payloads upon contact."

His orders were carried out.

"Commander, we're receiving a planetary broadcast communication from Nerva," Triflan said.

"Put it onscreen," Kladomaor said.

The broadcast header contained the seal of the Nershal Global Congress. After a moment, the vast congressional chambers appeared. Nershal global leaders and representatives crammed into the large octagonal structure. Kladomaor remembered the congressional chambers well. The last time he'd been in them was over sixty cycles ago when the Nershals had decided to break their alliance with the Boxans. At least, that was how it was recorded by the Nershal chroniclers. The ruling caste at the time decided the Boxans hadn't acted in good faith within their Nershal alliance.

A lot of lives had been lost when the alliance broke. What the Global Congress didn't know was that the Xiiginns had been in contact with the Nershals and had helped orchestrate the whole thing. The Xiiginns even went so far as to take over a Boxan battle cruiser and fire their weapons on Nerva, killing thousands of Nershals. The Boxans had tried to communicate with Congress, but all ties had been severed. The fact that Kladomaor had brought his stealth ship here could be considered an act of war, and it was—just not with the Nershals.

The video broadcast panned through the chambers. Tall windows allowed sunlight to stream into the room. The chambers were adorned with gray ornate sculptures that showed a visual display of the cultural history of the Nershals. Kladomaor remembered the depiction of a pre-winged Nershal species from ancient times. They were a proud and beautiful race, and he hoped the Nershals would see the true intent of the Xiiginns before it was too late.

The broadcast focused in on the Speaker—a Nershal dressed in robes of an ancient dynasty that had once been a ruling family for generations. "This is an official public hearing regarding the proposed evidence of a violation of interspecies confederation charter section six: illegal genetic testing of a species. First, we'll show the footage that has been making its way through our networks. Then, we'll hear from Mar Arden of the Xiiginn Ambassador Office, who will address these charges."

The broadcast switched to the video message that the Human, Zack, had created for them. It showed the horribly disfigured Nershals being experimented on and forced to live in squalor. Smaller Nershals who could only be children were shown. The last was the Nershal-protokar hybrid that had been kept apart from the others. There were several images of Xiiginns appearing among those being held. Kladomaor had to admit that Zack had done a good job with the message, given the amount of time he'd had to work on it and the fact that they were in the middle of a firefight aboard a Xiiginn cruiser.

The broadcast switched views to Mar Arden. Kladomaor scowled as the pale face of the Xiiginn who had tortured him appeared on the holoscreen.

"My fellow members of the Confederation, we've reviewed the video surveillance data that was broadcast from a research facility located on Selebus. It pains me to admit that the video and the beings on it were part of a rogue research initiative at the facility. This was in violation of Confederation charter section six, subsection three. Since the broadcast, we've been actively pursuing all involved and have apprehended many who worked at the facility. Based on the testimonies we've gathered so far, we now have evidence of our own to present," Mar Arden said.

"Before you present your evidence, I have a question," the Speaker said. "What happened to the victims? Did you provide medical treatment?"

"They were all killed in an explosion while the facility was under attack," Mar Arden said.

The Speaker closed his eyes with a pained expression. "One more question before you continue. Were there, in fact, Xiiginns involved in these atrocious crimes at the facility?" the Speaker asked.

"Yes, there were," Mar Arden answered.

The Nershals in attendance voiced their outrage, and it took the Speaker a few minutes to regain order.

"We've also found evidence that there were Nershal scientists involved in conducting these experiments as well," Mar Arden continued.

"This is troubling news. There will be a motion for more frequent inspection of all the research facilities on Selebus," the Speaker said.

"We will cooperate with any action the Nerva Global Congress deems necessary," Mar Arden said. The Speaker nodded for him to continue. "During our investigation, it was brought to our attention that there was a third species involved," Mar Arden said.

"Identify this species," the Speaker said.

"Boxans," Mar Arden said.

Dead silence swept over those in attendance.

Kladomaor glanced at his tactical officer. "Is this a live feed?"

"Affirmative," Triflan said.

"How could there be any evidence of our involvement?" Ma'jasalax asked.

"I'm not sure what Mar Arden is playing at. We didn't know what was at that facility until we were already inside. We were there to get the alpha priority message that had been sent," Kladomaor said.

The Speaker cleared his throat. "I certainly hope you have compelling evidence of Boxan involvement. The Boxans haven't been to our star system since we rebelled against their tyrannical rule. There isn't a Nershal in this room who will believe the Boxans would work with the Xiiginns in any capacity. Your species has been at war with them for some time."

"I do have evidence of their involvement, and I present it now," Mar Arden said. The video shifted to more surveillance footage that clearly showed armored Boxans sneaking through the facility. The image on the holoscreen shifted back to the Nershal Global Congress chambers.

"This is hardly proof that they were involved with the experiments going on at the facility," the Speaker said.

"Awareness of the rogue facility was brought to light during a Boxan-led attack. They were there to clean up evidence of their involvement," Mar Arden said.

"That is conjecture, but your opinion will be noted. Since this event has taken place on Selebus, we request that you turn over all prisoners and evidence to our military," the Speaker said.

"We will cooperate in any way we can. The Xiiginns are here to assist in any capacity the Nershals require," Mar Arden said.

"We appreciate your cooperation," the Speaker said.

"There is one more thing I would like to say," Mar Arden said, and the Speaker nodded for him to continue. "We've had reports that there is, at this very moment, a Boxan military stealth ship in this star system. We haven't yet alerted Nerva Space Command because we were hunting for the ship in the outer star system. I've just received an update that one of our warships has taken damage from an armed attack beacon. This type of attack has been documented in the past as having been used by the Boxans. We request congressional permission to actively pursue this threat more aggressively."

Another Nershal in formal attire approached the Speaker.

Kladomaor moved to his command couch. "Navigation, be ready to execute micro-jump. Weapons ready."

"What's happening?" Ma'jasalax asked.

"The Xiiginns are preparing for an ion missile sweep of the area. They're asking for permission to fire their missiles where they think we are," Kladomaor said.

"Given the range of their missiles and the radius of the detonation, how would they ever find us?" Ma'jasalax asked.

"You're correct. Range is something they will need to contend with. As for the impact radius of a detonation, it depends on how aggressive they are. What I would do is use broad sweeps with low-level ion intensity until my target was located and then unleash my more powerful weapons," Kladomaor said.

"Do you think the Nershals would agree to such a thing? These ion sweeps would affect all their equipment as well," Ma'jasalax said.

Kladomaor didn't answer but instead turned his attention to the main holoscreen.

The Speaker called for order, and the conversations in the congressional chambers immediately died down. "You are authorized to coordinate your efforts with our military to investigate this threat. Following this hearing, the governing council of the Nershals will meet and inform you of the authorized operating parameters," the Speaker said.

Mar Arden frowned. "That course of action would normally be extremely wise, but the threat from the Boxans is imminent. Please reconsider allowing our warships to take a broader approach to apprehending the Boxans for you."

"Denied," the Speaker said.

The broadcast ceased.

"Commander, we can micro-jump at your command," Varek said.

"We're running out of time. Take us to the inner system," Kladomaor said, and brought up his own tactical display console.

"What are you going to do?" Ma'jasalax asked.

"I'm checking our armament for close-quarters combat," Kladomaor said.

Ma'jasalax frowned. "You think the Xiiginns will attack anyway?" she said.

"Without a doubt," Kladomaor said.

"Why would they risk it?" Ma'jasalax asked.

"I'm surprised you're asking me this. I would have thought a Mardoxian priestess would have seen the outcome of this already," Kladomaor said.

"Perhaps I just want to know your intentions without them being clouded by outside influences," Ma'jasalax said.

"They have Zack, so the Xiiginns already know there's a new species. The footage they showed in the hearing only showed Boxans, but we had the crew of the Athena and Nershals with us, so the Xiiginns don't want the Nershals to know about the Humans yet. The Xiiginns understood what we were doing with the Nershals all those years ago. They know we're looking for a way to withstand the Xiiginn influence. I'm willing to bet Mar Arden will figure out that we reached out to another species before destroying the listening station in this star system," Kladomaor said.

Ma'jasalax's green eyes widened. "You said 'we.' We both know it was I who reached out to the Humans."

"Doesn't matter now. The Humans are here, and we must stand together. We can only deal with what happens from here on out," Kladomaor said. "The other thing is that I truly believe the Nershals are starting to question the Xiiginns more. Their alliance will continue to crumble because it's built on a stack of lies."

Ma'jasalax glanced over at the star system chart on the main holoscreen. All the known ships were marked, with one exception. "There are a lot of warships in the system."

Kladomaor nodded. "And one very outclassed Human vessel in the midst of it all. We have to find them and get them out of there now."

"Incoming missiles, Commander. Looks like they're firing blind, but it will be close," Triflan said.

Kladomaor turned his attention to his own tactical console. The Xiiginn warships were moving into the inner system as well. "Set condition Trident. Battle stations. Keep countermeasures on standby," he said, and opened a comms line to the entire ship. "Boxans, our enemy knows we're here. This is what we train for. We've bloodied them, and we'll keep on doing so. Our first priority is to buy as much time as possible for the Athena to retrieve their missing crew member. The Humans are counting on our support. Then we all get out of here."

Kladomaor closed the ship-wide comms.

"Commander," Triflan said. "Close-quarters combat will put us in close proximity to Nershal battle cruisers."

Kladomaor nodded grimly. "My orders stand. We do not engage the Nershal ships. If they detect us, we are to raise them on comms and announce our intentions. If they open fire upon us, we will return fire. That is the protocol," Kladomaor said, and turned his attention back to the console. The ion missile sweep was spreading out. No detonations were confirmed yet, but it was only a matter of time. Their minimal shielding was not enough. Their ship was a stealth ship and was not designed for trading blows with Xiiginn warships.

CHAPTER SIXTEEN

ZACK AND ETANU had emptied the supply cache of all the canisters. The giant mutant quickly consumed the contents of its prized green canister and then stayed near them. It always kept Zack in its field of vision, and the only outward show of aggression occurred if the approaching mutants became too overzealous in their pursuit of the supplies being distributed. Having witnessed the death and carnage of a previous feeding time, Zack thought this was a marked improvement. The glitch in the plan was that the supply cache was nearly depleted, and there were still so many mutants that hadn't received anything. The Xiiginn system necessitated the death of some of the mutants in order to control the population.

Zack stared at the giant mutant. He'd had the vague impression he was being watched earlier but couldn't think about that at the moment.

Etanu came over to him. "What now?" he asked.

Zack frowned and glanced over at the wall behind them. "I don't know. I wasn't sure they would all cooperate," he said.

Zack used his implants to check the passive scan he had running to try to connect to the pit's network. So far he had nothing.

"Let's go check out those cables at the wall. Hopefully our big friend will continue to watch our backs," Zack said, and picked up a couple of the metal canisters, bringing them along.

The blind mutants continued to harass the silent hunters. The giant mutant followed Zack and Etanu over to the wall, and the remaining mutants closed in on the remnants of the supply cache, picking it clean.

The area by the wall with the exposed cables looked as it had before, with cables running up into the wall. Zack reached down and felt along the edges with his fingers, seeking a release. He found a small depression and pressed down on it, releasing a large panel, which he and Etanu pulled open. The cables ran to a junction on the wall.

"What do you intend to do?" Etanu asked.

"These are power cables. If I can get one of these canisters to bridge the connection between two of the wires, they'll overload," Zack said.

"I see. The problem is, how can we do that without hurting ourselves?" Etanu said.

"Can I borrow your stick?" Zack asked.

Etanu handed Zack the long staff he'd been using to fight off the mutants. Zack raised it up and slammed it down on his leg, intent on snapping the stick in half, but the staff bounced off in a bone-jarring halt. Zack swore. As if he needed another damn bruise. Etanu asked for the staff, took it over to the wall, and pressed his foot against the middle of it. The staff snapped and gave way. Etanu handed the two halves to Zack.

"Thanks," Zack said.

He placed the two halves on the ground so they crossed each other about six inches from the top, then ripped off the sleeves of his shirt. He tied the crossed sections together and left some slack so the metal canister could be easily secured to it. After a few minutes Zack lifted his makeshift contraption off the ground, trying to quell the voices in his head that told him how stupid this idea was. He worked his hands back so they were at the far end of the sticks and glanced at Etanu. The Nershal intently watched what Zack was doing and gave him a single nod.

Zack blew out a breath and steeled himself for what he was about to do. He pushed with all his might, fighting the urge to let go of the sticks in order to keep from being electrocuted, and missed the target completely. Zack took another deep breath and steadied his hands. This time he held the canister as close to the power cables as he could without making contact. With a sudden burst he forced the canister between two of the cables and leaped back, turning away.

Silence.

Zack opened his eyes and glanced back at the cables. The metal canister was firmly between two of the power cables, but there was no overload. Zack inched back and tentatively touched the ends of the two wooden shafts. He wiggled the sticks a little bit, working the canister in place, but nothing happened.

Zack frowned. "This should have worked," he said.

Etanu came over and grabbed the ends. The Nershal's face contorted with effort as he forced the canister to wedge further between the cables. Zack's eyes widened as the cable connectors began to buckle. A loud pop sounded and both Human and Nershal jumped back, but it wasn't the cables. They heard it again, followed by more. It sounded like it had come from beyond the walls of the pit. An alarm blared from above, and some of the mutants raced away. The giant mutant winced as if it had been struck and backed away, covering its ears.

Zack frowned and Etanu pulled him away from the wall.

"Xiiginns," the Nershal hissed.

They heard the whine of the engines from a Nershal battle sled as it crested the pit's walls and landed by them. Armed Xiiginn soldiers in full armor readied their weapons and hopped off the sled. Zack noticed that not all the mutants retreated. Most stayed and watched the Xiiginns from a short distance away.

Zack caught sight of Kandra Rene's platinum-colored hair as she leaped to the ground. She glanced over at the mutants before coming toward Zack. He glanced at Etanu, pressed his lips together, and raised his hands above his head.

The Xiiginn strode over to him, her pale face set in a grim mask, and there was an edge to her purple eyes. The alien's tail flicked to the side, and she had a white-knuckled grasp on a hand cannon. There was another loud pop from beyond the walls that sounded as if it were getting closer. Zack shared a look with Etanu, and the Nershal moved in front of Zack as the soldiers came to a halt and pointed their weapons at them. Nearby the giant mutant groaned, holding its head in its hands.

"Stop hurting him," Zack said.

Kandra Rene spared the briefest of glances at the giant mutant. "The creature should know its place isn't here. What have you done to make it stay?"

Zack shook his head. "I haven't done anything."

Kandra Rene glared at Etanu and raised her weapon. Zack gently urged Etanu aside, and the Nershal grudgingly gave way.

"Tell me about the others who came with you in the cruiser," Kandra Rene demanded.

"What makes you think I'll tell you anything?" Zack asked.

Kandra Rene raised her weapon and fired. The ground near Zack's feet exploded in a flash of light, and a two-foot crater appeared.

Zack felt the Xiiginn push against his mind. The buzzing intensified and pain lanced across his forehead. He cried out, collapsing to his knees.

"Tell me," Kandra Rene hissed.

Two soldiers grabbed Zack and hauled him to his feet.

"Tell me what I want to know or I will keep you in a state of permanent torture until there is nothing left," Kandra Rene said.

The agonizing pain in his head eased up but there was ringing in his ears. The soldiers let him fall to the ground. Kandra Rene waved them back and used the tip of her weapon to raise Zack's head.

"Alright," Zack gasped. "I'll tell you."

A sneering smile twisted Kandra Rene's face. Loud pops continued to sound from beyond the walls.

"My planet is full of people just like me who will never comply with the likes of you," Zack said, reversing his seeming compliance with an uncompromising stare of contempt.

Kandra Rene's jaw tightened and her nostrils flared. The Xiiginn spun, and her tail struck Zack on the face. Zack brought his hand up to his cheek and felt blood trickling down.

"Your kind isn't as infallible as you believe. Placing your trust in the

Boxans was a mistake. They once thought to defy us, too, and we took their empire away from them," Kandra Rene said.

"Is that why you're still at war with them?" Zack asked.

Kandra Rene stepped back. "I think you've outlived your usefulness. Do you really think anyone will care if I kill you?"

Zack sucked in a breath and ignored the hand cannon she was pointing at him. "I'm never going to tell you anything," Zack said, and glanced over at the wall. "And I think your time is running out."

"We have plenty of time. The rebels outside these walls cannot break through them," Kandra Rene said.

Zack watched as she went over to the giant mutant.

"Kill him," Kandra Rene said, pointing to Zack.

The giant mutant stopped struggling and turned its maddened eyes toward him. Howling, it took a step toward Zack. Then it brought its hands to its head as if it were fighting some unseen force. Kandra Rene's face was a mask of concentration. Zack glanced at the soldiers, but they were watching the thrashing mutant.

Seeing his opportunity, Etanu leaped forward and snatched the weapon from Kandra Rene's hand. The soldiers spun and were poised to attack, but Etanu held Kandra Rene and pointed the gun at the side of her head.

"Tell them to back off," Etanu said.

Kandra Rene stopped struggling. "You forget your place, Nershal," she said.

The soldiers stopped closing in.

With Kandra Rene distracted, the pressure in Zack's head vanished.

Etanu pressed the barrel of the hand cannon to the side of Kandra

Rene's head. "Listen up, Xiiginns. I want you to open these walls and let everyone go."

Kandra Rene laughed. "These creatures don't know how to survive outside these walls. They are less than animals."

"They're much more than that," Zack said. He looked at the Xiiginn, and even with a gun to her head, she showed no fear.

Kandra Rene smiled, then heaved forward, using her tail to pull Etanu off balance while knocking the hand cannon from his hand. The Nershal slammed his fist into the Xiiginn's face, following it with a crushing thump with his elbow. Kandra Rene shook off the blow and kicked out with her leg, but Etanu dodged the strike. The Xiiginn's tail sliced through the air, and Etanu leaped forward, absorbing the blow to his side. The Xiiginn spun and climbed atop the Nershal, locking her legs around his torso and rapidly landing blows to Etanu's head. Etanu brought his arms down, holding Kandra Rene's legs in place, and fell to the ground, pivoting so the Xiiginn bore the brunt of the fall. Escaping their grotesque embrace, Etanu scrambled away and readied himself to face the Xiiginn once more.

Zack watched as the alien combatants traded blows in a whirlwind of precise hits. Each used whatever advantage they could. Zack saw the hand cannon and dove for it. Kandra Rene saw where he was headed and broke off her attack on Etanu, charging toward Zack. He stumbled back and Kandra Rene jumped for him. Just then, a large shadow moved next to Zack, and the giant mutant caught the Xiiginn mid jump in one of its massive hands. It raised the Xiiginn high into the air. Kandra Rene frowned in concentration, and the giant mutant faltered. The Xiiginn thrashed against the giant mutant's grasp, trying to free herself. The creature roared and slammed the Xiiginn against the wall near the open panel. Kandra Rene was hardly affected, her battle armor absorbing the blow. Zack's eyes widened in astonishment as the giant mutant drew back its hand to slam her again.

Energy bolts seared into the giant mutant's back. The creature stumbled toward the wall, howling in pain, and dropped Kandra Rene. The surrounding mutants charged forward, and the soldiers turned their attention to the unarmed mutants. They fired their weapons, killing many of the mutants, but still they came. The Xiiginns were cut off from the sled. Zack watched as one of the Xiiginns shouted into his wrist comms for them to open the door in the wall. He glanced at the open panel where the canister was still lodged between the power cables. Etanu followed his gaze and the Nershal's eyes conveyed understanding. He grabbed Zack and threw him to the ground.

The door that was used to bring the supply caches into the pit started to open. There was an enormous crackle of energy that burned its way up the wall, speeding toward the tower. Zack felt the hot blast of thunderous explosions around them, and then something large landed on top of them. Zack gasped, feeling the breath forced from his lungs. Etanu coughed next to him. Zack struggled to push up and barely managed to gulp another breath of air. The explosions stopped.

"Etanu, are you okay?" Zack asked.

Etanu coughed and nodded.

"Something is on top of us. We need to push together," Zack said.

When Etanu was ready, Zack counted down, and they pushed together. Zack gritted and strained against the wreckage pinning them to the ground, to no avail, but suddenly there was the sound of groaning metal being bent, and the wreckage was pulled away. He poked his head up and saw the lumbering form of the giant mutant. Zack pulled himself out, and Etanu quickly came to his side. The giant mutant was hunched over, and one of its arms hung loosely by its side. Dark blood flowed from all its wounds, but its gaze softened when it looked at them.

Zack approached the giant mutant. "Thank you," he said.

Zack didn't know if the creature could understand him, but he hoped the sentiment somehow bridged the gap between them. The giant was covered with wounds. The glowing points of blue on its forehead grew dimmer, and it collapsed to the ground.

Zack swallowed hard. He didn't know what to do. "There's got to be a way we can help it."

Etanu looked at the giant mutant, his eyes reflecting his concern. The creature's harsh, labored breathing grew softer.

"You did help it. You freed it from the Xiiginn, and now it can die in peace. Look," the Nershal said, and gestured away from them.

Zack's mouth opened in shock. A large portion of the wall was blown away, and the formerly captive mutants were escaping through the gap. They were finally free of this place. More mutants burst forth from the trees and were bolting toward freedom. Zack turned back to the giant mutant and walked toward its head. The creature watched him with tired eyes. Zack could see traces of Boxan features mixed with those of a Nershal, but there were others, and he had no idea what they were. He reached out and placed his hand on the roughened, greenish skin, and the mutant's eyes slowly closed. Its labored breathing stopped, and Zack let out the breath he'd been holding, his throat thickening with emotion.

"Come, Zack, we can go now," Etanu said.

Zack stood up and glared up at the burning tower. Smoke billowed from the structure. He glanced at his forearm where the tracker had been placed.

"We can cut it out of you and then you'll be safe. The power is out, and the Xiiginns will be unable to transmit the signal that would trigger the device," Etanu said.

"The Nershal is correct. I'm not detecting any comms signals from the tower," the AI said, its voice coming through the speaker on his PDA.

"I heard sounds of fighting outside the walls. Let's go. Someone could be here to help us," Etanu said.

Zack nodded and glared at the tower. "She got away," he said.

"I don't know. It all happened so fast. All that matters is that we get out of here," Etanu said.

Zack followed the Nershal. Stragglers emerged from the pit and dashed through the broken wall. They were among the last to leave. Zack turned around, taking one last look, but the smoke-laden air blocked most of the view. He slowly shook his head in disgust. The horrors of this place would be with him for a long time, but he quickly blocked those thoughts and focused on following Etanu. The Nershal guided him out, and Zack allowed himself to be led. Soon they were away from the walls, and the AI picked up a Nershal comms signal.

"Send them a signal to let them know we're here," Etanu said.

Zack sent a signal, and within a few minutes Nershal soldiers closed in on their position. They wore brown battle armor and helmets that covered most of their faces. The soldiers fanned out around them, forming a perimeter, while an armored Nershal came up to them. He retracted his helmet, revealing a loose-skinned face with age lines tugging at the edges of his eyes.

"Father," Etanu greeted him.

Udonzari's gaze locked onto Etanu, and he pulled him into a firm embrace. Zack smiled and thought of his own father, who had passed away over ten years before.

Udonzari released his son and gave a slight bow of his head toward Zack. "We've been looking for you since the Xiiginn cruiser was destroyed."

"Have you heard from the others?" Zack asked.

One of the Nershal soldiers urged them to move out.

"They are alive. Let's get you out of here. Transport is close by," Udonzari said.

They didn't have to go far, for which Zack was thankful. Now that they were out of immediate danger, tiredness seeped into all his muscles, demanding that he rest. Etanu urged him along and helped him when he stumbled. One of the soldiers handed them something to drink. Zack began gulping down the liquid without a moment's hesitation, hardly tasting it.

"Slowly," Etanu said.

Zack stopped gulping and started to sip the liquid instead. He tasted hints of cinnamon, and his exhaustion was pushed back as he became more alert.

They climbed aboard the Nershal battle sleds. Etanu told them about the tracker, and one of the soldiers came over to examine Zack's arm. The soldier reached inside his pack and withdrew a small handheld device. He held it above the reddened, scabbed skin of Zack's forearm and activated it. An amber glow bathed his arm. It felt warm, and the itching he'd been ignoring finally diminished until it ceased altogether. Zack looked down at his arm, and the skin looked much less irritated than before. The soldier put the device away and rubbed a pale green salve into his skin. It felt cool.

"The tracker has been deactivated and the salve will help speed the healing process," Etanu explained.

"What is it?" Zack asked.

"It's made from a plant here on Selebus," Etanu said.

His arm felt much better. He could almost hear Brenda Goodwin chiding him for exposing himself in such a way, warning him about the dangers of physiologies and how theirs might react differently than the Nershals'. But Zack figured that with everything that had happened, he'd get a pass from the Athena's medical officer. That said, with everything he'd already been exposed to, it would be unfortunate indeed if he were to become deathly ill from the Nershals' efforts to try and heal him.

Once they were away, Udonzari came over to them.

"How did you find where they were holding us?" Etanu asked.

Udonzari glanced at Zack. "We received word from your ship. Ezerah is with them."

"Are they here?" Zack asked, eager to return to the Athena. It wasn't that he didn't appreciate Etanu's help, but he wanted to see the crew of the Athena again.

"They are on their way," Udonzari said.

Zack frowned. "Where are they?" he asked.

"They went to Nerva, our home planet. Your commander used a Mardoxian chamber there to find you. They were able to send a communication to us, and we came here for you," Udonzari said.

"Nerva," Etanu said. "There aren't any chambers there. The only one in this system was destroyed sixty cycles ago."

"That's what we all thought, but apparently we were mistaken. They didn't go into a lot of detail about that, but they did say it was kept in secret. It seems as if the Boxans were testing our species for the Mardoxian potential," Udonzari said.

"Did Kladomaor go with them?" Zack asked.

The old Nershal shook his head. "The Xiiginn sent four warships into our star system, ostensibly to assist in the recovery and investigation of their cruiser. Kladomaor used his own ship to draw three of the warships to the outer system."

"Where is the fourth warship?" Etanu asked.

"That one went to Nerva with Mar Arden, who was speaking at a global congressional hearing about what you uncovered at the research station," Udonzari said.

"It's worse, that place," Zack said, gesturing in the direction they'd come from. "The Xiiginns were performing more than genetic experimentation. They were creating hybrids across multiple species."

Udonzari's eyes widened in surprise and he glanced at Etanu, who then began to tell Udonzari about what the Xiiginns had been doing at the pit, their experiments with controlling the mutants, and

Etanu's theory that they were trying to breed soldiers. The more they spoke, the grimmer Udonzari's features became.

"Etanu saved my life in the pit, more than once," Zack said.

"It was you who saved us all," Etanu said. "You were the one who sought out the other mutants. You earned their trust, and we're both alive because of that."

"We worked together," Zack said, and looked at Udonzari. "He has fulfilled his vow."

Udonzari regarded them for a few moments, his gaze lingering on his son. He then called the soldiers to gather around them. "Etanu, my son, on this day I recognize that you've accorded yourself with honor and have fulfilled your vow in ensuring the safety of this Human. You are hereby welcome to return to the ranks and aid our rebellion against the Xiiginns as First Wing Commander."

The soldiers howled their approval, and when they quieted down Udonzari turned to Zack.

"Zack, of the Human species," Udonzari said, "your deeds with be sung into our history. You've helped uncover a dark vein of deceit, and it will be our mission to see that the rest of our species knows of this. We will remove the Xiiginns' blight upon us, and you have our gratitude. I will see to it that Humans are welcome in Nerva, but if there is anything you desire that is within my power to grant, you just need to ask."

Zack felt his cheeks flush. He had just been trying to get out of the pit alive. He hadn't been trying to make any grand gestures for the Nershals. Udonzari was waiting for him to speak. "You're welcome," Zack said, feeling foolish. "I was just trying to get us out of there alive," he said, glancing at Etanu.

Udonzari nodded. "I understand that, but your actions will have lasting consequences that will ultimately benefit the Nershals. That's what we wish to honor."

"Oh," Zack said. "I just want to get back to my ship."

Udonzari nodded.

"Father," Etanu said, "you honor me."

Udonzari shook his head. "No, son, it is your actions that have brought honor to yourself."

Etanu pressed his lips together. "I wish to stay with the Human. I want to see him safely delivered back to his ship and help them return to their own star system."

Udonzari's face registered surprise. "What about your duty to the Nershals? You are First Wing Commander now. You will command soldiers and become a valuable asset in our struggle to free ourselves from the Xiiginns."

"I *am* thinking about my duty to the Nershals. If the Humans remain here, they will be caught in the crossfire. It is our duty to see that they leave our star system safely," Etanu said.

"The Boxans—" Udonzari began.

"This is our star system. The responsibility falls to us. The Boxans will help, but the Nershals should be represented as well, and this is a small price to pay for all the Humans have done for us," Etanu said.

Udonzari considered this for a moment. "It shall be as you desire. After the Humans are returned safely to their home star system, you will return here."

Some of the soldiers withdrew, and Udonzari was surrounded by a few who needed his attention.

Zack walked over to Etanu. "What are you doing? You were free of me. I thought you just wanted to get back to your people and help them fight the Xiiginns."

"I do, but helping you and your crew is equally important," Etanu said.

Zack didn't know what to say, but he knew he should say something. "Thank you," he said.

Etanu's normally hard features softened for an instant. "You're welcome."

There was a flurry of activity on the deck of the sled. Zack glanced at the other sleds flying near them and saw Nershal soldiers racing around. Gunners scanned the skies.

Zack and Etanu went over to Udonzari.

The old Nershal was issuing orders and turned toward them. "We have incoming. Xiiginn scouts were picked up on our scanners. Go arm yourselves."

Zack's mouth went dry. "They're after me," he said.

"He's right," Etanu said. "If we can get Zack off-planet, we can draw them away."

Udonzari nodded. "We have a couple of slip fighters not far. We'll get you to one, and you can escape in that."

Etanu turned, crossed the deck of the sled, and descended a narrow stairway. Zack followed. Etanu turned right and entered a small room where there were several weapons mounted on racks. Etanu glanced at Zack and then picked up one of the smaller, bronze-colored rifles.

"This is a pulse rifle. It shoots three-round bursts and is easy to control," Etanu said, handing Zack the weapon.

Zack took the pulse rifle. It seemed well balanced, and there was a metal sheath that surrounded the trigger.

"There's a button on the side to activate it, but don't press it in here. Wait until we're outside," Etanu said.

"Just aim and fire?" Zack asked.

Etanu closed his eyes and took a breath. "Just keep your head down and let me worry about shooting. If it comes to it then, yes, just point and shoot."

Etanu moved down the rack and hoisted one of the larger rifles. Checking the readout on the side, he nodded to himself and moved over to a tall locker where he found a couple of Nershal battle-mesh shirts. He tossed one at Zack.

"Put this on. It will adjust to your size," Etanu said.

Zack leaned the pulse rifle against the wall and held up the shirt. The dark brown sleeves looked a good six inches too long for him, and the bottom went down to his thighs. The shirt opened in the back and had four long slits cut into it. He glanced at Etanu, who was already putting the battle-mesh shirt on. He saw the shirt conform to Etanu's size, and the slits neatly compensated for the Nershal's wings.

Zack removed the tattered remnants of his old shirt, which was filthy, covered in dirt and dried blood. He slipped his arms into the battle-mesh shirt and pulled up the sleeves so his hands popped out of the ends. The dense material hugged his wrists. Zack pulled the top over the front of his shoulders. The material activated, and he felt it shift along his skin. The latches on the back joined together, and it conformed snugly to his skin. Zack stuck his arms out in front of him and was surprised to feel hardly any resistance at all.

Etanu handed Zack pants that were made of the same material. The pants were already closer to his size than the shirt had been, and both were extremely comfortable. Zack kept the boots he'd worn on the Athena. The Nershals' feet had three large toes and were just too different from Human feet to make the shoes work.

"The battle-mesh will give you some measure of protection, but don't take any unnecessary risks," Etanu said and handed him a thick metal collar.

"Thanks. I'll follow your lead this time," Zack said.

A loud blast sounded from the deck above.

"Keep your head down and follow me," Etanu said.

Zack frowned at the collar not seeing a use for it. He left the collar on the bench and followed Etanu to the door. The Nershal paused at the doorway, checking the activity beyond, and then exited. Nershals manning the deck guns fired behind them. Zack glanced back and saw a group of battle sleds following.

Two of the battle sleds flying with them eased back to provide their sled some cover.

Their pursuers opened fire, and the sky came alive with bolts crossing the distance between them. Etanu led them over to the side and squatted down.

"The slip fighters aren't far," Etanu said.

"If they're firing on us, how are we going to be able to break off?" Zack asked.

There was a bright orange flash behind them, and one of their battle sleds was rapidly losing altitude. Zack noticed dark shapes diving off the crashing sled and taking flight. The flying Nershals fired their weapons at the Xiiginns in the pursuing battle sleds.

Etanu pulled Zack down and gestured for him to follow. Crouching, they crossed over the deck, heading toward the front of the sled. They came to a stop, and Etanu told him to wait. The Nershal raised his head and glanced ahead of them. Zack watched the Nershal soldiers fire their weapons at the Xiiginns behind. Several Nershals had fallen to the deck and were pulled from harm's way. Zack could hardly believe that a short time ago these same Nershals were cheering for Etanu.

"The slip fighters are straight ahead," Etanu said.

Zack nodded. "How are they going to slow down so we can get off?" he asked.

Etanu glanced back at the fighting and then looked at Zack. "They're not. We're going to have to jump."

"Jump!" Zack cried. "I don't know if you've noticed, but I can't fly, and one of your wings is damaged."

"I know you can't fly, and my wing is healed enough for this," Etanu said.

Zack's mouth hung open in astonishment.

Etanu glanced over the wall again. "No time," he said, and grabbed Zack.

Together they leaped over the side. Zack screamed. The wind roared past his ears, and he faintly heard Etanu counting down. They plunged toward the ground and the Nershal still hadn't opened his wings. The breath caught in Zack's lungs as the ground rushed up to meet them. Etanu locked his grip around Zack, and they jerked in the air, slowing down before crashing to the ground. Zack rolled away in a heap, eventually coming to a halt, and Etanu landed more gracefully behind him. Zack's breath came in gasps as he slowly came to grips with having survived. Etanu pulled him to his feet and glanced up at the sleds flying overhead.

"I don't think they saw us, but we've got to hurry," Etanu said.

Zack couldn't get his feet to work right. He tried to go straight, but he kept leaning to one side. His equilibrium was off because of their freefall. Etanu glanced at him, bewildered.

"I'm fine. Let's go," Zack said, shaking off his dizziness.

Etanu led him toward several large mounds, but the Nershal stopped before they reached them. Etanu pulled Zack behind a small rocky formation and gestured for silence. The Nershal pointed above them, and Zack heard the whine of a sled's engines approaching them. Zack waited while Etanu stuck his head just above the rocks to get a better view. After a few moments he sat back down and glanced at Zack as if weighing his options.

"There are three Xiiginns approaching in one of the smaller sleds," Etanu said.

"Can we get to the slip fighter without them noticing?" Zack asked.

Etanu shook his head. He checked his weapon, and Zack's mouth went dry. "We don't have a lot of time. I want you to stay here while I scout to the side and try to flank them."

"You want me to just wait here? Isn't there something I can do to help you?"

"Calm down," Etanu said. "Stay here and keep your head down. If they get too close, use the pulse rifle."

Zack nodded and his stomach started to clench.

"I won't be far. I'm going to take them out before they get close to you," Etanu said.

The Nershal crawled along the ground away from him. There weren't any trees nearby for cover, but the Nershal made good use of the tall grass. Zack couldn't see Etanu after a few seconds, even with the augmentation of the implants. Zack clutched the pulse rifle to his chest and switched off the safety, then inched up the wall to get a better look. The sled was much smaller than the one they'd used. It only had room for a few people. The whine of the engines grew louder, and the sled slowed down. The three Xiiginns wore black armor. He couldn't tell if Kandra Rene was with them. Could they be tracking them somehow? What if there was another tracker on them that they didn't know about? The Nershal medic had scanned them and hadn't detected anything. Zack queried the AI.

::No traces of foreign elements reported,:: the AI said.

Zack turned over so he was on his stomach and pointed the pulse rifle at the approaching sled. His hand shifted near the trigger, and a three-round burst shot forth. Zack gasped. He'd hit the front of the sled, and something had broken off. A small tendril of smoke was trailing the sled. The Xiiginns shifted position and were heading straight toward him. They fired their weapons, and Zack ducked back down. Rocks shattered above and pieces rained down on him. *Oh crap,* Zack thought. He glanced to the side, weighing his chances of running, and shook his head. If he ran, they would have a clear shot at him. The sled closed in on his position and hovered over the ground as he crawled to the edge of the rocks he was using for cover.

There was a loud pop, and a small crater appeared a few feet in front of him. The shots came closer to him, and Zack shot to his feet, holding the pulse rifle up above his head in surrender.

Two of the Xiiginns dropped to the ground, leaving one in the sled.

"Throw down your weapon," a Xiiginn soldier commanded.

As Zack dropped the pulse rifle in front of him, the sled exploded. The two Xiiginns on the ground spun around, and the one who had stayed on the sled dropped to the ground with a large hole through the chest. Zack scrambled for the pulse rifle, and one of the Xiiginn soldiers turned to shoot him. Another shot rang out, and the Xiiginn collapsed to the ground. The remaining soldier dove to the side before Etanu could take him out. The soldier positioned himself so Zack was between him and wherever Etanu was hiding. Zack grabbed the pulse rifle and fired at the Xiiginn, but his shots went wide, missing completely. The Xiiginn aimed his weapon at Zack just as a shot whipped past Zack's head and took out the soldier.

Zack's breaths came in gasps. The whole encounter had lasted only seconds.

Etanu ran over to him.

"Come on before others arrive," Etanu said.

Zack forced himself to look away from the dead Xiiginns and follow Etanu. The Nershal brought up his wrist and entered a few commands. The mounds they'd been heading for shimmered and faded, revealing a dark metallic shape. There was an elongated midsection that had lower wings toward the front, with elevated rear wings. The engines on the wings were glowing as the power came up. There was a hiss as the front canopy opened.

"That's how we're going to get you back to your ship," Etanu said.

Zack peered inside. There were two seats side by side, separated by a center console. "This is a slip fighter?"

Etanu nodded. "Highly agile and quick. A squadron of these can wreak havoc on our enemy."

"Yeah, but there's only one here," Zack said.

Etanu gave him an exasperated glance. "If you're going to persist in stating the obvious, I may just hand you over to the Xiiginns."

"I'm just saying. I'm sure it's fast," Zack said, and looked up at the battle sleds trading weapons fire. "Can we help them?"

Etanu followed Zack's gaze. "They'll be fine," he said.

"But—" Zack began.

"I know you're not a soldier. The fighting here is only just beginning. Soon it will spread, and there is little difference we can make in one slip fighter," Etanu said.

They climbed aboard, and Etanu quickly showed him how to strap in. Zack glanced at the instrument panel.

"Don't touch anything," Etanu said.

Zack's hand recoiled, but he instructed the AI to connect to the ship's systems.

::No connection possible.:: The AI's words appeared on Zack's internal HUD.

Zack brought up his interpreter so he could try and understand what the controls did. It didn't help. Zack was no pilot. It might have made sense to Kaylan but not to him. There were two sticks conveniently placed in front of him.

"What are the sticks for?" Zack asked.

"They're for the rear weapons systems. Hopefully we won't need them—" Etanu was saying when a comms channel chimed. It was Udonzari.

"We've just received a notification that there is a Xiiginn warship en route to Selebus," Udonzari said.

"Understood," Etanu answered. "Are any of our ships out there?"

"There were two Nerva-class battle cruisers already here, but they might not realize what the Xiiginns are doing down there," Udonzari said.

The canopy sealed shut and Zack heard the whine of the engines. A screen switched on in front of him. There were several flashing dots heading directly for them. Zack was about to ask what they were when the slip fighter lifted off the ground and rocketed into the air. The ground passed by in a blur and then fell away as Etanu took them higher into the air.

"How are we going to find the Athena?" Zack asked.

"I was hoping the AI you're so proud of would help out with that," Etanu said.

"I'm sure it would, but it's not able to gain access to your ship's systems," Zack said.

Etanu grinned. "That's by design. Just enter the communications protocol into the console in front of you and then send a signal to your ship."

The color drained from Zack's face, and Etanu glanced over at him.

"You do know the communication protocols?" Etanu asked.

Zack frowned. "Of course I do. I just don't know how to feed that information into your ship's computer," he said.

The slip fighter passed through the atmosphere, entering outer space. Zack glanced at his PDA, which looked like it was barely holding together.

"Zack," Etanu called.

"Just give me a minute. I'll come up with something," Zack said.

"We've got incoming. Hang on," Etanu said.

Zack couldn't see anything but the HUD overlay that showed approaching vessels.

Oh crap, Zack thought.

CHAPTER SEVENTEEN

MAR ARDEN PACED on the bridge of the warship, and the commander of the ship glanced over at him. A Xiiginn of Mar Arden's stature should never show anything but unwavering leadership, and his pacing could be interpreted as weakness that would invite others to challenge his authority. Mar Arden came to a halt near the communications console. The comms specialist hardly turned to look and kept working, as was expected of her.

"What's the status from Nerva Space Command?" Mar Arden asked.

"We're still waiting on clearance to leave," Hoan Berend said from the commander's chair and gave Mar Arden a meaningful look.

Mar Arden moved away from the comms specialist and returned to stand near Hoan Berend. As first ambassador, he outranked the commander, but Mar Arden saw no reason for him to give up his seat just because the first ambassador happened to be on the bridge.

"First Ambassador, there's a priority alpha message for you. I've transmitted the challenge authentication key to your comms channel," the comms specialist said.

Mar Arden stepped over to a vacant console and used his implants to authenticate. Tetran protocols had been in effect since the incident with the research station. If his authentication failed, the alpha priority message would be deleted from the system. Anyone who failed to authenticate properly was immediately pulled from the duty roster and questioned. Unlike the cruiser that had been destroyed, this warship had only Xiiginns operating within it. There were no Nershal soldiers to complicate matters.

Mar Arden's inbox appeared on his internal HUD. There were two alpha priority messages waiting. He glanced at the comms specialist, but her back was to him. She had already gone on to her other duties.

He opened the first message, and Kandra Rene's face appeared. She had several wounds on her head and neck. Evidence of quick healing was already evident, and Mar Arden wondered how extensive the wounds had been before she'd received healing.

"The Human has escaped and is in the hands of the Nershal terrorists on Selebus. I've dispatched all available resources to pursue and bring him back. In the event that recovery is not possible, they've been instructed to take out the target. Awaiting your orders." Kandra Rene's message finished.

Mar Arden clenched his teeth. Questions tumbled through his mind, and he immediately categorized them in order of importance. His protégé had reported the facts and what she was doing to solve the problem. A lesser commander would be consumed with laying blame and bringing the guilty parties under his wrath. Kandra Rene knew she had failed him, and however brief her existence might now be, she was working to rectify her failure. Mar Arden knew there were other Humans here. No species sent just one of their number out into the void—at least none that they had encountered so far.

The second message was an alert that contained the spectral analysis of a suspected Mardoxian signal coming from Nerva. Mar Arden frowned. If he accepted the intelligence analyst's report, that would mean there was a Mardoxian chamber somewhere on the Nershal home world. His mind raced with the implications of that. What would compel the Boxans to risk returning to Nerva to use the Mardoxian chamber? The Xiiginns hadn't been able to detect the Boxan stealth ship, and he very much doubted that a battle commander such as Kladomaor was hiding on the surface of the planet. The Boxan relished his freedom too much for that. There was a connection between the Boxans and Humans, but he didn't understand it fully at the moment. Mar Arden put the Human element of the problem to the side and focused on why the Boxans had returned to the Nershal star system in the first place. They were trying to get the Nershals to rebel against the Xiiginns, which was a marked change in their tactics. And it was working. The Nershals were becoming increasingly more difficult to control. It might be time for them to reevaluate their alliance with the Nershals.

Why would the Boxans bring the Humans here? There was little doubt that the Mardoxian priestess was in Kladomaor's hands, but why would they need to use the chamber? He brought the intelligence analyst's report to the forefront and took a closer look at the readings. If it had been a deep-space communication, the signal detected didn't match the known vectors.

Mar Arden glanced at the commander. They were still awaiting clearance to leave the planet. Mar Arden suppressed his urge to order Hoan Berend to take them out of there at once, regardless of their clearance status. He didn't want to press the Nershals any more than necessary. He knew the Boxans were still in the system, and he had three warships hunting for them in the outer system. If only Kandra Rene hadn't let that Human slip through her fingers.

A thought blazed like lightning through his mind. Humans! The answer to the question was Humans. They were the reason the Boxans were still here. They were trying to find their missing crew member. The Xiiginns had taken steps to prevent the Mardoxian priestess from determining where the Human was being kept, but the use of a Mardoxian chamber changed things. The priestess could have used the Mardoxian chamber to find the missing Human.

"Commander," Mar Arden said. "I want best speed to Selebus."

"First Ambassador, we still don't have clearance," Hoan Berend said.

"Noted. When the Nershals initiate communication, inform them we are investigating an emergency situation on Selebus," Mar Arden said.

"That stall tactic will only work for so long," Hoan Berend warned.

"We don't have that much time," Mar Arden said.

Hoan Berend began issuing orders to the crew. As expected, Nerva Space Command wasn't happy with their abrupt withdrawal, but they had their hands full with the political unrest on the planet at the moment.

"Engage scanners," Mar Arden said.

"What are we looking for?" Hoan Berend asked.

"Something we haven't seen before. An unknown ship, probably something smaller," Mar Arden said.

Hoan Berend frowned. "I'm going to need more to go on than

that," the commander said.

"Look for evidence of a smaller power output, something a more primitive species would use," Mar Arden said. "And also scan for Cherubian drive signatures. I suspect there will be a gravity well for a wormhole detected soon."

Hoan Berend nodded.

Mar Arden quickly recorded a message for Kandra Rene. He opened a specially crafted secure channel so not even the Boxans would be aware and sent the message.

*****

Kladomaor watched the main holodisplay. The Xiiginn ion missile sweep had taken out most of the beacons they had planted throughout the system. When the missiles detonated, an ion wave expanded, disrupting systems that kept things like stealth in place. The beacons had no protection against an ion wave, but a Boxan dreadnaught had shielding in place that would take more than an ion wave to disrupt. The effective range of the ion wave was limited in that the wave rapidly lost strength as it expanded. But the ion missiles were a good tactic at flushing out enemy ships in stealth.

The negative effect of this tactic came with their use in populated star systems. The ion wave was designed to disrupt the electrical systems of any target, and the Nershals had a fair number of mining platforms and scientific research facilities throughout the star system. The use of the ion missile sweep would cause significant impact to those platforms. Kladomaor hoped the Nershals working at those facilities were up to date on emergency procedures to reduce the potential risk for loss of life. The Xiiginns would deem the loss of those facilities acceptable, but given the state of their relations with the Nershals, Kladomaor didn't think Nerva Space Command would agree. The Xiiginns' blatant use of the ion missile sweep could be construed as a violation of their alliance with the Nershals, but even if the Nershals finally broke their alliance with the Xiiginns, the Boxan fleet couldn't just conveniently show up to assist. Kladomaor had provided the rebel Nershals, like Udonzari, with a way to reach the Boxan fleet if Nerva Space Command required assistance in expunging the Xiiginns from this system, though he doubted they would use it.

Kladomaor glanced at the main holodisplay on the bridge. Another beacon went offline. The Xiiginns were systematically eliminating targets, but Kladomaor knew that for a few of those Xiiginn warships it was already too late. The Xiiginns had presumed the beacons had been deployed just to throw them off the Boxans' trail, and that was part of his strategy, but the primary objective of the beacons was to entice the warships to approach. When they did, the passive suite of detonators would latch onto vulnerable parts of the warships, and, once activated, the Xiiginns would be in for a surprise.

He glanced at Ma'jasalax, who sat at a nearby console with her eyes closed. She had been that way for a while, and Kladomaor knew she was trying to locate the Athena. He had instructed his comms specialist to monitor for any type of communication from the Athena, but nothing had been sent. At least Kaylan understood the need for stealth, but it was frustrating to be in the dark, and it required them to be ready to assist at a moment's notice. Things were probably going to heat up quite a bit before they could get away.

"Multiple ship signatures detected around Selebus. All are Nershal Space Command ships, Commander," Triflan said. The Boxan frowned at his console. "There is a Xiiginn warship en route to Selebus, and it looks like it came directly from Nerva."

"Mar Arden!" Kladomaor growled. "The game is almost up. Best speed to Selebus."

He pulled up the Cherubian drive status, which had been on standby with power levels hovering on the borderline of detection.

Ma'jasalax sucked in a deep breath and opened her eyes.

"I hope you were able to find them because I think the Xiiginns have finally figured out that the Humans have a ship in this star system," Kladomaor said.

Ma'jasalax glanced at the console. "They are almost to Selebus."

With all the ships gathering around the planet-sized moon, there was little chance of either of them being able to escape undetected. Kladomaor shoved those thoughts aside. He couldn't trade blows with a Xiiginn warship and survive for long, but if he could strike at the right moment, it might be enough to tether the Athena to their ship and jump from the system. Kladomaor authorized the use of their armament and saw the consoles around the bridge change colors to reflect this. The bridge crew remained focused. This is what they had trained for. The parameters of the Boxan mission may have changed, but they would all give their utmost in their war against the Xiiginns. Kladomaor hoped he had been clever enough to get them through this alive. The pieces were in place, and the endgame was fast approaching.

CHAPTER EIGHTEEN

ZACK'S MIND RACED into overdrive. The HUD overlay showed another ship approaching that was vastly larger than the Nershal battle cruisers.

"Is that big one the Xiiginn warship?" Zack asked.

Etanu switched through the console. "Yes. It looks like it came straight from Nerva. Have you figured out how to reach your ship yet?"

Zack frowned as he tried to think of what the implications would be if he did reach out to the Athena. "Are you able to contact your people's ships? Can we send them a message?"

"It will alert the battle cruisers to our presence if they don't already know, but we can send them a message," Etanu said.

Zack opened the interface on his PDA and crafted a dataset of all the raw data about where they had been held. "Good. I want you to send this over to them. Do you know if there are Xiiginns serving aboard the cruisers?"

Etanu shook his head. "Not many. The exchange program was for Nershals to serve on Xiiginn ships. What's in the message?"

"I had thought Udonzari would be reaching out to those ships, but he might be busy at the moment. It's all the information I have about the facility that held us—the different species, the location, everything. I'm hoping they'll stall the Xiiginn warship so we can find the Athena," Zack said.

Etanu nodded and opened another interface. A flurry of alien symbols went by too fast for Zack's interpreter to process.

"Message sent. I included my personal identification," Etanu said.

"One day you're going to have to tell me where your family fits in the Nershal hierarchy," Zack said, but quickly refocused on the task at hand. "I have the Athena's communication protocols ready."

"Send them over," Etanu said.

Zack took one more look at the collection he'd put together, which consisted of the comms protocols used by NASA. He just hoped someone on the Athena would be checking the comms station on the bridge.

There was a flash of light, and the slip fighter lurched to the side. Etanu's hands flew to the controls. Alarms flashed on the fighter's HUD. Etanu changed their course to head directly for the Nershal battle cruiser.

"What was that?" Zack asked.

"We're taking fire. It looks like some of the Xiiginns borrowed a few slip fighters to use against us," Etanu said.

The Nershal flipped a switch, and the controls in front of Zack lit up. A HUD appeared directly in front of him.

"You're a gunner now. I need you to control the rear cannons," Etanu said.

Zack grabbed the two sticks and saw four slip fighters behind them.

Etanu pulled up, and the slip fighters disappeared from view. Zack waited for the fighters to appear again and squeezed the trigger. Bolts rapidly fired, but the fighters dodged out of the way. Zack instinctively moved the sticks, and his combat screen moved to follow. Etanu banked to the side and quickly went back again, causing one of the slip fighters to plunge into a stream of bolts coming from their rear cannons. The fighter was destroyed instantly, and pieces of that fighter peppered the other fighters. Zack frowned in concentration as he tried to hit another one, but they were frustratingly quick. Whoever was flying those ships wouldn't fall for the same trick twice.

Etanu flipped their fighter over, and Zack's world went upside down. The Nershal fired the forward cannons, taking the slip fighters by surprise. Zack couldn't tell if they had taken any damage, but they did scatter. Etanu flipped back around and sped quickly away. Another alarm blared on the main HUD.

"They've fired missiles," Etanu said, "and they're locked on us."

"Can you outrun them?" Zack asked.

"Impossible. You have to take them out," Etanu said.

Zack tried to line up the sights, but the missiles were so small. He fired the rear cannons and didn't even come close. Blazing bolts belched from the rear cannons, sweeping the area behind them, but the missiles executed evasive maneuvers. The sticks felt slippery in his sweaty palms.

The missiles raced toward them.

"I can't hit them," Zack said, his voice rising in panic. "Etanu!"

The Nershal hit one of the controls, and the cockpit blasted away from the fighter. The missiles closed in, and their slip fighter was blown to pieces, but they rocketed away, safely beyond the broken remains of their craft.

Zack's brows knitted together. "I'm sorry. I couldn't get the targets to line up," he said.

"Don't be," Etanu said. "Taking out missiles without any training was too much to ask."

The lights and HUDs in the cockpit went out. They could see out of the canopy above them, but that was it. Etanu tried to get the power back on.

"What happened to the power?" Zack asked.

"We must have taken damage. I can't get it back on," Etanu said.

Zack glanced around the small cockpit and didn't see helmets. "Are there any helmets? What if the canopy breaks?"

Etanu looked over at him, his eyes straying to Zack's neck. "Where is the neckpiece that goes with your suit?"

Zack's mouth went dry. "What neckpiece?" he asked, his hands rising instinctively to his neck.

"This one," Etanu said, and pointed to a gray metallic collar around his own neck.

"I don't have one of those. Please tell me that's not the helmet," Zack said.

Etanu turned away and began checking the different storage panels in the cockpit.

"Etanu," Zack said. "Does that collar somehow become a helmet?"

Etanu frowned. "You asked me not to tell you," the Nershal said.

"That was sarcasm."

"Oh, well then, yes it is. Why didn't you put on all the clothes I gave you?" Etanu asked.

Zack clenched his jaw. "It was bulky. I didn't know the collar was needed. It's not like we had a lot of time to get into it. Is there another one on the ship or some type of emergency helmet I could use?" he asked.

"That's what I'm checking for, but it appears all the spares are gone," Etanu said.

Zack's stomach clenched. He was going to die because he didn't put on some stupid collar. "How much air do we have?"

"Normally we would have plenty, but without power there's nothing to scrub the atmosphere. It won't last long," Etanu said.

"What about those other fighters?" Zack asked.

"Without power to the pod, they might believe they've destroyed us because their scanners won't be able to detect us," Etanu said.

The Nershal continued to pull open panels and check the components inside. They didn't know how bad the damage to their escape pod was, and Zack didn't have much hope of figuring out how to turn the power back on. He glanced down at his PDA and used his implants to communicate with the AI.

::Start broadcasting on any frequency the Athena could be monitoring,:: Zack said.

::Acknowledged, but I should warn you that the range is severely limited,:: the AI replied.

::Understood. Do what you can,:: Zack replied and said a silent prayer for the others to find them. He didn't know how he could get to the Athena without a spacesuit, but hopefully between them and

Kladomaor they could come up with something.

*****

Kaylan was on the bridge while the Athena closed in on Selebus. She'd searched for the place where Zack was being held and found it a smoking ruin. She'd told the others.

"That's a good sign," Hicks said.

"How is that a good sign?" Redford asked.

"It means they've escaped. If the facility had been fully intact when we got there, we would have had to go in and break them out," Hicks said.

"Now we just need to figure out where he is," Kaylan said.

Gaarokk stood at the back of the bridge, his bushy brows pushed forward in concentration. The AI had given the Boxan access to their systems so he could help.

Kaylan glanced at the holodisplay over at the conference table, which showed the nearby ships orbiting Selebus. There was a Xiiginn warship that had followed their trajectory from Nerva. It seemed that the Xiiginns had finally figured out they were here. She checked the comms status for any frequency Zack would use to contact them, but it was silent.

Abruptly, the comms channel chimed into the silence, drawing everyone's attention.

"Athena, this is Kladomaor. Have you found him?" the Boxan asked.

"The facility where Zack was being held has been destroyed. We're closing in on Selebus now," Kaylan said.

"Understood. We're on approach to Selebus but on the far side from your position. We have hostile warships following. By now you must realize that their warship is tracking you. Whatever you intend to do, do it fast, and we'll support you as best we can," Kladomaor said.

Kaylan raised a brow and felt the beginnings of a smile. "Thank you. We're going to—"

"Commander," the AI said. "The Xiiginn warship is accelerating."

"The Nerva battle cruisers are calling for the warship to stand down," Gaarokk said.

Kaylan brought up the navigation interface and checked their approach vector. The Athena was using every ounce of speed available, and they would need to fire breaking thrusters soon. She glanced around the bridge at the crew. Their lives were in her hands, and the next decision she made would affect all of them.

"Kladomaor, are you still there?" Kaylan asked.

"We're here," the Boxan replied.

"We're going to make a pass over the vicinity where Zack was being held. If we can't get a signal, we'll need to leave quickly," Kaylan said, her chest tightening as the words left her mouth.

"We'll make sure you get as much time as we can possibly give you. We've reached out to Udonzari, and his forces are in the same area. Zack might be with them. The comms chatter indicates there's fighting on the planet's surface," Kladomaor said.

The comms channel closed, and the bridge was silent.

"I don't get it," Redford said. "Why the sudden change of heart from Kladomaor?"

Kaylan glanced at Katie, who was hovering at the back of the bridge. Neither of them wanted to think about leaving Zack behind, but they might have to.

"We can question it later," Hicks said. "We just need to know they're doing everything they can to help us, so now we have a chance to find Zack. We should get to our stations. Vitomir and Brenda, you're with me in the shuttle."

"I'll be in the Beagle," Katie said.

Kaylan nodded and the others left the bridge.

Ezerah came to her side. The Nershal had been quietly observing them since they'd left Nerva. Kaylan glanced at Ezerah. After experiencing how the male Nershal soldiers behaved, the females seemed to her to be more reserved. At least that was the case with Ezerah.

"That must have been difficult for you to do," Ezerah said.

Kaylan swallowed away the thickening of her throat. "It was the right call," she said.

"That is the burden of being in command," Ezerah said.

The status on the main HUD showed the breaking thrusters firing, but they didn't feel a thing on the bridge. The blue-green planet loomed in the window and looked so peaceful from up there.

"We're in position," Hicks said.

"Beagle is ready to go," Katie said.

Kaylan acknowledged and brought up the different comms interfaces. They were all flat-lined. Kaylan sighed. *Come on, Zack, I know you're out there.*

Gaarokk cocked his head to the side, his eyes going wide. Bright flashes from beyond the ship snagged her attention.

"The Nershals opened fire on the Xiiginn warship!" Gaarokk said.

Kaylan brought the camera feeds onto the display. She magnified the image as much as she could. Bright beams of energy were coming from the two Nershal cruisers, tearing into the larger warship. The Xiiginn warship rolled to its side and fired a massive energy beam. Gaarokk gasped. The beam tore through the Nershal battle cruiser and emerged on the other side. Smaller orange flashes came from the cruiser, and it stopped firing.

Kaylan's lips parted.

The second ship kept firing at the warship while maneuvering away from the beam.

Kaylan opened all of the comms channels and patched the others in so they could listen. "Zack, if you're out there, please respond," she said.

Garbled static was the only sound. Kaylan kept repeating herself, her voice growing a little more desperate with each iteration. Kaylan gripped the table, her muscles going rigid and her head bowed. She wanted to scream. Her eyes became misty and she squeezed them shut, trying to listen for some sign that Zack was there. The Nershals were dying in the start of a rebellion against the Xiiginns, and the Boxans were ready to face death so the Humans could have this chance to rescue Zack. He had to be there. She sucked in a deep breath and forced down the ache in her chest so she could focus.

The garbled static rose in pitch for a moment, and Kaylan's eyes snapped open. She scanned the comms channels to see which one had the signal. A channel spiked again.

* * *

*****

Zack watched as Etanu tried to restore power to their escape pod. The Nershal had put on his helmet so their oxygen would last longer. Zack glanced at the PDA wrapped around his wrist. The silver casing had cracked and he hardly dared touch it for fear it would stop working altogether.

The pod slowly spun, and their view changed from that of the blue-green planet with the gas giant looming nearby to that of deep space. He glanced out the canopy, squinting to get a better view.

"You need to take a look at this," Zack said.

Etanu looked up and out of the canopy. Bright flashes blazed like a lightning storm in space. "There's a battle being fought."

Zack glanced back at the Nershal, wondering what he must be thinking, but Etanu looked down at the exposed guts of the slip fighter's electrical systems.

"None of the primary systems respond. I don't think I can fix this from inside," Etanu said.

"And you can't get outside because of me," Zack finished.

They were silent for a few moments, and Etanu wouldn't look at him.

"Faint comms signal detected," the AI said from Zack's PDA.

"Is it the Athena?" Zack asked.

"Unable to confirm at this distance, but it is highly probable," the AI said.

Zack took control of the comms system. "Athena, this is Zack.

Please respond."

He closed his eyes and focused all his attention on the static. With no power to their escape pod, his PDA with its measly capabilities was their only lifeline. The static pulsed, and Zack opened his eyes.

"Athena, if that's you, we can hardly hear you," Zack said.

The static in the comms signal became louder as the signal became stronger.

"Zack, this is the Athena," Kaylan's voice said over comms.

Zack shared a look with Etanu and cried out. Warmth filled his chest and he felt his eyes become misty. "Kaylan, I'm so glad to hear your voice. We're in trouble. We're in an escape pod, but it doesn't have any power. My PDA is damaged, and I'm not sure how long it will last," Zack said.

Zack had to repeat himself a few times because of the weak signal, but they were on their way, and his heart felt as if it would burst out of his chest when the silver-and-white hull of the Athena came into view. He couldn't stop smiling and could hear the relief in Kaylan's voice.

Etanu watched the Athena come closer to their position and frowned. "*That* is your ship? It doesn't look big enough to house a Cherubian drive."

"I don't know what that is," Zack said.

Etanu glanced at him. "Never mind. We still need to get you aboard your ship."

Zack nodded. "Athena, I don't think the escape pod is going to fit in the airlock. Any ideas on how we can get aboard?" He explained that he didn't have a spacesuit and warned them about the slip fighters in the area.

The flashing from the space battle stopped, drawing their attention. Kaylan told them about the Nershal battle cruisers engaged with the Xiiginn warship.

"Can your ships beat the warship?" Zack asked.

Etanu swallowed and shook his head. "It would take more than two of them."

Zack felt his stomach drop. The Xiiginns were likely on their way here right now. He opened a comms channel to the Athena. "We don't have much time, do we?"

He heard the sound of hushed voices for a moment. "No, we don't," Kaylan said.

Etanu gestured toward Zack's PDA, and he nodded his permission for the Nershal to speak. "Athena, can you position your craft so we're as close to the airlock as possible?"

"What good will that do?" Zack asked.

"The closer we are, the better the chance we can jump from the pod to the airlock," Etanu said.

"Are you insane? If we open that canopy, I'm dead!" Zack said.

"We'll be dead if we don't," Etanu said.

"The Athena isn't designed to maneuver that way," Zack said.

"He's right, Etanu. We can't move the Athena like that, but we can move the pod to our airlock," Kaylan said. "Katie?"

"Already on my way," Katie said.

"You guys seem to be forgetting that I don't have a helmet," Zack said.

"Calm down," Etanu said. "You will not die instantly. The battle-mesh will protect your body. If we're quick, you will survive."

The Beagle 4S swooped into view. It was a small, one-man spacecraft developed for satellite salvage and repair. Zack took in the sight of the white hull and tried to slow his racing pulse. The Beagle leveled off, and he had a clear view of Katie Garcia in the cockpit. She smiled at him.

"Hey, you. We'll get you aboard in a minute," Katie said.

Zack's breathing became shallow. With the Athena being so close and Katie right outside, he wasn't sure if he could keep it together.

"Zack," Katie said. "Look at me."

He looked at her.

"You're going to be fine. You can do this. Etanu is right. You won't die from brief exposure to space," Katie said.

Zack swallowed hard and took a deep breath. "How much time do I have?"

"Not more than fifteen seconds," Katie said.

Zack's mind worked through the calculations, taking into consideration the distance they needed to be from the airlock. There was hardly any room for error.

"Understood," Zack said.

"Athena," Katie said. "Confirmed, the pod will not fit in the airlock."

"Acknowledged," Kaylan said. "Get them as close as you can. Hicks and Brenda will be ready to receive you."

The Beagle 4S rose, disappearing from view, and a few moments later Zack heard something latch onto the back of the pod. He knew there were three robotic arms that extended from beneath the pilot's seat, and he waited for the other two to latch on.

"I've got them," Katie said. "Nice and easy now."

Zack tried to glance behind them but couldn't see anything. The escape pod was slowly being pushed toward the Athena. Etanu reached to the side of his seat and pulled out a container. He opened it and took out some dark green fabric that was rolled together.

"What's that for?" Zack asked.

"They're healing packs. The microfiber will offer you some protection from the vacuum of space. I need you to wrap it around your head, and be sure to cover your eyes," Etanu said.

Zack took the fabric. It felt spongy and dense. He vaguely remembered from his astronaut training that minimizing exposure to the vacuum of space could mean the difference between life and death. He wrapped the squishy fabric around his neck, working his way up. It felt cool against his skin, and he felt all his little cuts and scrapes tingle. The tension melted away from his forehead and neck, and Zack wondered if the healing packs had some type of painkilling effect. He didn't cover his eyes yet, wanting to keep his sight until the last possible second. He had just enough fabric to circle it around his head twice more, and he imagined he looked like some type of green mummy. Zack looked over at Etanu.

"Good," Etanu said. "Here, put on your gloves."

Zack heard the sounds of his own breathing, and he tried to keep it slow and steady. The others were waiting for him. He knew that if there were any other way to safely get him aboard, Kaylan would have insisted. He trusted them.

"I'm ready," Zack said.

230 | THE STAR ALLIANCE

"Not long now," Katie said.

The Beagle 4S guided the pod toward the airlock near the top of the ship, and Zack recalled that this was nearest to the med bay. The pod was guided above the ship, and Katie brought them to a halt at an angle. Once the canopy opened, they would have a clear shot to the airlock. Hicks waved to them from inside the airlock, and the door opened.

Zack glanced beyond the ship, and his heart was in his throat. "Watch out!" Zack shouted in a half-startled cry.

Barreling toward their ship was the biggest ship he'd ever seen. Black scorch marks were peppered across the massive gray hull. The Xiiginn warship was like the leviathan of the skies—a behemoth, with angular planes and gun turrets strewn throughout the hull.

Etanu reached over and shook him. "Cover your eyes. When I tell you to exhale, you must expend all the breath in your body."

Zack nodded and wrapped the fabric around his eyes, closing off his view of the warship.

"Katie, get out of here," Zack said.

"Don't worry about me. I'll just make sure you get to the ship. Etanu, let me know when you open the canopy. I'll use the thrusters to hold the pod in place. The little bit of atmosphere in the pod should give you a boost," Katie said.

"Understood," Etanu said.

Zack heard his breath push against the fabric. "Wait, Etanu," Zack said. "If something goes wrong, don't try any heroics. Get yourself on the Athena."

Etanu was quiet for a moment. "I will get you onto your ship.

Remember to exhale at the end of the countdown."

Zack nodded and unbuckled himself from the seat, hearing Etanu do the same. He felt the Nershal climb in front of him, so his back must have been to the canopy. Etanu grabbed both of Zack's arms.

"Three."

Zack sucked in a deep breath and blew it back out.

"Two."

Zack sucked in another breath and forced every bit of air from his lungs. He squeezed his eyes shut and his body went tight with anticipation.

"One."

There was a loud snap-hiss as the canopy blew open. Zack's body was thrust forward into a wall of cold that slapped his skin. The spongy fabric went rigid, and Zack fought the urge to suck in a breath. He couldn't hear anything, and for a few moments they were sailing through space. His lungs burned, and every instinct inside him demanded that he take a breath. He slammed into something hard, and the last thing he felt was the intense burning on his face and neck before passing out.

*****

Kaylan's eyes were locked onto the video feed from the airlock. Two dark shapes burst into the airlock and slammed against the interior door. The breath caught in her throat as she waited for the airlock doors to shut. Seconds dripped past and Kaylan's heart pounded in her ears. The indicator lights around the door changed to red and the vents opened, flooding the room with air. One of the dark figures began to move. That must be Etanu. Zack lay motionless on the airlock floor. He had something wrapped around his head. The interior door opened, and Brenda and Hicks ran inside.

"Did they make it?" Katie asked from the Beagle.

"They're aboard," Kaylan replied.

"Is Zack okay?" Katie said.

"Brenda is checking him. Katie, dock the Beagle. I'll give you an update as soon as Brenda tells me something," Kaylan said.

Kaylan fought the tremendous urge to run to the medical bay. More than anything she wanted to make sure Zack was okay, but the Xiiginn warship closing in changed things.

She needed to wait for Katie to dock the Beagle before they could attempt to get away. She tried to raise Kladomaor, but the Boxan didn't reply.

"He's coming," Gaarokk said. "He won't risk an open comms channel now."

Kaylan had a course ready to execute the moment Katie docked her ship. She glanced at Gaarokk, and his flaxen eyes were focused on the holodisplay. The Boxan hardly blinked. Ezerah was there as well. For as much time as the two aliens had been aboard the Athena, it still wasn't a sight Kaylan was used to.

Efren sent an update that the engines were ready.

"I'm docked," Katie said over comms.

"Execute course alpha," Kaylan said.

The Athena's engines flared to life, and they started to move away from the warship. Gaarokk had advised her to use the planet to their advantage—both to try and keep the planet between the Athena and the Xiiginns, and to use the gravity from the planet to assist in their acceleration. The Xiiginn warship changed course to pursue, and another ship signal appeared behind it.

"It's the second battle cruiser," Ezerah said.

Kaylan's heart pounded as she glanced at the Nershal. She'd been told the cruiser would be no match against the warship. Flashes of light could be seen from the Athena's windows. Kaylan had no idea what the Xiiginns were using for weaponry, but she knew the Athena wasn't designed for that type of punishment. It was a science vessel designed for exploring Earth's solar system. Their only defense was to put as much distance as possible between themselves and the battle.

The sensors showed the Xiiginn warship gaining on them.

The door to the bridge opened and Hicks came in, walking to Kaylan. "Brenda is still working on him," he said, and glanced at the holodisplay.

"They're going to try to capture this ship," Gaarokk said.

"How?" Kaylan said.

"The same way we did before with the use of a gravity tether. The tether will hold the ship in place," Gaarokk said.

"Yeah, but we were able to break free of that, thanks to you," Hicks said.

"You don't understand. Kladomaor let us go. The damage to the Athena would be too great if we were to repeat what we did before," Gaarokk said.

An alert chimed on the holodisplay, and three more ship signatures appeared in their direct path, albeit a good distance from them. After a moment the AI identified them as Xiiginn warships.

Kaylan's mouth went dry. "Four of them," she said.

The display put the approaching Xiiginn warships' velocity in orders of magnitude above anything they could do. They would be on them in minutes. She glanced at Hicks and saw the same resignation on his face. They weren't going to get away. Kladomaor had repeatedly said their stealth ship couldn't take on a single Xiiginn warship, let alone four of them. Her heart sank to her stomach. She had done this because she had refused to leave Zack behind. Now he was on the ship, and she wasn't even sure if he was alive. The price they paid for her foolishness would be the ultimate price.

"I'm sorry," Kaylan whispered.

Another ship detection alert chimed on the holodisplay, cutting off Hicks's reply. It was almost on top of the Athena and matched her velocity. Kaylan glanced at Hicks, and the comms station on the Athena lit up.

*****

The stealth field surrounding the Boxan ship dissipated, allowing them to bring their weapons system to full power.

"Send detonation signals," Kladomaor ordered.

"Signal sent, Commander," Triflan confirmed.

Multiple readouts updated as their electronic warfare suite utilized a full sensor sweep of the surrounding ships.

"The Nershal battle cruisers exacted a toll on the closest warship. Target the hull breaches with our missile package," Kladomaor said.

Multiple missile tubes opened on the Boxan stealth ship, and within moments a mixed armament group spewed forth. The distance between the ships was short. The first wave of missiles carried a destructive payload capable of breaching the Xiiginn warship's defense capabilities; however, the Boxan stealth ship could only carry so much ammunition, and that amount was insufficient to take out a warship. The second wave contained ion missile warheads. Kladomaor only sought to blind them enough that they could get away.

"Confirm detonations on all three warships. Two of them are decelerating," Triflan said.

Kladomaor kept his gaze locked on the closest warship. Mar Arden was aboard that ship, and he yearned to destroy it, taking his former captor with it, but he couldn't. He glanced at Ma'jasalax, and the Mardoxian priestess gave him a single nod.

"Ready the gravity tether and lock it onto the Athena," Kladomaor said.

After a few moments, Triflan said, "Tether locked."

Alarms blared across the bridge.

"They're returning fire, Commander!"

"Deploy countermeasures and engage the Cherubian drive," Kladomaor said.

*****

Kaylan reduced the acceleration of the Athena's engines and watched as the Boxan stealth ship shielded them.

"Gravity tether is locked onto us," Gaarokk said.

A comms channel opened from the sensor array at the top

observatory. "Commander," Redford said. "Detecting gravity anomaly dead ahead of us. A wormhole is opening."

Just then a comms channel opened up, but Kaylan couldn't tell where it came from. A loud screeching noise sounded through the Athena's speakers. Kaylan winced and covered her ears, using her implants to cut the signal. The Athena increased its velocity, closing in on the wormhole. Kaylan glanced out the window at the Boxan ship. Bright flashes made her wince and turn away.

Their view of the stars folded away from them as if they were riding a huge wave. Lines of starlight rippled past the windows. The last time the Athena had gone through a wormhole, the ship had felt as if it were going to fly apart, but not this time. The gravity tether must be protecting them somehow. The two ships barreled through the wormhole, leaving the Nershal star system behind. Kaylan gripped the table and held on. The edges of the wormhole rippled and pulled away from them. There was a loud metallic clang and the Boxan stealth ship dove ahead of them in a slow spin. The ship turned over, revealing several gaping holes venting gases into space.

The streaming stars returned to normal, and proximity alarms blared on the bridge. They were going to crash into the Boxan ship. Kaylan dashed toward the pilot's seat and tried to steer clear, engaging the bottom thrusters to pull them away from the other ship.

"Grab onto something!" Kaylan screamed.

Those on the bridge scrambled for a handhold.

The side thrusters engaged, but the edge of the Boxan ship clipped one of the lower decks. Those decks were immediately sealed. Thankfully, no one was near the damaged sections. Kaylan engaged the breaking thrusters, and the Athena began to slow down.

Farther away, the Boxan stealth ship leveled off and came to a halt. Kaylan was gasping as she glanced around the bridge. The others appeared to be fine.

"What happened?" Hicks asked.

Gaarokk was catching his breath. "I think the wormhole became unstable. That can only happen if the Cherubian drive fails. We were lucky both ships weren't torn apart."

"Athena," Kaylan said. "Can you reach the other ship?"

"No reply, Commander," the AI said.

Kaylan walked over to the holodisplay and glanced out the window, but there was nothing nearby—no planets, no stars, nothing. She opened the comms throughout the ship, asking for everyone's status and a damage report. The reports came in, and the crew ran preliminary diagnostics. They hadn't heard from Redford, and she sent Nikolai to go check on him.

"Go on," Hicks said to her. "Go to the med bay. I'll let you know if anything comes up."

Kaylan hesitated. This was her ship.

"The ship isn't in immediate danger. You can take a few minutes to go check on Zack. I'll monitor from here," Hicks said.

Kaylan swallowed hard and nodded. "I'll be right back."

She slowly walked from the bridge, but the farther she went, the quicker her pace became until she was found that she was running. Before long she stood outside the medical bay doors. She took in a deep breath and opened them.

"We can't risk unwrapping his head until the heat lamps have had a chance to work; otherwise, we could risk damaging his skin," Brenda Goodwin was saying to the others as Kaylan walked in.

Zack lay on one of the beds. Above him, heat lamps were blasting their warmth. She couldn't see his face. It looked as if his head were in some sort of green cocoon. She glanced at his chest and saw the steady rise and fall of his breathing.

"Has he awakened yet?" Kaylan asked.

"He started to, but I sedated him," Brenda said.

Katie Garcia was at his side. "He's going to be alright," she said with a tired smile.

Kaylan slowly approached the bedside. Zack wore one of the battle mesh suits she'd seen the Nershal soldiers wearing. She turned and saw Etanu standing off to the side. The Nershal didn't immediately meet her gaze, and Kaylan didn't know what to say to him, but he had helped save Zack's life.

"Welcome aboard the Athena," Kaylan said.

"It is an honor to be here, Commander," Etanu said.

"Now, what exactly is it that you had Zack wrap around his face?" Brenda asked.

"It was part of the healing kit we had on the slip fighter. It's meant for wounds. I had Zack use it to provide some protection around his face," Etanu said.

"Is there a problem?" Kaylan asked.

Brenda shook her head. "No, I think Etanu did the right thing, but we can't know for sure until he warms up a bit. The rest of Zack's body appears to be fine."

"Where are we?" Katie asked.

"I'm not sure. Something happened that pulled us from the wormhole. We haven't been able to contact Kladomaor yet," Kaylan said.

She glanced at Zack and wanted to stay, but she knew she was needed elsewhere.

The doors to the med bay opened and Nikolai and Vitomir carried in Redford's unconscious body. They laid the astrophysicist on one of the other beds.

"We found him unconscious in the observatory where he likes to work," Nikolai said.

Brenda leaned over and started to examine him.

Hicks reached out to Kaylan over comms, saying she was needed on the bridge, and she told him she would be right there. She took one last look at Zack, as if needing to convince herself he was really there. She wanted to see his face, but Brenda was right to be cautious. Katie said she would stay and help Brenda. Kaylan nodded and left for the bridge with Nikolai and Vitomir following.

Chapter Nineteen

ZACK HEARD SOMEONE call his name, but they sounded muffled and far away. He felt something press against his face and took a shallow breath. The skin on his face stung. He tried to open his eyes, but something was keeping them closed. He started to panic when he tried to raise his hands and couldn't.

"Hold still, Zack. It's Brenda. Don't try and talk yet. Just squeeze my hand if you can hear me."

Zack felt someone take hold of his hand, so he squeezed.

"Good," Brenda said. "We're about to unwrap the Nershal healing packs from your face."

Zack squeezed Brenda's hand again.

Brenda let go of his hand, but someone else grabbed his other one.

"I'm right here," Katie said.

Zack gave a slight nod, and a shaky breath left his throat. He felt something cold and hard press against the side of his neck.

"We're cutting through the fabric, and then we're going to pull it off of you," Brenda said.

Zack tried to lay as still as possible while the fabric was cut away. The stinging became worse as his skin was exposed to the air, and he bit back a wince. Brenda cut away faster, and the fabric fell away from his face. He slowly opened his eyes and saw Katie and Brenda peering down at him. He tried to think of something witty to say, but his mind was overwrought with seeing them again. He felt his lips quiver, and the stinging faded to a dull ache.

Brenda inspected his head, her own face a mask of intense concentration. After a moment she smiled, relieved. "You were very lucky," she said.

Zack smiled, and the sensitive skin on his face and neck ached. The warm lamp above him felt good. He looked at Katie. "Hi," he said.

"Welcome back," Katie said.

Zack glanced off to the side where Etanu stood. "Are we even yet?"

Etanu regarded him for a moment. "I'm no longer keeping count."

Zack snorted and winced. "Thanks," he said.

Katie handed him a cup of water, which he gratefully drank. He tried to sit up, but Katie pressed him back down.

"Just rest," she said.

Zack heard someone groaning from one of the other beds and saw Redford sitting up. He held his hand to his head, rubbing the back of it. Brenda went over and examined him.

Redford allowed himself to be examined. The astrophysicist knew when it was hopeless to try and dissuade the Athena's medical officer from doing her job.

"I'm fine, I just bumped my head," Redford said, and looked over at Zack. "Mr. Quick, I'm glad to see you've made it back to us."

Zack was so happy to be alive that he was even glad to see Jonah Redford. "Thanks," he said.

Redford stood up. "I think I'll head to the bridge and see what our next move is. Are you coming?" he asked and glanced at Brenda.

"Yeah, I think everything is under control here," Brenda said.

Etanu gave Zack a nod and followed the others to the bridge.

Zack looked over at Katie where she sat beside him on the bed. He didn't know what to say. He had imagined getting back to the Athena and seeing everyone again. He felt all the emotions he had pushed to the side return stronger than they had been before, demanding to have their due. He swallowed hard. "I don't know where to begin," Zack said, sagging back against the bed.

"It's okay. Begin wherever you want," Katie said. Her long black hair was tied back and hung over one shoulder.

Zack felt his throat thicken as he looked into her dark eyes. "I kissed Kaylan," he said. "I did. I thought I was going to die. And I didn't want her to be trapped on that ship because of me."

Katie blinked and she gave a slight nod. "We're not married, Zack. You and Kaylan have a history. We were just having fun."

Zack was clearly surprised by these words. "Katie, I . . . this thing between us wasn't just fun for me. I care about you."

"But . . ." Katie said.

"I would be lying to you if I said I didn't have feelings for Kaylan as well," Zack said, and looked away from her.

"Hey, I understand," Katie said softly. "I get it. I've known there was something between the two of you since we first got aboard the ship. I kissed you that first time because I liked you. We had fun, and it doesn't have to be any more than that."

Zack felt his stomach tighten. He felt like Katie was pulling away from him, as if she knew what he had hardly admitted to himself. He opened his mouth to speak, but Katie silenced him.

"You may not be ready to admit to yourself how you feel about Kaylan, but I can read your actions as clear as day. You threw yourself into danger to protect her without thinking about what would happen to you—both on the planet and on that ship. If that's not enough for you to admit how you feel about her, then I don't know what would be," Katie said.

"I just feel like I've betrayed you," Zack said.

Katie's lips lifted into a small smile. "You're a good guy, Zack," she said, and left him alone to rest in the med bay.

She walked down the corridor, away from Zack, and sagged against the wall. She felt tears in her eyes and quickly wiped them away. Katie couldn't make Zack stay with her. It wouldn't have been fair to either of them. She felt a deep pang twist in her chest. She hadn't lied to him—their relationship had started off as something fun—but she cared deeply for the computer-hacker-turned-astronaut, deeper than she cared to admit. But if he loved someone else, she'd much rather see him happy. Katie sucked in a quick breath and headed toward the bridge.

*****

Kaylan was reviewing the Athena's diagnostic reports of the ship's systems on the bridge, and Etanu had joined them a short while before. Kladomaor had sent a message that they were assessing the damage to their ship. The Athena was in surprisingly good shape.

They had sustained minimal damage, which she had told the Boxans. She also offered assistance in case they needed it. She doubted Kladomaor would take her up on it, but at least the offer was there.

"Commander, I wish to say something to you," Etanu said.

A hush swept over those on the bridge, and Kaylan nodded for the Nershal to continue.

"I must apologize for my treatment of you and the rest of the crew when we first met on Selebus. I thought strict adherence to our traditions was the best way to deal with any situation. I have since learned a great deal about your species from my time with Zack. Although he and I don't agree on many things, his unwavering loyalty to all of you is inspiring," Etanu said. The Nershal went on to recount their imprisonment on Selebus, being trapped in the pit and the torture Zack had endured at the hands of a Xiiginn who called herself Kandra Rene. "I had thought your species to be weak and couldn't understand why the Boxans would put such a high value on so unworthy a race, so when Zack saved my life, I hated him for it. I was wrong. Even in the pit, surrounded by mutants, Zack was strong. I know he doesn't view himself that way, and he was at times both weak *and* strong, but it was him who was determined to free every single mutant trapped in that pit. I was still only looking to fulfill my vow to save Zack's life. My actions in the pit were enough to satisfy that vow, but I'm not finished with him. That's why I requested leave to see that Zack and the rest of you are taken safely back to your home star system. I'm here to help you however I can."

Kaylan felt herself tear up as Etanu recounted the events they'd endured in the pit. She had glimpsed the facility where they had been held but could hardly imagine what it must have been like to be trapped there. Kaylan had caught sight of Zack's PDA, and it was barely holding together. It had been extremely unlikely that they would have been able to find Zack and Etanu at all, and her relief was overwhelming. She thanked Etanu and welcomed his help.

Kaylan noticed that Ezerah had been silent for the duration of Etanu's recounting, which she found curious. The female Nershal appeared to be considering something.

The door to the bridge opened and Katie walked in. Her eyes were slightly glassy, as if she'd been crying.

"He's resting," Katie said.

Kaylan nodded. "The diagnostics show we're in pretty good shape, but I want a visual inspection of the damaged section. I don't want us to be underway and discover a problem that could have been prevented before turning into a much bigger problem."

They organized into groups and set out to perform their assigned tasks. Kaylan thought about going to see Zack again, but there was so much to do. She promised herself that once she was sure the ship was in good shape, she would go to him.

CHAPTER TWENTY

CRITICAL ALARMS FLASHED on the bridge of the Boxan stealth ship. Kladomaor studied them on his private console, prioritizing them in his mind. Their ship had sustained heavy damage during their brief encounter with the Xiiginns, but they had survived. Their preparation for an encounter with a vastly superior force had only been made possible by a superior strategy. Unfortunately, that strategy didn't extend to their engines escaping damage caused by the Xiiginn warship's weapons. Mar Arden was many things, but a fool in battle wasn't one of them. The Xiiginn knew precisely where to hit him. They had only escaped because the window of opportunity for the Xiiginns to exact the maximum damage was reduced by the disarray they'd caused the other warships. Mar Arden must have assumed they would surrender in the face of four of their warships. Kladomaor was happy to disappoint the Xiiginns, but the momentary elation quickly faded to smoldering disappointment that he hadn't been able to take out his former captor.

The Boxan crew was working to restore full communications capability, along with their sensor array. They needed them both to figure out where they were. The wormhole had become unstable due to the damage they had taken during battle. It was a miracle that both ships hadn't been torn apart. They were light-years away from the Nershal star system and had been en route to their own colony entry point before transitioning to the actual colony where remnants of the Boxan fleet were. He had hoped to get support for the Humans there. The council would have been eager to learn of another species with the Mardoxian potential. According to Ma'jasalax, Kaylan's talents would be counted as "gifted" among the Mardoxian sect.

A comms channel from Engineering chimed.

"Go ahead," Kladomaor answered.

"The sensor array should be up soon, but we'll have limited communications for a while. The engines can operate at twenty-five percent capacity, and we currently don't have Cherubian-drive capability," Triflan reported.

"Understood, carry on," Kladomaor said.

Ma'jasalax frowned, looking at the console. "This complicates things," she said.

"That it does," Kladomaor said.

"What's your plan?"

"To repair what we can and figure out where we are," Kladomaor said.

"Being without the full use of our engines will limit what we can do. Without communications we can't call for help if we need to," Ma'jasalax said.

"All true, but we were en route to the transition point before heading directly for the colony. We should be near a known star system where we still have a presence," Kladomaor said.

Ma'jasalax nodded.

"The engines are what concern me the most at this point. We may need to limp on for a while," Kladomaor said.

"Could the Xiiginns have tracked us here?" Ma'jasalax asked.

"I don't think so. They might have gleaned some information from their sensors prior to the wormhole destabilizing, but they were also fending off our attacks. So I think we're relatively safe for the moment —as safe as we can be stranded in the great expanse," Kladomaor said.

"With our sensor arrays still down, have you considered asking the Athena for help?" Ma'jasalax asked.

Kladomaor frowned. Being so focused on his own ship's repairs, he hadn't considered it.

"It could give us some much needed insight. Wouldn't you agree?"

Kladomaor nodded. "I will reach out to them," he said.

If anything, the Mardoxian priestess was relentless in her determination that Humans and Boxans should be working together. He conceded the point, but it just hadn't been at the forefront of his mind. He opened up a comms channel and waited for them to respond.

"Athena here," Kaylan's voice answered over comms.

Kladomaor gave her an update of their current status on the ship and paused.

"Kaylan," Ma'jasalax said, "how is Zack?" she asked, giving Kladomaor a meaningful look.

"He's stable and recovering from his brief exposure to space. Brenda says he should be up and around in no time," Kaylan said.

Kladomaor pressed his lips together and glanced at Ma'jasalax.

Kaylan had been so insistent on finding Zack that he was a bit surprised at the neutrality of her tone.

"He'll need time," Kladomaor said. "The wounds the Xiiginns inflict may not be visible on the surface."

"I'll be sure to let Brenda know that," Kaylan said.

"Our sensor array is being repaired. Right now I was hoping you would be able to help us with the use of your own sensors," Kladomaor said. The Human ship had rudimentary sensors, but as Ma'jasalax had pointed out, some information was better than none, which was what they currently had.

"I can have the AI open a data feed to your ship that will allow you to see what we've learned so far," Kaylan said.

"That would be greatly appreciated," Kladomaor said.

As the data was transferred, Kladomaor routed it to the navigation computer. After a few minutes, the nav computer was able to triangulate their position, and the results showed on the main holodisplay.

"Is that right? The Carnarvon system?" Ma'jasalax said.

Kladomaor sucked in a deep breath and gave her a solemn look. "It's right," he said.

"Commander," Triflan said. "Limited communication has been restored. I'm detecting a Boxan signal from that system."

Kladomaor's brows drew up in consternation. "There shouldn't be anyone in that system," he said.

"Can you fill us in?" Kaylan asked.

"The Carnarvon system used to be home to a primitive race of beings that fell victim to the Xiiginns. This system was our first documented instance of Xiiginn intentions," Kladomaor said.

"What happened?" Kaylan asked.

"The Xiiginns exploited them to gain access to their manufacturing capabilities. Though the species was considered primitive by Confederation standards, they were adept at creating resilient materials on a massive scale. The Xiiginns stole their technology and incited global war between the dominant factions. Their planet is now a wasteland. The Xiiginns then used what they learned to create their current fleet," Kladomaor said.

"Triflan," Kladomaor said. "Try and hail them. See if they can help us."

A few moments went by as Triflan attempted to communicate with whoever was out there. If they had full communications capability, they would be able to follow the protocols that would make the information his tactical officer was trying to obtain unnecessary.

"Commander, there is an asteroid outpost in the area under the command of Prax'pedax. They are insisting that you send your authorization; otherwise, they'll open fire on our ship," Triflan said.

Kladomaor seized the comms channel on his console and entered his unique battle commander ID, along with the authorization codes provided by Boxan Space Command.

"Are we in danger?" Kaylan asked.

"No," Kladomaor said. "This is standard protocol when a certain level of secrecy must be maintained."

"Coordinates have been transmitted," Triflan said. "I've informed them that we're in need of their assistance; however, with our current engine capabilities, it will be at least a week standard before we can reach the asteroid outpost."

Kladomaor shook his head. "That won't do. If we push the engines like that, we might do further damage."

"Commander, this is Gaarokk. I have a suggestion," the Boxan's voice said over comms.

"Go ahead," Kladomaor said. He hadn't spoken directly to Gaarokk since he'd gone aboard the Athena. The scientist likely believed Kladomaor was angry with him, and he *had* felt betrayed but had come to accept what his scientist friend wanted to accomplish.

"If the reactors aboard the ship can handle it, I would propose the use of the gravity tether. We can then use the Athena's engines to take some of the burden off your ship's damaged engines," Gaarokk said.

"Won't that put too much of a strain on the Athena?" Kaylan asked.

"Not necessarily. There's a gravity field that's being maintained. The only resistance the engines would receive is from that field. And you can use the stealth ship's engines to help compensate," Gaarokk said.

Kladomaor ran through the calculations in his head and reached out to Thraxu with Gaarokk's suggestion. "Thraxu thinks this could work. It will still take us the better part of a day to reach the outpost, but that's better than a week," Kladomaor said.

"Can Prax'pedax send help from the outpost?" Ma'jasalax asked.

"Not until we get closer. His mission supersedes our need for assistance, it seems," Kladomaor said.

Ma'jasalax slowly shook her head.

"I'll coordinate from here, and we'll monitor the Athena's hull integrity for irregularities," Kaylan said.

"We'll let you know when we're ready to move," Kladomaor said.

* * *

*****

Mar Arden was furious, but he resisted the urge to have his entire bridge crew executed on the spot. The truth of the matter was that none of this had been their fault. The failure had been his and his alone.

At least his suspicion of a Boxan presence in the Nershal star system had been confirmed. He wasn't sure what was worse—being outmaneuvered by the Boxans or that fact that he had effectively let a new species slip through his grasp. He glared at the holodisplay, which showed the three warship commanders who had also failed to capture the Boxans.

"How exactly did one Boxan stealth ship manage to disable three of our warships?" Mar Arden asked.

"They utilized beacon suites," Deng Arel said.

He was the most senior of the commanders, and Mar Arden had expected him to reply first.

"Go on," Mar Arden said.

"We swept the outer system and kept receiving anomalous ship detections in multiple locations. We broke apart to investigate. It wasn't until the ion missile sweep that the frequency of detections increased. Since we were there to flush them, we had to investigate all of them. We detonated the ion warheads where we could and investigated the rest, working our way into the system. I think it's safe to say the Boxans have improved their stealth capabilities," Deng Arel said.

Mar Arden clenched his teeth, but he couldn't find fault with Deng Arel's mission report. Doubtless the detailed report would be without flaw as well, with the exception that the Boxans had out-thought them. And their alliance with the Nershals was collapsing. Two Nershal battle cruisers had opened fire on his ship. He'd destroyed one and disabled the other. Nerva Space Command was mobilizing. Despite the tactical advantage their warships gave them, the Nershals would throw themselves against them. Once the Nershals committed to an action, they rarely changed course.

"We've analyzed the damage to our ships," Deng Arel continued. "The Boxan beacon suites contained drones that attached themselves to our hulls. The drones were concentrated on communications arrays and external power couplings to the engines. They knew exactly how to hit us. All they had to do was wait for the opportune moment."

Mar Arden sighed. "And the damage this ship sustained from the Nershal battle cruisers allowed them to disable us, allowing them to escape," Mar Arden finished. He glanced at the damage reports and critical system statuses on the commander's console. "Continue with repairs. We need to be ready to deploy as soon as possible. I want you to meet with your own staffs and work out a counterstrategy against this new type of stealth warfare the Boxans used."

"What about the Nershals?" Deng Arel asked.

"I'll deal with them, but let's move farther away from Selebus," Mar Arden said, and cut the comms channel. They had their work to do.

The bridge doors opened and two Xiiginns entered with an armed escort. Kandra Rene and Sion Shif came before him. He had seen Kandra Rene's mission report on the events that had taken place on

Selebus. She met his gaze and waited for him to speak.

"Sion Shif," Mar Arden said. "Before the Boxans escaped, you ordered that a compulsion signal be beamed at the Boxan ship. I'm curious as to what you hoped to accomplish. To my knowledge, aside from Kladomaor, none of the Boxans aboard had been subject to compulsion."

"The signal was directed at the Human vessel," Sion Shif said.

Mar Arden glanced at Kandra Rene. "I thought you were unsuccessful with that technique?"

"It didn't work on him. Sion Shif exerted his influence on another," Kandra Rene said.

"Is this true?" Mar Arden asked.

"When they attacked our cruiser, I was part of the team sent to where we were holding the Mardoxian priestess. During the firefight, one of the Humans had become separated. On a hunch, I tried compulsion," Sion Shif said.

Mar Arden pressed his lips together and his tail hung lazily behind him. "I'm afraid I don't understand. Did it work?"

"That's the thing. I'm not sure. It definitely affected the Human. I just told it to return to the others and it did," Sion Shif said.

"And what was in the signal?" Mar Arden asked.

Sion Shif's eyes widened hungrily. "The rudimentary protocols to send a signal to us here."

"A sleeper agent," Mar Arden said.

"I thought it was fitting. If it works, we should hear from them soon and will be able to jump to their location," Sion Shif said.

Mar Arden smiled, and he nodded. Perhaps the Boxans and

Humans were within his grasp after all.

Chapter Twenty-One

KAYLAN WAS ON the bridge, reviewing the latest engine performance reports. Between the Athena's engines and the limited capability of the Boxan stealth ship, they were due to arrive at the Boxan space station in a few hours. The day before, Hicks had insisted that she get some rest, and after checking on Zack's status with Brenda, she'd gone to her room and passed out. She slept so hard that when she woke she wasn't sure how much time had passed. She had set an alarm, but she wouldn't put it past Hicks to kindly ask the AI to override it so she could get more sleep.

She was alone on the bridge for once. Gaarokk was spending time with Redford, and Efren was going over the particulars of the gravity tether. Kaylan understood the basic concepts and would have liked to know the specifics of how it worked, but there had been very little time for her to do so. Michael Hunsicker had made running the Athena look easy, and she sometimes found herself wondering what he would have done differently if he'd been here.

"Commander, I have an update," the AI said.

The Athena's artificial intelligence made all of their lives easier. She really had to focus to remember a time when they had functioned without it.

"Go ahead," Kaylan said.

"There has been increasing comms activity between the Boxan ship and the space station," the AI said.

"Hardly surprising. What is it that you find interesting?" Kaylan asked.

"I'm unable to monitor those transmissions. I can detect when they occur, but I don't have the necessary clearance to decode the actual contents," the AI replied.

Kaylan chewed on the inside of her lip for a moment, considering. "The Boxans are entitled to some privacy," she said.

"Of course, Commander. I was merely bringing it to your attention."

"Understood, and thank you," Kaylan said.

Both Ezerah and Etanu looked askance at the Athena's AI having so much unrestricted access to the ship and had been slightly amused that the Humans showed any type of courtesy to a software construct. Kaylan didn't see it that way. The AI had proven to be a valued member of the crew, even if they had first gotten off to a rocky start. She treated the AI like she would anyone else, and she'd learned at a young age that a little professional courtesy could go a long way in building effective teams.

The door to the bridge opened and Vitomir walked in, followed by Nikolai. The young cosmonaut had made it his personal mission to monitor Vitomir's every move since they had learned of his actions at Titus Station, which had resulted in four people dying, including Vitomir's wife. Kaylan had reluctantly given Vitomir some freedom because they needed everyone to contribute if they were going to survive. Vitomir had helped them, but she still wondered if at some point he would betray them again. But the guilt of his actions for sabotaging Titus Station so he could join the original Athena mission still seemed to weigh heavily on him. When not busy, he had a haunted look in his eyes.

Vitomir walked over to her. "Commander, may I have a word with you?" he asked quietly.

Kaylan regarded him for a moment before nodding.

Vitomir glanced at Nikolai. "Please, would you give us moment?"

Nikolai glanced at Kaylan.

"It's fine," Kaylan said.

Nikolai walked over to the comms station.

Vitomir pressed his lips together, and his thick gray brows wrinkled in concern. "I realize that advice from me is probably the last thing you want to hear, but I would like to give you some, if you're willing to hear it," he said.

"Go ahead," Kaylan said.

"One thing this journey has taught me is that every moment is precious and there is no way to know if the next moment that comes will be your last. I've done horrible things that will bring me shame for the rest of my life. I would give anything to hear Natalya's voice one last time," Vitomir said, swallowing hard. "She's dead because of me. I can see it in your eyes, and you're right. What I wanted to tell you is to take the time for things that are important beyond the work, because you never know when those moments will slip by, never to return."

Kaylan gave Vitomir a long look and then nodded. Vitomir stepped away from her, and the bridge doors opened. Hicks walked in. Kaylan glanced at Vitomir, whose back was to her. She hated what he'd done, and she was mad at herself for listening to him, even if what he was saying was exactly what she needed to hear. She'd been avoiding Zack and had hardly seen Katie since Zack's return. She had been giving Zack some space, but she needed to know where things stood between them. Part of her was afraid to find out, but Vitomir was right, she was burying herself in her work.

Hicks came over to her.

"Would you mind covering things here for a bit?" Kaylan asked.

"Take your time," Hicks said.

Kaylan headed to the med bay. The door opened, and she saw Brenda standing at her console.

"I was just about to go help Emma with analyzing the data Gaarokk provided about the Xiiginns," Brenda said.

"Oh, okay, that's good. I've been meaning to follow up with her, but I came here looking for Zack," Kaylan said.

"He said he was going to one of the observatories," Brenda said.

Kaylan rested her hand on the door. "How is he?" she asked.

"Time will tell. He's been through a lot. His body will heal just fine, but he was a prisoner of the Xiiginn. That would take its toll on anyone. I've spoken to both Katie and Hicks to see what they had to say about it. I figured the military would have given them training that could offer some insight on how to best deal with it. They said we just need to be here for Zack, and take it one day at a time," Brenda said. "You should go to him. I'm sure he'd like to see you."

Kaylan nodded and thanked Brenda, then decided to head to the port observatory. It was the place Zack would go to when he was avoiding Redford. As she made her way through the ship, she kept thinking about their last moments together on the Xiiginn cruiser. She'd reviewed everything that had happened in meticulous detail, and when she grew tired of that, she would move on to before they'd even gone to Selebus that first time. She hadn't been honest with herself then, but she was determined to be so today.

Kaylan rounded the corner and opened the door to the port observatory. Zack was sitting on one of the small couches, gazing out the window. He wore a white shirt and blue sweatpants. The Boxan stealth ship was on the opposite side of the Athena, so he had a clear view. As she walked in, he turned toward her and smiled. His face had sharper features, as if there were more of an edge to him than there had been before.

"Brenda told me you were here. Do you mind if I join you?" Kaylan asked.

"Please," Zack said quietly and gestured next to him.

Kaylan walked over and sat. The side of his mouth drew down as he pressed his lips together, which was what he often did when weighing whether or not he should speak.

"I'm sorry I haven't come sooner," Kaylan said.

"You've had your hands full," Zack said. "The others filled me in on everything you did to find me. I don't know how to thank you."

"Thank me?" Kaylan said. "Zack, you saved my life. Yes, you did," she said when he started to protest.

Zack shifted in his seat. "Anyone else would have done the same," he said.

Kaylan frowned. "Really?" she said. "Someone else would have kissed me and then locked me in an elevator because they thought they were going to die?"

Zack swallowed and met her gaze. "They tried to get me to do things and tell them about all of you. I fought them as hard as I could," he said.

"You were their prisoner," Kaylan said. That reason alone was more than enough for anything he could have said to the Xiiginns.

"I told them some things. She tried to control me," Zack said.

"Etanu told me what happened," Kaylan said.

"They had video surveillance on their ships, and she kept showing me the part of the video where I kissed you while they did things to me," Zack said.

Kaylan reached out and rubbed his shoulder. "I'm so sorry for what they did to you," she said.

Zack took her hand in his. "I'm not a soldier. I know there are other people who would have done things differently, but I would do it all again to keep you safe."

Kaylan's breath caught in her throat. "You keep saying how weak you are, but your actions tell a different story. No one else could have achieved what you did, and I don't mean just saving my life. You fought for all those prisoners."

"I had to. What was being done to them was wrong," Zack said.

"That's what makes you the strongest person I know and why I love you," Kaylan said. Her throat thickened, but she felt a great weight lift from her shoulders, as if she were finally free of everything she had pent up inside. "I know you're with Katie, but I needed to tell you, to say it out loud."

Zack was clearly taken aback, and she watched as he tried to form words. "We're not together, Katie and I. She, uh—knew my heart belongs to you."

Kaylan's eyes became misty, and her breath hitched. Zack started to say something else, but she cut him off. "Shut up and kiss me, you idiot."

Zack pulled her toward him, and her lips parted as she melted into his arms. Heat coursed through her veins and she glowed inside. For the first time it felt like it was just the two of them on the ship. Her lips sank into his and she held him to her, losing herself in the press of his lips.

"I could kiss you forever," he whispered.

Kaylan smiled. Zack's eyes widened with surprise as she took off his shirt and then removed her own. She wanted this, and so did he. Her heart raced, and she moaned as their bare skin came together.

A short while later they lay naked on the couch, and Zack glanced behind them.

"Aren't you afraid someone is going to walk in here?" Zack asked.

Kaylan shook her head. "No, I locked the door," she said.

Zack frowned in confusion.

"Neural implants, silly," Kaylan teased.

Zack snorted.

"You're probably right though. We should get dressed," Kaylan said.

Neither one of them could stop smiling. She hoped they could manage some semblance of control because they weren't exactly in the clear. The Xiiginns could still find them, and they were light-years from home.

Zack looked at her and, for a moment, seemed uncertain.

"Day by day," Kaylan said, placing her hand on his arm.

Zack nodded, and his gaze narrowed playfully. "Just so I'm clear, do I need to call you Commander while we're alone?" he asked with a smirk.

Kaylan punched him in the arm, and he used it as an excuse to pull her in for another kiss.

"I'm just kidding," Zack said with a grin.

Kaylan pulled herself away from him. "We'd better get to the bridge. I expect we're getting close to the space station," Kaylan said.

"I'll meet you up there. Can't show up at the bridge dressed like this," Zack said, gesturing to his sweatpants and T-shirt.

They left the observatory, and Kaylan returned to the bridge. She felt like her lips couldn't stop smiling, and there was more of a spring to her step than there had been before. She opened the door and saw Gaarokk, Ezerah, and Etanu on one side of the conference table, with Hicks and Redford on the other. She greeted them and asked to be brought up to speed.

Gaarokk sat hunched over, with his thick, dark hair hanging down his chest. The Boxan never complained about the tight quarters he found himself in, but Kaylan imagined it must get a bit uncomfortable after a while.

"There are two escort ships that are going to guide the stealth ship to the dock at the station," Gaarokk said.

"What about us?" Kaylan said.

"They will have you dock near our ship. Kladomaor insisted," Gaarokk said.

Kaylan shifted her feet. "Is there a problem we should be aware of?" she asked.

"I don't know for certain. This station and the work being done there is highly confidential. Kladomaor told me they haven't even shared with him what they're doing. The good news is that we should be able to repair the ship, and from there we can take you before the council," Gaarokk said.

"How do you think they'll react?" Kaylan asked.

"Excuse me, Commander, but Kladomaor is hailing us," the AI said.

"Put him through," Kaylan said.

"Greetings. Before the Athena docks, they'll scan your ship to determine if it will be allowed to enter the space dock. Once we're aboard the space station, we'll meet with the station commander by the name of Prax'pedax," Kladomaor said.

"Prax'pedax is no mere station commander," Gaarokk said.

"Who is he?" Kaylan asked.

"Technically, he's my superior. He's what you would call a fleet admiral, which means the work being done here is vitally important. We may have stumbled into something," Kladomaor said.

"What else is new?" Hicks said with a wry grin.

"Indeed," Kladomaor said. "Just be aware that there will be heightened security protocols in effect."

"Understood," Kaylan said.

The gravity tether was disengaged, and Kaylan put some distance between the Athena and the Boxan stealth ship so it could be safely guided to the asteroid space station. Two smaller, rectangular-shaped ships moved into position on either side of the Boxan ship and guided it away. The rectangular ships were dark gray and shuttle-sized. Another of those ships approached the Athena, and a comms channel opened from it.

"Greetings, Human vessel Athena. We will guide your ship into the space dock," a Boxan's deep voice said over comms.

"We'll follow you in," Kaylan said.

"We will first commence scanning of your ship. Please disengage any countermeasures that might interfere with an accurate reading."

Kaylan glanced at Gaarokk.

"Standard protocol," Gaarokk said.

The Boxan ship flew a quick circuit around the Athena and came back to its position in front.

"Scan complete. You are cleared to dock. Please follow us in."

"Understood," Kaylan said.

She climbed into the pilot's seat and took control of the Athena's thrusters. Their sensor feed was piped into the holodisplay at the conference table so the others could see what Kaylan was seeing on the HUD.

The space station had been built into a large asteroid over a hundred kilometers in diameter. The chunk of space rock had a hollowed-out central structure that went through the whole thing, and there was a deep amber glow coming from inside the central structure.

"That glow is just the resonance coming from the shield. Once we're inside, there will be sections where an atmosphere is maintained," Gaarokk said.

"What about the smaller, tower-like structures spaced across the outer surface?" Kaylan asked.

Gaarokk peered over her shoulder at the HUD. "They're weapon systems," he said.

Kaylan glanced up at him.

"We've been at war for a long time. Any type of work beyond the safety of the colony requires that measures be taken for our protection," Gaarokk said.

Kaylan nodded. She brought the Athena to a halt, allowing the Boxan stealth ship to limp into the space dock first. Then Kaylan eased the Athena forward and passed the threshold of the cavernous interior of the asteroid.

"How many Boxans are here, do you think?" Zack asked.

"Probably a few thousand," Gaarokk said.

"Remarkable," Redford said. "Absolutely remarkable."

The astrophysicist's wide-eyed gaze was alight with wonder. Kaylan glanced at him and saw Redford wince.

He noticed her watching him. "It's just a headache," Redford said, and pointed to a bruise on his forehead.

The interior of the asteroid was lined with a metallic infrastructure. Gaarokk informed them that there were tunnels and facilities throughout. The asteroid was both an efficient use of resources and effective camouflage for a space installation. The Boxan stealth ship moved into position, and docking arms secured the ship in place.

"Now it's our turn," Kaylan said.

"Athena," the Boxan pilot said through comms, "position your ship at the next slot, and the docking arms will do the rest."

Kaylan took a deep breath. Docking any type of craft back home had required patience and skill. NASA pilots practiced for months before being able to dock a real ship. Trusting the docking arms to do their job was difficult for Kaylan.

Gaarokk nodded encouragingly.

"You got this," Hicks said from the copilot's seat next to hers.

She moved the Athena into position and used the lateral thrusters to move the ship toward the dock.

"Excellent," the Boxan pilot said. "Just hold position."

Kaylan brought the Athena to a stop. Docking arms extended from the space dock and moved into position. The docking clamps didn't actually come into contact with the ship but used a gravity field to hold the ship in place.

Kaylan thanked the Boxan pilot for his help, and he advised them that transport to the actual dock would be provided at an airlock of their choosing.

"Will we need our spacesuits?" Zack asked.

"No," Gaarokk said. "There's a breathable atmosphere maintained now that we're inside the space station."

Zack nodded, and Kaylan noticed him glance at Etanu. The two had bonded during their imprisonment. Etanu had helped save Zack's life, which made Kaylan inclined to give the Nershal a second chance.

This time the entire crew would be leaving. No one wanted to be left behind, and the crew was abuzz with excitement at seeing the Boxan space station. Use of an asteroid for a space station had been considered by the various space agencies of Earth since humanity had first started reaching into space. They had scratched the surface with mining installations but nothing like what they were about to see. They filed to the airlock.

"I'll look after the ship, Commander," the AI promised.

The airlock doors opened, and a floating platform moved into position. There were three Boxans on the platform, with two in powered armor. Glowing cyan lines marked the edges of the chest piece and legs.

"Please come aboard," a Boxan said.

The crew stepped onto the platform. Gaarokk stretched to his full height and let out a big sigh.

"We'll need to consider your height and build when we design future ships," Kaylan said.

"I do like the Athena's design. It's quite capable, but I would very much appreciate more space," Gaarokk said.

The platform worked like the one they had used on Nerva, but it was definitely in better working condition. Kaylan glanced over the side and didn't relish the thought of plunging to the depths below. Zack glanced at her questioningly.

"We used something similar to these platforms on Nerva," Kaylan said.

Their transport brought them to the main docking area near the ship, and Kladomaor was already there with Ma'jasalax. They exited the platform and greeted Kladomaor and his crew. Some of his crew wore their powered armor, which made Kaylan wonder if they were in more danger than they'd originally thought.

Large doors opened and a contingent of Boxan soldiers headed toward them. They were led by a large Boxan who wore a green uniform that reminded Kaylan of the battle mesh the Nershals wore.

Kladomaor saluted, and his soldiers followed suit. "Thank you for your help with our ship, Prax'pedax."

The large Boxan approached, and Zack whispered that it was like they were surrounded by giants. Kaylan smiled and saw some of the others grin softly. It was good to have the crew back together.

"We couldn't leave you floating in the great expanse," Prax'pedax said, and looked at Etanu and Ezerah, bowing his head. "It gladdens my heart to see the Nershals among the Boxans once more."

Etanu and Ezerah gave Prax'pedax a slight bow of their heads in return, and the Boxan station commander turned to Ma'jasalax.

"Our station is at your service. We had no idea one of the Mardoxian sect was in the Nerva star system," Prax'pedax said.

"A new development, Commander," Ma'jasalax answered.

Prax'pedax turned to address the crew of the Athena. "Kladomaor's report mentioned the discovery of a new species. It is an honor to stand before you."

The crew of the Athena bobbed their heads respectfully.

Prax'pedax turned back to Kladomaor. "Your mission summary said you took on four Xiiginn warships in the Nerva star system."

"That is correct," Kladomaor said.

Prax'pedax let out a booming laugh. "I was on the approval board for your mission to Nerva. Nowhere did it say that you expected to have open conflict with the Xiiginns, except on the ground, of course."

Kladomaor glanced pointedly at the crew of the Athena. "We had more than a few surprises. I am happy to report that the Nershals are actively rebelling against the Xiiginns. I'm not sure whether they will reach out to the council, but I've left several of their leaders a means of doing so."

Prax'pedax nodded and his expression turned serious. "Which of them was held captive by the Xiiginns?" he asked.

Kaylan noted that the surrounding Boxan soldiers seemed to stiffen at this. Zack stepped forward and was quickly joined by Etanu.

"The Nershals have proven to be resistant to the Xiiginn influence, and you are therefore excluded from this," Prax'pedax said to Etanu, then gestured toward Zack. "Human, it is my understanding that you were a prisoner of the Xiiginns?"

"Yes," Zack said.

Prax'pedax gestured to two Boxan soldiers, who approached. "Apologies, but I must put you in a holding cell."

"What's the meaning of this?" Kladomaor asked.

"Our work here is too important to risk falling into the hands of the Xiiginns. At this point, it is unknown whether the Humans can resist the Xiiginn influence," Prax'pedax said.

"I'm not being controlled by the Xiiginn," Zack said.

"Forgive me if this appears harsh, but that is exactly what someone who is under their influence would say," Prax'pedax said.

"Commander," Etanu said. "I can vouch for Zack. The Xiiginn did try to control him with compulsion, but he not only resisted them, he defied them. This I saw with my own eyes."

"It's all right," Zack said. "Go ahead and detain me."

"No, it's not all right," Kaylan said. "Zack is a member of my crew. We're supposed to be guests here. In fact, the only reason we're here at all is because of the monitoring station you built in our own star system. Zack just escaped from a Xiiginn research facility and prison. I'm not going to stand idly by while you try and stick him in another one."

No one actually moved, but it felt as if the crew of the Athena inched closer together.

Prax'pedax's jaw set and his muscles tightened.

"Perhaps a compromise," Ma'jasalax said. "To address your concerns, assign an armed escort for Zack. This way you can monitor where the Human goes. Would that work for you?"

Prax'pedax's features softened. "The wisdom of the Mardoxian is always welcome. It will be as you say."

The Boxan looked at Kaylan, and she nodded.

"Now, if you'll follow me, I shall give you a brief tour of our station, and then we can plan our next move," Prax'pedax said.

As the Athena crew followed the Boxans out, Hicks leaned in so only Kaylan could hear. "Good job, Commander."

She flashed him a smile as they followed the others to the station's interior.

CHAPTER TWENTY-TWO

KLADOMAOR WAS RELIEVED they had been able to find the asteroid station; otherwise, they would have been in real trouble. And he wasn't at all surprised by Prax'pedax's attempt to have Zack detained. If he'd been running the station, he would have done the same. The Human appeared to be fine, but Kladomaor still had his suspicions where Zack was concerned. He knew firsthand what the Xiiginns could do to someone. On the flip side, he was also impressed with Kaylan's argument for Zack not to be detained. It was the mark of a good commander to defend their crew.

The short tour was as much for Prax'pedax to form an opinion of them as it was for their benefit. They saw that repairs of their ships were already underway, which was a good thing. The sooner the repairs were completed, the better. Kladomaor had left Triflan aboard the stealth ship to oversee the repairs and get the ship resupplied.

There were thousands of Boxans serving on the station, and Kladomaor experienced mixed feelings about being around so many of his own kind. Despite his reputation earned during their war with the Xiiginns, he was a bit of an outcast. Once a Boxan had been subjected to the Xiiginn influence, very few were able to retain their sanity if they ever became free of them. Most Boxans were trained to recognize the signs that they were coming under Xiiginn influence and begged to be killed, like one of his own crew had done. Death was a mercy, because for most Boxans, there was no cure for the Xiiginn influence. Kladomaor's case was the exception, and it was only because of Ma'jasalax that he was able to serve in the Boxan military at all. Most Boxans were leery of working with him, but as he proved himself, the requests to join his division steadily grew.

Their group split up, with some of the Athena crew going on to explore more of the station.

Prax'pedax guided the rest of them to a room where they could speak openly and stopped before the entrance. "I don't recall that Humans have been admitted to the Confederation."

"The Confederation of Species is unaware of their existence," Kladomaor said.

Prax'pedax glanced at Kaylan and the others for a few moments. "How did they come to be in the Nerva star system?" he asked.

"I will explain once we're inside," Kladomaor said.

"Before we do that, I would like to know your intentions for them," Prax'pedax said.

"I intend to take them before the council and petition support for their home planet. The Xiiginns have learned of their presence and will now actively seek them out. I would spare the Humans becoming slaves to the Xiiginns," Kladomaor said.

The Boxan station commander considered this for a few moments. "You're proposing that we form an alliance with their species outside the Confederation?"

"The Confederation has all but cast us out," Kladomaor said.

"Interesting," Prax'pedax said, "considering that this is coming from you."

"The Humans have proven worthy of an alliance with us, and even if they weren't, we're responsible for them being here," Kladomaor said.

"Commander," Ma'jasalax said. "You might agree that our former stance on diplomatic relations with other species could do with some improvement given the current state of affairs."

Prax'pedax nodded. "I look forward to hearing more about this alliance you are going to propose," he said, and gestured for them all to come inside.

The rocky walls of the station's interior were a stark reminder that they were in an asteroid. The furnishings were a step above what they had on the Athena but nothing like what they had left behind on their home world.

"Please, sit," Prax'pedax invited.

The circular room they were in was meant for information gatherings, and the furnishings were able to accommodate them all.

"Why have you returned here?" Kladomaor asked.

"The Qegi was the first species to fall victim to the Xiiginns," Prax'pedax said. "This was where it all began, where we learned of their true intentions. The planet is a nuclear wasteland, and it will be many thousands of years before life will return to this star system. One of the reasons we came back was because this was one of the systems where there was a strong probability of finding a species with the Mardoxian potential."

Kladomaor glanced at Kaylan and the others but didn't say anything. He had left the Mardoxian potential in Humans out of his report. This wasn't because he didn't trust Prax'pedax, but he wanted to avoid any record of it until they'd returned to the colony.

"The Xiiginns had no idea; otherwise, they might have taken greater care when exploiting this species," Prax'pedax said.

"That can't be the only reason," Kladomaor said.

Prax'pedax eyed Kladomaor for a moment but didn't say anything.

"You've made a discovery," Ma'jasalax said, "beyond the history here."

Prax'pedax nodded. "We've found evidence of another spacefaring species that had been to this star system before."

"What have you found?" Kladomaor asked.

A holoscreen came on and showed the partial remains of a ship that appeared to have crash-landed. The images magnified, and something about the ship's design tugged at the back of his mind.

"The Drars?" Kladomaor asked. "You think this is the remains of a Drar ship?"

Prax'pedax nodded.

"But that's impossible. We've found hardly any trace of them beyond our own home system," Kladomaor said.

"Who is to say they didn't leave more of their technology behind for other species to find?" Prax'pedax said.

Kladomaor frowned.

"Who are the Drars?" Kaylan asked.

Kladomaor glanced over at her. She was flanked by Hicks, Emma, and Zack. The rest had gone on to explore the station.

"Do you remember when I told you about how my species observed an interstellar war that began snuffing out entire star systems? Well, the Drars were one of those species that fought in that war. The name is derived from a partial data cache we managed to find while first exploring our own star system. Their technology is the basis for the Star Shroud," Kladomaor said.

Zack frowned. "When you say basis, do you mean the Star Shroud was based on some other race's design?"

"That is correct. The Drars had constructed a device that could protect entire star systems from attack. We only found reference to it, along with some prototype designs. We perfected it into the Star Shrouds as they are used today," Kladomaor said, and turned toward Prax'pedax. "What were you able to learn from the wreckage?"

"We may have found out where they went," Prax'pedax said.

Kladomaor glanced at Ma'jasalax, and the Mardoxian priestess was just as surprised as he was.

"Why is this so important to you?" Hicks asked.

"This was a species that was involved in one the most destructive interstellar wars we've ever come across. We've resisted resorting to practices that the Xiiginns have no qualms about employing—things such as genetic engineering and system-wide destruction. If the Xiiginns could harness the power of an entire star system, what's to stop them from forcing the entire galaxy into submission?" Kladomaor said.

"Are you saying you could do such a thing?" Hicks asked.

Kladomaor shook his head. "We know it's possible but won't explore researching such a thing," he said.

"Why not? You could turn the tide of your war with the Xiiginns," Hicks said.

"Like me, you're a soldier, and your first impulse is to protect your species, but when you engage in conflict you influence the battle by the way you choose to fight it. As with any war, there is also a risk of the weapon you use falling into enemy hands," Kladomaor said.

Hicks nodded. "Yeah, but if your survival is at stake then . . ."

"That's just it. We choose to fight our war with the Xiiginns on our own terms and prefer not to put the galaxy at risk as it once was," Kladomaor said.

Hicks slowly nodded.

"There is more," Prax'pedax said. "We might have deciphered the path the ship took to this system. If our analysis is correct, it came from a previously unexplored part of the galaxy."

Kladomaor's brows rose. "You're hoping to follow them," he said.

Prax'pedax nodded.

"Excuse me," Kaylan said. "What is the connection between the Mardoxian species potential, the Drars, and the species that originally resided on the planet in this system?"

Prax'pedax glanced at Kladomaor, intrigued. Kaylan may not have had Ma'jasalax's training in the Mardoxian sect, but she certainly had a keen insight.

"We believe the Drars may have set the conditions for the Mardoxian trait to be possible throughout the galaxy. Until now, the Boxans were the only species to have a strong inclination toward this trait," Kladomaor said.

Prax'pedax looked sharply at Kladomaor and then at the group of

Humans. "Are you saying the Mardoxian potential is present in Humans?"

"Beyond the shadow of a doubt," Kladomaor said.

Prax'pedax glanced at Ma'jasalax. "This is unprecedented, and now I can see why you're so keen to keep them out of Xiiginn hands, but I'm afraid this complicates things."

Kladomaor narrowed his gaze. "How?"

"I'm afraid I can't allow you to leave for the time being," Prax'pedax said.

"You have no authority to stop me," Kladomaor said.

"In this you're mistaken. The nature of this mission gives me a certain amount of autonomy. Finding anything remotely related to the Drars could help us take back our home and cure all those who were afflicted by the Xiiginns. This station is operating under blackout protocols. The only reason we answered your hails was because you were in trouble," Prax'pedax said.

Kladomaor was about to reply, but Ma'jasalax spoke first.

"Give us some time to discuss this new development so we may come to a resolution that is satisfactory to all," Ma'jasalax said.

"Of course. Take all the time you need. We'll speak more later," Prax'pedax said.

The station commander left them, but two of the station's soldiers were posted outside the doors.

"So that's it? They're just going to keep us here?" Kaylan asked.

Kladomaor was silent while his mind whittled away at the possibilities.

"How much time are we talking about here? Is there any possibility the Xiiginns could track us here?" Hicks asked.

"Highly unlikely," Kladomaor said. "Prax'pedax is right about the blackout protocols. If he's truly onto something about the Drars, he can temporarily hold us here."

"I think we should learn all we can while we're here," Ma'jasalax said. "In the meantime, I can try to reason with him."

"And if he won't see reason?" Kladomaor asked.

"Then you'll do what you do best," Ma'jasalax said.

"I could help if we're looking to try and get out of here," Zack said.

"No!" Kladomaor said. "They're already suspicious of you. I don't want to give them any reason to treat us more firmly."

"What do you suggest we do then?" Kaylan asked.

"We're his guests. Let's see what they've discovered. After that, we'll take you before the Boxan council and then back to Earth," Kladomaor said.

Kaylan nodded.

Considering all that had happened, Kladomaor thought the Humans were coping quite well. They had proven to be a highly resilient species. He needed to check on the ship repairs just in case he had to take matters into his own hands. If that were to happen, the Humans might have to leave their ship here, which they wouldn't like. Kladomaor left them to check on Triflan and the repairs.

CHAPTER TWENTY-THREE

REPAIRS TO KLADOMAOR'S ship would be completed any time now. They still didn't have clearance to leave, but having a working spaceship brought them a lot closer than they had been before.

The now-familiar stomping that followed Zack throughout the ginormous space station came to a halt when he did. Over the past two days he had tested the boundaries by quickening his stride to see how far away his escorts would let him go. It was slightly amusing to him when the heavy footfalls of the Boxan soldiers quickened to catch up with him; it was less amusing when they shot some sort of beam that froze him in place. At least he'd learned something by having a bit of fun at the Boxans' expense, even if they'd had the last laugh.

Zack had arrived at the conclusion that the Boxans as a race were quite standoffish when they couldn't meet you on their own terms. Their presence here on this asteroid space station was a prime example. Zack had been in enough situations to know when he was being barely tolerated. There were exceptions of course. Gaarokk was quite easygoing and open with them, and Etanu had pointed out that the Boxans had suffered a great many disappointments since they had been cast out of the Confederation.

"That's just it. I'm not sure I believe their being cast out is their greatest upset," Zack said.

Etanu was with him, along with Emma, Kaylan, and Efren. They were at the docking area and within sight of the Athena. Their ship was tiny compared to the other ships at the dock.

"Are you saying you think the Confederation isn't important to them?" Etanu asked.

Zack shook his head. "No, it's important to them, but it's the Xiiginns' and the Boxans' own place in the universe that are more important to them. They feel responsible for what the Xiiginns have done, but without the Confederation, and perhaps if they abandon the Star Shroud program, what will they do then?"

Kladomaor's time was mainly spent in meetings with Prax'pedax, but he'd managed to take Hicks, Redford, and some others around the dock, showing them the different ships. Redford had hardly slept since they'd been here, and Zack thought the astrophysicist had seen more of the station than anyone else.

Gaarokk waved over to them as he approached.

"Indeed, what will we do?" Gaarokk said.

Zack blanched. "You heard me from all the way over there?" he asked.

"We have excellent hearing," Gaarokk said.

Zack glanced at his soldier escorts and wondered if they had heard some of the things he had said about them earlier. "Good to know," he said.

"How much longer will they keep us here?" Kaylan asked.

"I don't think it will be that much longer—certainly not for any extended period of time. Finding evidence of the Drars is an astonishing discovery. They were an advanced civilization that existed well before any of us," Gaarokk said.

"Yeah, but they fought an interstellar war and were never heard from again," Zack said.

"That is true. Some Boxans believe our fate is tied to theirs, so it's important that we learn all we can about them," Gaarokk said.

"What have they learned so far?" Zack asked.

Gaarokk was about to answer when a nearby door opened and a group of Boxan soldiers headed in their direction. Zack had a sinking feeling they were there for him. The two soldiers that were assigned to watch him closed in from behind.

The Boxans came to a halt and their leader gestured toward Zack. "This one will come with us," the Boxan said.

Without waiting for a reply, his soldier escorts prodded him forward. Zack was sure the nudge had been gentle by Boxan standards, but his shoulder ached nonetheless.

"What's the meaning of this?" Kaylan asked.

The rest of them were following along.

"The commander wishes to speak with him," the Boxan said.

Kaylan walked by Zack's side. "Did you do anything?"

"No, I swear," Zack said. "Those two have been with me the whole time."

Zack glanced at Gaarokk, and the Boxan told him not to worry. Zack wasn't reassured.

They were led through a series of rock-walled corridors, and the Boxans they passed all seemed to be quickly making their way somewhere. They brought Zack to the large room that was the command center for the entire station. Boxans were working at various workstations throughout. Zack caught sight of Kladomaor by Prax'pedax's side, and neither Boxan appeared to be happy to see him. They were on an elevated platform so they could oversee the command center. Zack recognized some of the Boxan soldiers as being part of Kladomaor's crew.

The Boxan soldiers guided him to a small circular platform and had him stand on it. The platform glowed amber, and Zack found that he couldn't move his legs. He looked at Kaylan, alarmed.

Kaylan rounded on Prax'pedax. "We've been nothing but cooperative with you. Why are you holding him?" she demanded.

"Cooperative! Then tell us why a wormhole has been detected on the edges of this system," Prax'pedax said.

Kaylan looked at Kladomaor. "The Xiiginns are here?" she asked.

"We've found that a signal has been broadcasting our position since shortly after we arrived," Kladomaor said.

"I didn't do anything," Zack said.

Kladomaor's lips pressed together, and he looked at Kaylan. "He may not even realize he's under their influence."

"He's not," Etanu said, stepping closer to Zack. "The Xiiginn, Kandra Rene, tried many times to control him, and every single time she failed."

Kladomaor shook his head. "She might have been wearing away his control, learning the best way to apply her influence."

"If that's the case," Zack said, "anyone here could be under their influence."

"We thoroughly examined him," Kaylan said. "Our medical officer compared his brain scans from before he was captured to after, and there were no anomalies that could be explained as having been caused by the Xiiginn influence."

Prax'pedax narrowed his gaze. "How do you know anything about the effects of the Xiiginn influence?"

"I told them," Gaarokk said. "They have a right to know what they're facing, and given the fact that Zack was their prisoner, it was prudent that they be equipped with a way to determine if he was affected."

"The only problem is that the effects can be different, depending on the species," Prax'pedax said, and looked over at Kladomaor. "Is this the one who deciphered the Star Shroud protocols?"

Kladomaor nodded. "He could have done this. He could have configured a broadcast signal to tell the Xiiginns right where we are."

"I'm telling you I didn't do this," Zack said.

Prax'pedax's stony gaze took them all in. "We have no choice. Take the Human into custody and put him in one of the holding cells."

Etanu started to move toward Zack. "Don't," Zack said. He didn't want them to start fighting with each other, not with the Xiiginns coming for them.

"You don't have any proof," Kaylan said.

"The safety of this station comes first. We'll investigate—" Prax'pedax was saying when Kaylan interrupted.

"How are you going to have time to investigate?" Kaylan said. "If the Xiiginns are attacking, you won't have the time. He's a member of my crew. I'll confine him to the Athena and assign one of the crew to remain with him at all times. You can even post guards outside the ship to make sure he doesn't leave."

Zack watched Kladomaor glance at him as if trying to figure out whether he was lying. He knew he hadn't consciously done anything, but someone had. How else could the Xiiginns have followed them here?

Kladomaor turned toward Prax'pedax. "As his commander, she has the right to investigate the alleged actions of one of her crew."

Prax'pedax's mouth drew downward and his flaxen eyes went cold. "So be it. However, I want all the Humans to return to their ship immediately."

The amber glow from the platform beneath Zack's feet went out, and he was able to move again.

"I'll have my soldiers see to it," Kladomaor said.

The Boxan soldiers surrounded them, and they were ushered from the command center.

CHAPTER TWENTY-FOUR

THREE XIIGINN WARSHIPS emerged in the Qegi star system. The signal they'd received had come from this area, and Mar Arden first believed it was a Boxan trap. Hoan Berend, the commander of the warship, argued that they couldn't afford not to investigate. The paltry signal was their only lead for following the Humans. Mar Arden used the fact that they had to repair their ships to see how long the signal would persist. Sion Shif had taken up the comms post and was monitoring for any signals in the system. After they had received the initial signal from the Qegi star system, the young Xiiginn had firmly believed it came from the Human. But in Mar Arden's experience with compulsion, there were certain degrees of resistance a species could exert. Most species they'd encountered couldn't resist them, with the exception of the Nershals. Never before had they encountered such conflicting results when trying to control another species as they had with the Humans. Kandra Rene, who was quite gifted at compulsion, had failed to get their Human captive to do anything except experience pain. That Human had been defiant from the onset. Sion Shif, on the other hand, appeared to have successfully brought at least one of the Humans under his influence. It was a problem he looked forward to exploring when they found the Human home world.

One of their warships was too damaged to make the trip and had to remain in the Nerva star system. Reinforcements would arrive there soon to lend support.

"Why would the Boxans come here?" Hoan Berend asked.

"This was where they discovered what we were doing to Qegi. To them, this is where the war started," Mar Arden said.

"The Qegi were too primitive a race to be allowed to join the Confederation. They likely would have killed themselves off anyway, but without them we wouldn't have been able to build our fleet," Hoan Berend said.

"Commander, I'm getting a massive Boxan detection on the scanner," Sion Shif said.

"Onscreen," Hoan Berend said.

Mar Arden frowned. "That's much more than a stealth ship."

"I think we've stumbled onto something here," Hoan Berend said.

The scanners indicated that the Boxans were inside a massive asteroid.

"They know we're here," Mar Arden said.

Hoan Berend nodded. "Let's see if we can keep them from escaping."

Mar Arden narrowed his gaze. It couldn't be pure happenstance that had brought the Boxans here. They were up to something, and for them to put an asteroid space station in this system, he was willing to bet it was something pivotal to their war effort.

"Attack now," Mar Arden said.

*****

Kladomaor watched as the Humans were led away.

"I would have thought that you, above all, wouldn't shirk in the face of doing one's duty," Prax'pedax said.

"I'm sorry you think so, but they're right. You have no proof that Zack did anything."

"The Human was held by the Xiiginns. That's proof enough."

"No, it's not," Kladomaor said. "We can't afford to be fearful and at each other's throats. The real enemy is out there."

"I looked up the initial report you filed after Ma'jasalax sent that unsanctioned signal to the Human home world. You said they were primitive and power hungry, territorial and warlike," Prax'pedax said.

"They are also loyal and compassionate. The same situations that would drive other species apart brings them closer," Kladomaor said, and for a moment he couldn't believe he was actually defending the Humans.

"With the Mardoxian potential present in their species, if the Xiiginns harnessed that capability—or worse, brought the Humans to their side—it could be worse for us than when the Nershals decided to side with our enemy," Prax'pedax said.

"The Humans are a decidedly stubborn race. They would rather fight than be subject to another species' rule. We would be counted lucky if they were to ally with us against the Xiiginns, despite their current level of advancement. I've seen soldiers freeze at the moment of battle, but even the Human noncombatants show courage under fire."

Prax'pedax frowned. "Someone sent that signal. Are you prepared to deal with that when we find out who the perpetrator is? Because you won't be granted clearance to return to the colony otherwise."

Kladomaor understood what was at stake. Prax'pedax would let them leave, but he would also send his own report back to Boxan Space Command, informing them of the potential compromise to their colony. Kladomaor would never get clearance to go anywhere near the colony.

Alarms blared in the command center.

"We mark three Xiiginn warships in the system—make that six," a Boxan said.

The count went up to eight, and Kladomaor gasped. Prax'pedax issued a station-wide alert.

"You have to get out of here. There's no way this station can stand against eight Xiiginn warships," Kladomaor said.

Prax'pedax glared at the consoles in the command center. The Xiiginns had divided their forces and were approaching from opposite attack vectors. Unlike the limited attack protocols in the Nerva star system, there would be no repercussions for unleashing their full armament here.

Kladomaor watched as Prax'pedax glanced at the small console in front of him showing the remains of a Drar ship.

"This is too important," Prax'pedax said.

"You have to destroy it so the Xiiginns will never learn why you were here. There are thousands of Boxans here depending on you to get them to safety," Kladomaor pressed.

Prax'pedax's eyes grew distant. Kladomaor was about to speak again when Prax'pedax ordered his tactical officer to fire a missile at the wreckage.

Kladomaor glanced at the main console that showed the Xiiginn warships closing fast. Soon they would be within firing range.

"Bring up the station's electronic warfare suite. Firing solution clean sweep," Prax'pedax said.

Kladomaor was stunned. Clean sweep was used to provide covering fire for all escaping ships but had limited tactical capabilities. "You're not leaving?" he asked.

"There isn't time to move this station. I will stay and give the evacuation as much time as I can," Prax'pedax said.

"Authorize the station's AI to defend itself and evacuate with the rest," Kladomaor said.

Prax'pedax shook his head. "You know the protocol. When there's evidence of Xiiginn compromise, we need to operate under the assumption that all systems have been compromised."

Kladomaor knew the protocol, but he also knew High Command couldn't afford to lose someone like Prax'pedax. The commander was ordering fire teams to the defense towers. Using his neural implants, Kladomaor set his sidearm to stun and fired at Prax'pedax. The station commander's surprise was still on his face as he crumpled to the ground, and Kladomaor caught him as he fell.

"It's not your time, my friend," Kladomaor said.

Some of the soldiers in the command center raised their weapons and pointed them at Kladomaor.

"Take your commander to one of the escape shuttles," Kladomaor said.

"You shot him," a soldier said.

"Do you want to stand here and argue with me or get out of here and live?" Kladomaor said.

Two Boxans came over and carried their commander away. Kladomaor strode over to the comms officer.

"Issue the evacuation order and get out of here," Kladomaor said.

He sent a general recall message to the tower defense teams. If they hurried, they might reach the Evac units in time.

The ground commander opened a comms channel to Kladomaor.

"Where is Commander Prax'pedax?" Ground Commander Tolpan asked.

"He's on his way to an escape shuttle," Kladomaor said.

"He wouldn't abandon this station," Tolpan said.

"You're right; he wouldn't. I had to stun him so he would leave. There are eight Xiiginn warships coming to lay waste to this station," Kladomaor said.

There was silence for a few moments.

"The tower defense squads will knock that number down and help provide cover for the evacuation, Commander," Tolpan said.

Kladomaor wanted to tell them to abort, but he knew they stood a much better chance with the defense towers operational. They would be needed to take out the slip fighters heading their way.

"Your sacrifice will never be forgotten," Kladomaor said.

The comms channel cut off, and Kladomaor's neural feeds showed that the defense towers were engaging the enemy. Kladomaor used his implants to authenticate with the station's systems and headed toward the space docks. He monitored the Xiiginns' approach and authorized the missile defense system to fire. Squadrons of Xiiginn slip fighters were already attacking the station's exterior.

Throughout the station, Boxans ran to their designated escape vehicles. They moved with a practiced efficiency that would have made any commander proud. Discipline was what saved lives and was a core tenant in Boxan society.

He came to the space dock doors, and beyond them ships were fleeing the asteroid station, engaging their Cherubian drives after clearing the station.

The floor quivered beneath his feet. The Xiiginns were firing on the station, hammering away at their defenses. The soldier in him wanted to inflict as much damage as he could, but this wasn't his time to die either. They were running out of time. Kladomaor authorized the self-destruct protocols to engage. The timers had to be set for maximum deployment; otherwise, part of the station could remain intact, and he couldn't risk it falling into Xiiginn hands. The self-destruct signal would send a warning to all remaining Boxans on the station. Kladomaor raced toward his ship and saw some of the Athena's crew clustered together on the space dock. *Why haven't they gotten to their ship yet?* He closed in on them and saw that his own soldiers held their weapons ready.

"We don't have time for this," Kladomaor shouted.

"Commander," Triflan said. "We've found the saboteur."

Kladomaor glanced at the group of Humans. Their medical officer was hovering over someone. The soldier Hicks had his weapon aimed at the person on the ground, but the female soldier had her weapon pointed at his own soldiers.

"Lower your weapons," Kladomaor ordered his soldiers, and craned his neck to see who was on the ground. "Let me see."

Katie stepped aside, and Kladomaor pressed his lips together. On the ground was the Athena's astrophysicist, Jonah Redford. His blackened arms were covered in blood. He glanced at Triflan.

"They found him trapped in one of the comms towers. The broadcast signal he was sending caused a power surge."

Redford's face was twisted with pain and the unmistakable madness of one who was under the Xiiginns' control.

"Make it stop! Make it stop! I have to send the signal. They have to know we're here," Redford said.

Kladomaor's eyes blazed as he pulled his sidearm out and took aim.

Kaylan put herself between them. "He needs our help, not execution," she said.

"He's under their influence now and is beyond our help," Kladomaor said.

"You also thought Zack was the one under the Xiiginns' control, and you were wrong. I won't stand by and let you execute him. If you want to get to him, you'll have to go through me," Kaylan said.

The Athena crew gathered around their commander, each with a solemn but defiant expression. Kladomaor knew what he had to do. All his training and experience demanded that he execute those afflicted with the Xiiginn influence on the spot. The risk of them roaming free was too great.

Ma'jasalax caught his gaze, and the Mardoxian priestess's expression pleaded with him for reason. If he pulled the trigger, any hope of an alliance with the Humans would be extinguished. He sucked in a breath and holstered his weapon.

"We have to get out of here, now. Then we can talk about what to do with him," Kladomaor said.

Kaylan's eyes widened, and the rest of the Humans sagged with relief. A large explosion plumed on the other side of the vast station interior.

"Get on your ship," Kladomaor said.

The Humans scrambled to one of the transport platforms and raced toward their ship.

Kladomaor headed toward his own ship, and Ma'jasalax stayed by his side.

"You did the right thing," Ma'jasalax said.

"That remains to be seen. We still need to escape this place," Kladomaor said.

He sent one last command through his implants, authorizing the electronic warfare AI to unleash its full armament at the Xiiginn warships regardless of their proximity to the space station.

They entered the ship and Kladomaor raced toward the bridge.

"The station is breaking apart," Varek said.

Kladomaor scanned the consoles. Any escape shuttles that could get away were gone. There would be Boxans trapped here, and he could do nothing to save them. Their deaths would be remembered.

"Engage the Cherubian drive. Set a course for dark space," Kladomaor ordered.

Opening a wormhole in the station's interior would be catastrophic, but it was their only shot.

"Take us alongside the Athena and bring up the gravity tether," Kladomaor said.

"Tether engaged, Commander," Varek said.

"Drive ready," Triflan called out.

"Execute," Kladomaor said.

An explosive chain reaction flooded through the station's interior as the artificial wormhole expanded into being. The Boxan stealth ship lurched forward with the small Human vessel at its side. Kladomaor clenched his teeth as they raced toward the event horizon. The confines of the asteroid station streaked away as they barreled through space.

"Influx of energy detected. Wormhole is becoming unstable," Varek said.

Unstable wormholes could send shockwaves that would tear them apart if they didn't escape. Kladomaor's eyes locked onto the countdown. To prematurely exit a wormhole could also result in both ships being destroyed.

"Wormhole integrity deteriorating. Gravity tether will be compromised," Varek said.

"Divert auxiliary power to the tether," Kladomaor said.

The station's destruction would be racing after them through the wormhole and was causing the influx of energy. The countdown dwindled to target, and the star lines faded. Their ship immediately stabilized and the gravity tether returned to normal. An orange inferno chased the two ships beyond the entry point but quickly dissipated in the vacuum of space. They were free from danger, but they were out in the void, away from any system. Kladomaor hoped the station's destruction would be enough to cover their escape. Regardless, they were free of the Xiiginns for the moment.

*****

Kaylan glanced over at the others and sighed. "We're through," she said.

"Never a dull moment, is there?" Zack said.

A notification chimed on his PDA, and he turned his attention to it.

The Athena's AI put up a star chart, and they gathered around the conference table. They were at a point between stars. A comms channel chimed from the med bay.

"Redford is stable for now," Brenda said. "I've sedated him."

"How could we have missed this?" Kaylan asked. The question wasn't just for Brenda but for the entire crew. "Was Jonah acting strangely at any point?"

"He was always excited about the alien technology," Zack said.

"Commander, his brain scan is different now," Brenda said. "I checked us all when we first got back to the Athena and compared the scans side by side. Jonah's was the same as everyone else's, only now it's different. If I didn't know better, I'd say he was suffering from some type of infection."

Kaylan glanced at Emma. "Can you take a look at what Brenda found? See what we can learn from it?"

"Of course," Emma said, and left the bridge.

"We need to figure out our next move," Kaylan said. "Athena, can you open a comms channel to Kladomaor?"

The Boxan's actions had surprised her. She'd thought for sure Kladomaor would kill Jonah rather than allow him to live.

"Go ahead, Athena," Kladomaor said.

"I think we need to meet to discuss our next move. May we come aboard?" Kaylan asked.

"Yes, I think that would be a good idea," Kladomaor said.

The comms channel closed.

"Holy crap," Zack said.

Kaylan glanced over at him and saw that he was looking down at his own console.

"What is it?" Kaylan asked.

Zack glanced up at them. "When they brought me back to the ship, I had Athena search the station's systems for information on the Drars. I think we need to bring this over to them."

Kaylan nodded. "Let's go."

A short while later she was aboard the Boxan ship along with Zack, Hicks, and Vitomir. Katie had insisted she stay on the Athena in case there were any problems with Redford. Gaarokk met them once they were beyond the airlock, and they followed him to a meeting room that was near the bridge.

Kladomaor and Ma'jasalax were already inside, and they were soon joined by Etanu and Ezerah. The room had various green plants along the edges, and the air smelled moist and fresh.

"Thank you for coming," Kladomaor said.

Kaylan informed the Boxans of Redford's status.

"So it appears that some of you, at least, are not able to resist the

Xiiginn influence," Gaarokk said.

"Emma said she would need time to study it and run more detailed comparisons to Zack, since he was able to resist them," Kaylan said.

"As long as he is alive, there's a risk he'll betray you to the Xiiginns," Kladomaor said.

"Understood, but it's our risk," Kaylan said.

"Our laws forbid us from taking anyone who is afflicted by the Xiiginns to the colony. I will be sending a report about recent events that will eventually make it to High Command. I would like to offer you the option of speaking on behalf of your species," Kladomaor said.

Kaylan was startled by this offer, and she glanced at the others. "I'm not authorized to negotiate an alliance on behalf of humanity."

"We understand that," Ma'jasalax said. "It's more an introduction."

"Oh." She glanced at Zack, who nodded enthusiastically. "Okay then."

"I have something I'd like to share with you," Zack said, and gestured toward the wall screen.

"At least he asked permission this time," Gaarokk said to Kladomaor.

"Go ahead," Kladomaor said.

Zack looked at the Boxans and raised a brow. "Now don't be angry, but I managed to download the research data on the Drars before we left the station."

Kladomaor narrowed his gaze, and Ma'jasalax leaned over to whisper something.

"It's what he does," Kaylan said.

Zack snorted. "I'm not keeping it or anything. Here, it's yours. Didn't you keep saying how important this was to the Boxans?"

Kladomaor sat up straighter. "What do you want in return?"

"In return?" Zack repeated. "Nothing. You're already helping us get home. We're alive because of you. This is just my way of saying thanks."

"Gaarokk," Kladomaor said, and the Boxan scientist examined the data on the screen.

"He's right. It's the research data, and Prax'pedax was correct. They look like coordinates, but it's beyond anywhere we've ever been before," Gaarokk said.

Kladomaor glanced away from them in thought and his brow furrowed.

"You're afraid the Xiiginns will get their hands on this data," Kaylan said.

The Boxan nodded.

"Well, then, you'll have to go to wherever this place is and check it out. You can't let those bastards get there and take this from you," Zack said.

Kaylan glanced at Zack. While he was very much his old self, there were times when he showed a dangerous edge. Even though he had more reason to hate the Xiiginns than anyone else on the Athena, it still worried her.

Kladomaor cleared his throat. "We promised to return you to your star system, and it's a promise I intend to keep."

Kaylan felt a surge of happiness at the thought of going home. Things had been so much simpler then, but if the Boxans took precious time to send them home, they might miss an opportunity to learn about the Drars. "What if we helped you?" Kaylan said.

Kladomaor frowned. "What do you mean?"

"What if we went with you to investigate the Drars? I would need to discuss it with the rest of the crew, and we would need to vote on it, but what if we were to help you?" Kaylan asked again.

She glanced at the others. Zack was already nodding, and after a moment Hicks did as well. At their hearts, they were all explorers.

Kladomaor glanced at Ma'jasalax and then rose to his feet. He bowed his head to Kaylan in respect. "The fact that you're willing to forgo going home to aid us with this speaks volumes about your race. Perhaps it's something we've forgotten or needed to be reminded of again. Let this be the beginning of an alliance between our two species. Anything we find—be it a discovery or technological advancement—will be shared equally between us."

As much as Kaylan wanted to go home, she knew this was the best path forward. She had no doubt the Boxans would help Earth stay safe from the Xiiginns, but the fact of the matter was, the Boxans were losing their war, and humanity needed time to ascend. Perhaps taking this risk would allow them to survive what was to come. Ma'jasalax gazed at her in a knowing way, and Kaylan wondered if the Mardoxian priestess had arrived at similar conclusions, because she didn't seem surprised by any of this. Together they would plan and have disagreements—of that Kaylan had little doubt—but they would work together not only because they needed to, but because they chose to.

How would future generations look back at this moment as

humanity took its first steps into a much larger universe? Would it be a moment of wisdom to carry them forward? Or would it become a profound moment of sorrow—one where the whispers of the dead rose from a hushed celestial graveyard where the people of Earth once thrived?

CHAPTER TWENTY-FIVE

GARY HUNTER FELT like he'd been at the mission control center in Houston forever. Making NASA history required a lot of hours, sleepless nights, and hardly ever going home, but at least he got to shower every so often and had a change of clothes brought to him. Truth be told, he wouldn't have had it any other way. Michael Hunsicker had been his friend for over twenty years, since he'd first joined NASA.

He glanced at his watch. It was the middle of the night, which was inconvenient for those who preferred to work during the day. However, it just happened to coincide with the best time for communications from Pluto. Gary had his team running through various diagnostics so the president's call with the alien on Pluto would go off without a hitch. He had Edward Johnson's personal phone number on speed dial, and Gary was surprised the Dux Corp representative hadn't shown up yet. He knew Ed was much more than a representative. Anyone the president requested a meeting with wasn't just a company rep but someone actually important. He rubbed the weariness from his eyes and poured himself another cup of coffee.

Gary looked up at the main wall of screens that dominated the mission control center and saw the comms status get pinged with an incoming transmission. He frowned at the display because it didn't have a known source.

"Hey, Sally, am I reading that right?" Gary asked.

Sally Tyler sat in the area designated for communications to monitor transmissions from their deep-space missions.

"The instrumentation is fine. That's a valid signal," Sally said.

"Where the hell is it coming from?" Gary asked.

"I'm not sure, but if the header is any indication, the data coming through is big—like orders of magnitude big," Sally said.

Gary set his coffee down. The rest of the people who were on duty tonight were all focused on the main wall screen. The initial data dump completed and then another one started.

An astronaut video message opened onscreen, and Gary's breath caught in his throat as he recognized the face.

"Houston, this is Kaylan Farrow, acting commander of the Athena. A detailed mission report will follow this initial transmission about where we've been and where we're going. At this point, we have chosen not to return to our solar system. Instead, we are going to help the Boxans on a very important mission. The initial alien signal sent to Earth sixty years ago contained a warning. What you'll learn from the mission report is that the threat of the Xiiginns is very real. They will come to Earth, but we're not alone. In the near future, a Boxan emissary will arrive at Pluto and then will come to Earth to meet with world leaders. I cannot emphasize enough the danger the Xiiginns represent—so much so that we cannot risk returning to Earth at this time. Since the Athena left our solar system, we've been in contact with three alien species, and there are many more. The Boxans have no illusions about us or what we're capable of. I would advise anyone who negotiates an alliance with them to be a person of integrity. The Boxans will not tolerate the petty differences we've lived with for so long.

"Make no mistake, the Xiiginns will come to Earth. I've seen firsthand what they do to primitive species. Our best chance for survival is to work with the Boxans. I hope that after you review all the mission reports, you'll arrive at the same conclusions."

A solemn silence took hold over everyone in mission control as the transmission ended until Gary tore his eyes from the screen. "Okay, people, it's time to wake up the world."

ABOUT THE AUTHOR

I'm Ken Lozito, and I write fantasy, science fiction, and thriller adventure stories. The only thing I enjoy more than reading a great book is writing them. My main focus is to write books that I would like to read and I hope you enjoy them as well.

If you would like to get an email when I release a book please visit my website at **KenLozito.com**

One Last Thing.

Word-of-mouth is crucial for any author to succeed. If you enjoyed the book, please consider leaving a review at Amazon, even if it's only a line or two; it would make all the difference and would be greatly appreciated.

Discover other books by Ken Lozito

Ascension Series:
The Star Shroud (Book 1)
The Star Divide (Book 2)
The Star Alliance (Book 3)

Safanarion Order Series:
Road to Shandara (Book 1)
Echoes of a Gloried Past (Book 2)
Amidst the Rising Shadows (Book 3)
Heir of Shandara (Book 4)
Warden's Oath (Short Fiction)

ACKNOWLEDGEMENTS

First my thanks to you dear reader and to anyone who has reached out to me about the series. Your words of encouragement mean a lot to me and I am eternally grateful.

Next up is my family, you've all been the cornerstone to my foundation. To my children, who with silent demanding, dared me to be better than I thought could be.

My editors, Myra and Tamara, thank you for all the feedback and words of encouragement.

Friends and family who provided feedback and encouragement. Thank you so much for your time and support.

Made in the USA
Columbia, SC
15 January 2018